W9-BBD-113

RIM OF THE DESERT

BOOKS BY

ERNEST HAYCOX

ᛠᛠᛠ

RIM OF THE DESERT

SADDLE AND RIDE

THE BORDER TRUMPET

MAN IN THE SADDLE

SUNDOWN JIM

DEEP WEST

TROUBLE SHOOTER

TRAIL SMOKE

THE SILVER DESERT

ROUGH AIR

RIDERS WEST

STARLIGHT RIDER

WHISPERING RANGE

CHAFFEE OF ROARING HORSE

FREE GRASS

RIM OF THE DESERT

BY

ERNEST HAYCOX

BOSTON

LITTLE, BROWN AND COMPANY

1941

RIM OF THE DESERT appeared
in *Collier's* under the title of THE DRIFTER

COPYRIGHT 1940, 1941, BY ERNEST HAYCOX

ALL RIGHTS RESERVED, INCLUDING THE RIGHT
TO REPRODUCE THIS BOOK OR PORTIONS
THEREOF IN ANY FORM

FIRST EDITION

Published January 1941

PRINTED IN THE UNITED STATES OF AMERICA

CONTENTS

RIM OF THE DESERT

I

OLD SIGNALS RISE AGAIN

HE entered town late in the day, stabled his horse at Connoyer's and crossed to the hotel; and when he came to register he held the pen motionless awhile, as though the recollection of his full name were an unfamiliar act. On his features, brown-burned by all the years of outdoor life, lay that grave and attentive sereneness of a man long accustomed to his own company, to his own resources and solitary whimsies. He signed, "James T. Keene, Dalhart, Texas," in a broad angular hand and waited for the key.

The clerk said hopefully, "Long way to come."

Keene's bland "Yes" closed the clerk out. He took the key and turned to the stairs. Dust silvered his clothes, weather had faded them. His hair lay thick and black and ragged against his temples, there was no mark or scar or shadow of any worry on his face. His mouth was broad below a heavy nose, his eyes were of that shade of gray which is almost blue. Riding had trimmed him, had limbered all his muscles so that his boots made almost no noise on the stairs. At the upper landing he looked back with a sudden flip of his head and caught the clerk's following glance, and at that moment his eyes were nearer black than gray, with glass-sharp splinters of interest in them. Thus catching the clerk's off-guard curiosity, he was a man hard and fine-drawn by the habits of his life; the next moment he erased that impression with a smile and entered his room.

In this room's stale warmth every ancient odor of a frontier hotel lay as a musty remembrance. Once there had been crimson roses in the pattern of the shabby carpet. A pine bureau held its pitcher and bowl; there was an iron bedstead whose enamel was chipped by the roweling of countless spurred boots, a rocking chair, and on the wall a lithograph of an old Indian scout belly-flat beside a desert waterhole. Day's last clear light came through the single grimed window and through a bullet hole in the wall, autographed by the maker as follows: "Ventilated by Smoky Jules from Medora. 1882. Forty-four barrel on a forty-five frame. Never bet aces in another man's game." Some other weary-wise traveler, incited to public comment, had added: "Plenty of livestock in this bed. If I was a rustler I'd get rich."

It was one more hotel room in one more prairie town, but for Jim Keene it was the first night beneath a roof in sixty days. He stripped to the waist, scrubbed away the dust of long travel, and shaved in a growing twilight. Standing by the window later he had a better view of the town.

The main street was a crooked river of silver dust running from a yellow depot at one end of Prairie City to the out-scatter of sheds and corrals at the other. Keene looked down upon single-story buildings sitting shoulder

to shoulder, on board awnings shadowing the street
walks, on alleys leading to rear compounds. A wagonload
of barbwire rolled past, driven by an obvious homesteader with a square-cut beard. In front of a saloon
which advertised itself as the Cattleman's Palace cow
ponies stood heads down and half asleep.

There was something wrong with the town; he had
caught the smell of that at first entry. He considered the
street — the saddle shop, the Cattleman's Palace, the
grain-and-feed store, the sign which said, "Worsham
and Ross, Gen'l Mchdse," the flimsy bank building, the
courthouse. He made a picture in his head of it, for to
Jim Keene the real world was made up of stray words
overheard and the odd change on people's faces, of prints
in the sand and houses sitting empty in the middle of
sagebrush, of bullet holes in a hotel wall, of a man enormous in every physical detail standing now in the doorway of the Cattleman's Palace watching the homesteader
and his load of barbwire.

The wagon stopped, the homesteader got down and
started for the hotel. As he did so the man at the saloon
— a man nearly as tall and as broad as the saloon door
— moved into the street. When he passed the homesteader he swerved aside deliberately and his elbow
caught the homesteader and knocked him off balance to
the dust. The big man walked on, never looking back,
but immediately a small crowd of cowhands appeared in
front of the saloon, watching this scene with a narrow
amusement. The homesteader got up from the dust and

stood still, staring at his feet; in a moment he continued on to the hotel, slightly limping.

Jim Keene rolled a cigarette, watching the big man turn back to the punchers gathered at the saloon door. The big man had made his play for the entertainment of the punchers; now he grinned and waggled a hand and the whole group passed into the saloon. Keene lighted the cigarette. He took one deep drag of smoke into his lungs. To his face came the wry tightness of distaste and a feeling, the old feeling over which he had never had any control, ripped through him. He murmured to himself: "Always something like that," and went downstairs.

In the dining room he saw the homesteader again. The homesteader was at a corner table with his wife and a grown son and two small children. It appeared to be a holiday for them, a break in the hard work and loneliness of some sagebrush quarter-section a long way from town. They were all cheerful except the man himself, who sat at the head of the table without appetite or interest. Keene thought, "He didn't tell them about the knockdown."

Rising from his finished meal, Keene left the dining room. He was fed and at ease, his muscles were idle after the long ride and every sound and sensation of this town pleased his hungry senses; yet a cool wind was blowing from his errant past, that wind which governed his life no matter what wisdom his mind might hold. He felt it and regretted it, but nevertheless it pressed softly against him and it made him smile as he crossed to the doorway. In the smile was some regret. In it also, though he never knew this, was a hopeful anticipation.

He stood on the street to watch the crowd flow by. Ranch outfits came in and sent the street dust high as they wheeled before the Cattleman's Palace. They moved along the street with a salty arrogance; the razor-sharp appetites of rough living propelled them into the saloon. Their voices came back to Keene, high and quick and cheerful. Homesteaders entered town and wagons and buggies were banked wheel to wheel against the walks. Along these walks families cruised and grouped up with other families and moved idly on. Lamplights turned the steady street dust to a film of gold.

He heard a man say: "You see Jesse Morspeare knock Spackman down?"

Keene crossed the street and was caught in the slow-drifting stream of the crowd. On a wall of the saddle shop he saw a sign which read: "Re-elect Sheriff Ben Borders," and beside it a second sign said, "For Sher-iff — Jesse Morspeare. The Cattlemen's Choice." He paused by these notices, bracing himself against the steady push of people, and remembering what he had heard only a moment ago. Morspeare was the big one who had rammed his elbow into the homesteader. The homesteader was Spackman. At that moment the story of this town and the surrounding prairie was as clear to Jim Keene as though he had lived his life in it.

A wave of homesteaders broke against him and stirred

him out of his tracks and rolled on. A girl drove her rig against the walk and jumped to the street. She made a complete turn in the dust, saw Keene, and spoke. "Have you seen Dr. Ellenburg?"

Her hand touched his arm to stop him, bringing his attention down to the steady, gray alarm in her eyes; strain pushed the edges of her lips together. Keene removed his hat before he answered, and still delayed his answer. She was a tall girl whose hair had been whipped loose from fast riding. The touch of her arm was a weight and the tilt of her head was a picture in this noise and shadow and confusion. He said: "Sorry, but — " and saw her thrown backward by the collision of a man's blunt shoulder. The man had put his head down to make a way through this crowd. He was drunk and saw nothing, and he was laughing to himself as he shoved forward.

Keene caught the drunk by the coat collar and hauled him back. He whirled the man around and put both arms against his chest and slammed him against the saddle-shop wall.

The drunk cried: "Hey — Broken Bit!"

The girl straightened and tried to break away, but the crowd quit moving; it made a tight ring around Keene and the girl and the drunk. Men pushed down the street and somebody called out: "That you, Snap? Hey, Broken Bit! Hey, Red!"

"No," said Keene to the girl, "I haven't seen the doctor. I'm a stranger here."

The drunk planted himself firmly on his feet, bowed his head and butted Keene in the chest. Cowhands slid through the crowd and stood still, carefully watching. The drunk pushed against Keene, making no headway. He got rougher and angrier, he stamped his feet on Keene's boots, he swung his arms. Suddenly Keene slapped the drunk's face and straightened him up. Keene looked across the narrow circle, observing that one red-headed puncher looked at all this with narrow interest. Keene said: "You Broken Bit?"

"That's my outfit," admitted the redhead.

Keene caught the drunk under the arms. He called, "Here's your baby," and threw him at the redhead.

The redhead didn't care for that. He batted the drunk aside. "You're a little tough, friend."

The cool wind blew stronger and every piece of this scene was something Keene could repeat from memory.

Regret and pleased anticipation ran through him in equal strength, side by side. "Tell your partner to pull in his elbows, Red." Then he forgot about the redhead and he forgot about the drunk. "This lady is looking for a Dr. Ellenburg."

Somebody in the crowd called: "Up at the court-house."

The girl said: "Thanks." She had no reason for smiling, he thought, but still she smiled and murmured to him, "I'm sorry," and turned away. The crowd moved on. The drunk, having forgotten the last few minutes, rose from the walk and vanished, butting his way through the crowd.

The redhead remained, pushing his glance at Keene in a rough, half-aroused way. He was a long, freckle-faced man, never doubting himself. His red hair lay tight and short-curled against his head. He was bold enough for anything, but sufficiently smart to take his good time to read what he saw.

"You don't look like a homesteader."

"Don't let it worry you."

"Maybe I will."

"Suit yourself," agreed Keene. He was smiling, he was thinking back and remembering how this always went. It never changed. A man rode a thousand miles but the pattern caught up with him and now it was hard to know whether to be glad or sorry. He stood there, appraising the man in front of him. The redhead was a handsome rascal, and knew it. He was hard as iron and he knew that too. If he belonged to Broken Bit he would no doubt be the riding boss, for that air of bold assurance was on him. The homesteader, Spackman, came from the hotel with his family and stood in the street's lamp-stained shadows; and immediately a second family joined the Spackmans. A girl stood in front of Spack-man's grown son and touched his chest with her hand and laughed at him. Her lips were red and her brown-dusted face was stirred by that laughter and by the ex-citement of the night. Spackman's son looked at her with a solemn, disturbed interest. Keene noticed all this; and now he saw the redhead's glance strike across the street to that girl. His face changed, a flare of strong interest showed in his eyes. The two homestead families, now in one group, quartered across the street's dust. The girl's eyes lifted and saw the redhead and the smile left her lips; after she had gone by she looked quickly over one shoulder with a knowing darkness in her eyes, and by that obscure coquette's glance she raked up every hungry impulse in the redhead, leaving him with his tantalized hope. Keene saw all this.

Keene moved on to the saloon and walked into its full blast of noise, into its rolling haze of tobacco smoke. Piano music clanked steadily from the deep back end. Along the bar, which ran the whole distance from front door to rear door, men stood elbow against elbow and a back bar mirror flashed out its prisms of light and four barkeeps slowly sweated as they worked. Heads of deer and antelope and bear were mounted on the walls; two lamps bracketed a painting of a fleshy beauty lying on a couch, her heavy-lidded smile fixed on the poker tables below.

After the silence and long loneliness of the trail this noise and warmth and glitter, this odor of tobacco and whisky and clothes saturated with horse smell, comforted Keene. He found an empty place at a table and bought a stack. Somebody called through the saloon. "Where you been, John?" Looking toward the door, Keene saw the redhead enter the saloon with the giant Jesse Morspeare behind him. More outfits raced into

Prairie City, the sound of their arrival trembling through the flimsy walls of the saloon. A shot flatted along the night and the saloon doors swung ceaselessly back and forth to the inbound passage of the steady-flowing crowd.

Keene sat low in the chair, hat pulled down over his eyes. He ordered a drink and a cigar and he got the cigar evenly drawing between his lips, observing the deliberate manner in which Red John moved across the floor to take a seat at this table. Red John said: "A stack," and seemed to be amused at some joke in his head.

The old streaky feeling traveled through Jim Keene. All the ancient signals of trouble were rising in him and about him while he watched Red John's hard, rope-burned hands shuffle and deal the cards. They were fast hands; the fingers were supple. It was something to remember. He lifted his glance and caught the straight blow of the redhead's green-flecked eyes.

"You're no nester," murmured Red John.

"Maybe — "

Red John's voice cut in quickly. "Now, Snap was a little drunk. But that don't matter. If a Broken Bit man wants to use his elbows it's all right."

Keene said, "I pass," and laid his fingers on the table. He rubbed them along the felt table top, making short slow circles. Nothing ever changed. The quarrels of men rose from the same old reasons and moved through the same old pattern.

"I said it was all right," said Red John in softest voice.

That long wind had been blowing against Keene all evening; it strengthened now, it grew colder and stronger, coming up a thousand-mile trail. The player to his left took up the cards to shuffle them, but he laid them down again and said, "I'm cashing in," and left the table. Keene collected the cards and roped them between his hands.

"No haymow shuffles," said Red John. "You're a little queer on a lot of things, friend." He was talking in the same edged, amused voice, yet the ring of it flattened, it went out of key and his lids made a narrower frame around his eyes. Keene dealt and drew a long breath and felt the old current of wildness crowd him. This was what he had traveled so far and so long to escape. But the distance meant nothing; for a man carried his passport to hell in his heart wherever he traveled.

"It occurs to me — " he said.

Red John cut straight across the rest of it. "You're tough with drunks, friend. Which is an easy stunt."

Keene put down his cards and placed his hands at the edge of the table. He came out of his chair and flung the table in Red John's lap and watched Red John fall backward. Chips clacked along the floor. Red John's body made a squashing echo in the saloon and within the space of a breath there was no talk in the place and no sound except Red John's grunt as he wrenched himself to his feet. He took three backward steps and paused.

The other players at the table moved away at once and an open space appeared behind Red John, made by the withdrawing of men from the bar.

"When I'm talking," said Keene, "I don't like to be cut in."

Heat flared in Red John's eyes, the quick shadow of cruelty came to them; the man's lips drew down at the corners, they thinned in the center. Keene, waiting for what he knew would come, remembered how many other times he had watched this scene take shape before him. The memory made him smile and the smile was a rash signal on his face. He stood with his feet apart; he stood still, and though he had ridden a thousand miles to escape this kind of scene there was no regret in him now. This saloon was the Cattleman's Palace but it might have been the Drover's in Abilene or the Belle in San Antonio; it might have been a lot of other towns. If a man had pride and temper and if these were the things he cherished and would defend it made no difference how far he ran.

"Friend," said Red John, "I like to meet a tough man and try my luck."

That was it. That was the core and the meaning of the old story. A man had pride and pride took him into a fight. If he survived that fight his reputation grew and other men came along to say, as Red John was now saying, "I like to meet a tough man and try my luck." The time came when a man got weary of it and saw somewhere his own death in a last showdown and ran from it as he was now running. But there was no hope in running. For it was in the man, always.

So he stood there, still smiling, and said as he had said many times before: "All right, Red. Take a try."

Into the sibilant stillness of the room crashed the high scream of a woman, followed by the running scuff of heavy boots and the bubbling echo of a man's voice in pain. A puncher put his head through the door. He yelled, "Broken Bit!" and disappeared. The saloon crowd rushed at the door, pushing Red John aside, throwing him off his careful balance. Red John made a gesture with his hands, turned from Keene, and went out into the street. A floor man moved stolidly forward to pick up the capsized table and chairs. Then somebody said, "All right, Tonk," and the floor man moved away. Keene turned about, finding a man behind him whose eyes were brilliant green against an Irishman's crimson complexion. This man's eyes held a dancing light. They were approving Keene.

"My boy," he said, "be careful of that fellow. He's a Broken Bit man."

Keene said: "He's the boss?"

"He's the foreman. Grat DePard's the boss." Then the green-eyed man grinned. "Ah now, it would be a lovely fight between you. I think you're the one that might do it. You've got the mark. I'm Tim Sullivan and this is my place. Be careful of that crowd."

Keene crossed the saloon and pushed open the doors and was stopped by the solid crowd on the walk. In the middle of the street a ring of men, homesteaders and cowhands, stood around the Spackman wagon with its load of barbwire. Spackman's grown son and the two children were on the wagon seat. Mrs. Spackman stood by the wagon with an ax in her hand. Spackman was in the dust, now slowly rising; blood dripped from his mouth and dropped along his beard. He got to his feet and put up his hands in uncertain defense against Jesse Morspeare, who was a black and towering hulk in the stained lamplight and shadow of this night.

"Don't get in my way again," said Morspeare.

Mrs. Spackman screamed: "If you hit him again I'll use this ax."

Morspeare said: "Red, grab that old fool's ax."

Red John moved out of the circle, slow and careful; as he did so the Spackman boy jumped down from the wagon and stood beside his mother, and then Jim Keene saw homesteaders come slowly together, their faces black and stubborn yet half afraid. Red John was laughing. "You'll cut yourself with that ax, ma'am. Just put it down."

"Let her alone," said Spackman's boy.

Spackman spoke through his cut mouth: "No doubt you can do what you want with me, Jesse. But we'll still be out there on the Silver Bow flats when you're dead and gone. Now let me go home."

"Old man," said Morspeare, "don't ever get in my way."

"Then," said Spackman stubbornly, "stay out of mine."

"Go on back to Ioway and grub your land," called Morspeare. "Don't come here and spoil range grass."

"We'll be here," said Spackman, slow and weary and firm.

"Not long," retorted Morspeare, moving forward. Mrs. Spackman raised the ax, Broken Bit men edged forward, the homesteaders were a tighter, darker knot in the street. Red John laughed again, not moving. The homestead girl, having come to the wagon, put her hand on the shoulder of Spackman's boy. Now Red John watched her and Keene saw her stare back at Red John with a half-interested, half-repelled attention. Her red lips softened as she looked at the foreman.

Keene came against the crowd on the walk. He put his hands between the touching shoulders of two men and shoved them away. He hit them with a roll of his body and went through. He was in the street dust, pulling a Broken Bit man aside. The Broken Bit man flung himself around, resenting that roughness with a lifted arm. He looked at Keene, saying irritably, "Stop that!" Keene passed him and got behind Red John. The Broken Bit foreman stirred in his tracks, hearing trouble. He swayed and swung his head and found Keene, and he took a rapid step to the left and made a half turn. In the rounds of his eyes Keene saw the quick-roused flicker of cruelty again.

A voice quietly called: "Make way here." A gray and straight and severe old man walked inside the circle, saying: "Stop that, Jesse."

Morspeare let out a rumbling answer. "You won't be wearin' that star long, Borders."

"Long enough. You can go home, Spackman, or you can stay. It makes no difference. You Broken Bit boys just ease along."

A rider came up the street on a trotting horse, calling, "What's this — what's this?"

The crowd broke instantly to let him into the circle. He reined up before Morspeare and Borders. He sat heavy and square on a big horse, the burned darkness of his face shining like polished saddle leather in the saloon's outthrown light. He wore a cotton shirt unbuttoned at the collar and the muscles of his neck snapped straight and tight when he moved his head. He was big-chested, with a long flat nose and heavy lips loosely rolled together. He had a thick voice, the sound of it dropping like an ax stroke into the silence.

He looked at Morspeare, at Red John. He said: "When I want trouble I'll tell you. Get the hell out of town."

The huge Morspeare shifted on his feet. He lost his spirit immediately. "Ah, Grat — "

This, then, was Grat DePard. Keene considered the man with a widening attention, forming his own judgments. DePard sat like a soldier on the big horse, obviously accustomed to having his own way; on him was the air of a dry, aloof scheming. Jesse Morspeare dropped his head. Turning, he moved out of the circle, never thinking to question the order tossed so bluntly at him. DePard looked around at his crew. "Go on," he said. "Go on."

Mrs. Spackman spoke up. "Tell them to leave us alone."

Grat DePard dipped his head at her, giving her no comfort with his voice. "Take care of yourself. I didn't ask you homesteaders to come into this country and break up my range."

The Broken Bit men moved away in reluctance. Red John looked at the homestead girl, his desire sharp-calling over the dust. DePard stared at the old and serene sheriff. "Ben," he said, "these are my men. Don't order them around so quick."

"Hold them in hand then," said the sheriff.

"I'll do as it pleases me to do, Ben," announced De-Pard. He turned his horse. His glance touched Keene and remained steadfast a brief moment, the completely un-revealing glance of a player studying his hand. A moment later he followed his forming outfit down the street and soon left town.

Keene watched the crowd dissolve. The homestead girl rose to the seat with the Spackman boy, smiling up at him and speaking some soft, provocative word to him. The Spackman boy nodded soberly and put the team in motion. The outfits were running out and the home-steaders were departing, and presently Prairie City settled to its quiet hour and lights began to die and the street's silver dust glowed darkly through the settled shadows. Building corners made gaunt angles against the black sky.

Keene went into the saloon and stood up to the bar. The trade had dropped to a single steady game at one poker table; half a dozen men, other punchers from other outfits, remained at the bar. Pouring himself a drink, he watched the gray straight sheriff enter the saloon and walk toward him. This, he remembered, would be Ben Borders, who was running for re-election against the giant Jesse Morspeare.

Borders said: "Son, you make a wide splash."

"A drink?" offered Keene.

"One," said Borders, "one for an old man," and poured his drink. He had a slow and courteous voice, he had age's faded eyes. Behind the austerity of that long, disciplined face gentleness lay. "You're ridin'?"

"Just riding."

"It sounds natural," reflected the sheriff. "Just fancydancin' along the trail, admirin' the shape of your shadow. That's a nice time of life. Better than most times. Always something over the next hill."

"What's over it?" asked Jim Keene.

"Now that I remember back," said Ben Borders quietly, "it was the looking that was good, never the finding. But of course," and he added this with a perceptible regret, "I was a little headstrong and wanted too much. A man like that makes pictures in his head. The pictures are hard to fill."

"Why," said Jim Keene, "that's true. But a man's got to find the picture. If he took less, what would he have?"

"I thought that once," said the sheriff, and let his glance go far back into time. "But I was a young man then. Here's to the next hill, son."

"How," said Keene, and drank his whisky and left the saloon.

He crossed to the hotel and went to his room, but now he knew he couldn't stay. The walls were closing in on him and the night was flat and restlessness had its way with him. He went down to pay his bill. In fifteen minutes he had left the town behind.

It was then ten o'clock, with a coolness coming to the night. Somewhere he heard the sigh of wind through a lonesome juniper and somewhere the howl of a coyote floated along the stillness. To the rear and to either side lay the flat of the desert, and here and there he made out the distant wink of a homestead shanty; before him he saw the shapeless bulk of mountains. That was north, and toward the north he pointed, toward the hills he proposed to cross, one upon another, until the restlessness was gone.

Near midnight he made camp and built up a small sagebrush fire and cooked coffee; rolled in his blankets, he watched the fire die. Once he heard the distant drum of several horsemen. Starlight lay pale on the desert. This night, in Prairie City, his past had caught up with him and once more the old story had been played out in the saloon. A thousand miles wasn't enough to escape it; somewhere in the northern distance maybe he'd find a reason to put his pride away and be a humble man without a gun. Before he fell asleep he remembered the girl who had asked him about the doctor. Her face was oval and white and composed in his memory; around her eyes, he remembered, had been the hint of an iron resolution, but in her lips he had seen a contradictory thing.

II

AURORA BRANT

AURORA BRANT returned to the homestead shack with
Dr. Ellenburg at midnight. When he left half an hour
later he told her the worst of it in his bluntest words.
"Your father," he said, "can't last out another day."
She had known he would say that. The rest of the long,
black night she sat by the bed, watching her father move
through his fitful intervals of sleep, half dreaming of
death and half awake and aware of its coming.

Now it was day and he had fallen into a real sleep.
Aurora stood at the shanty door to watch strong light
move across a sea of sage and yellow grass. Prairie City
was a blur twenty-five miles southward. Here and there
at lonely intervals small square shanties, no different
than the one in which she lived, stood against the sun;
far away she saw a rider and his ribbon of dust. This was
the Silver Bow flats, on which the homesteaders were
settling. Only last year it had been free government land
used by the cattle outfits to graze their beef; the hatred
of the cattlemen at that intrusion was the one real fear
in the heart of every homesteader.

She saddled her pony in the shed, took a bucket with
a long rope, and rode toward the river a few hundred
yards away. The Silver Bow crossed the flats by means
of a deep lava-rock gorge and made a bend here and

came out of its canyon to provide the only suitable ford within twelve miles.

At the river she rode the horse into the current and dropped the bucket to the full length of the rope, thereby filling it. This was a device her father — a clever man who could do anything with his mind and nothing with his hands — had invented to save the labor of dismounting. While the horse had its long morning drink she looked across the river at the small, gray log cabin on the north side.

Beyond the ford two ridges formed the walls of a narrow valley — Cloud Valley — whose grass lay rich yellow in the sunlight; gradually as the valley ran northward the ridges pinched in and became the rough-tumbled chain of the Thunderhead Range, here and there touched by snow patches. All that valley was cattle graze, with the ranch houses of the big outfits — Broken Bit, Rafter T, and Cleve Stewart's Chain and Ball — hidden in small box canyons playing off from the valley. Every foot of that golden fifteen-mile meadow was free land, open to any homesteader who wished to file upon it. Only one homesteader had ever tried. He had built the log cabin across the ford. One night he had been shot dead and now the cabin stood as a stark warning to all other homesteaders.

She turned back. When she reached the yard of the shanty she heard her father calling with more strength than he had to spend. Dropping from the horse, she hurried in and saw the fear frozen in his eyes. He reached for her hand. "A man sees the sorry side of himself at a time like this. At this stage of the game you don't make excuses for yourself any more. I have never really been happy when alone. I can't even die alone."

"Don't regret anything, Dad. We've seen the world. We've had fun."

"If that were only all — "

He was very thin and in the last few years his hair had turned white at the edges, and he had hated that because he hated age. He was sixty but still kept the blue eyes of a young man; his face was without a line of worry. He had never worried, never worked very hard, never bound himself to any one place. Wherever they had moved he had always begun by saying: "This is our home at last. Here's where we make our fortune." But in a little while depression always came upon him and the orthodox pattern of life would bore him and then he would say: "It is not as I'd hoped it would be, Aurora. Let's try New Orleans. It is a lovely place." And so they would move. All her first memories were of trains and boats and coffee at midnight on ferries and stages rocking across lonely places. For him change was the breath of his life and regularity was death.

He held her hand and this too was as it had always been, for even as a child it had been her voice comforting him, her steadiness cheering him. It was her strength he fed on. He said: "One thing I regret. We never should have come here."

"It has been a lovely year, Dad."

She had the power to take his doubts away; now he was pleased to see that she believed in him. "Yes, it has been. And it was the cheapest health cure we could find." Then another thought turned him still and dreary and a pale shadow moved over his face and he spoke from the farther corridors of his strength: "How much money do we have left?"

Money was another responsibility he had never faced. She had been the banker. Now, as before, she lied to him to save him from one more gray fact he could never face. "About two hundred dollars."

"Enough to get you out of here. You can't keep this homestead. You wouldn't want to." He paused to struggle with his own conscience. "I have never cared for your mother's people. They disliked me when I married your mother and hated me when she died. But they're well off and they'll be good to you. I can think of no other way."

"All right, Dad."

It eased him to hear her approval. It took the last responsibility from his shoulders, he who could not bear responsibility. He smiled out of those blue eyes which held her love so securely. A little of the old gay boyishness came back to him and then, in accordance with his changeable mind and heart, it went away. He lay quietly on the bed and she knew he would be thinking of a poem out of Wordsworth or the glitter and laughter of some great party in his younger years, or perhaps he was thinking of tomorrow and the great day to come in another place.

"I leave you so little," he said. "Not even friends. We have never stayed anywhere long enough to make friends."

"Everything," she said, "has been lovely. Always."

"You must not be too serious, Aurora. Let the solemn ones grind out their souls by trying to shake the roots of the world. Life will break you if you let it. Don't let it. Be gay. There is never enough laughter, never enough laziness and dreaming. Remember one thing when people speak those dismal words about duty and usefulness and the necessity of making something great of your life. Remember that the heart of a rose contains all the meaning this world has for any of us. Its fragrance is yours for nothing. Go to your mother's people. Take a year in a finishing school. Marry well and have a great house and bring people to it who are wise and witty and full of pleasant nonsense."

"Yes," she said. "Yes."

But, watching her, he had his moment of insight. "I think I have made you old too soon. One of us had to do the worrying and you did it. You do not know yourself. You have the capacity for loving some man with your whole heart. If you find that man permit yourself to love him. Ask no questions and have no doubts. That is the one great adventure." And then, deeper and deeper along the black tunnel into which he steadily receded, he said in a changed and terrible voice: "Aurora — my life has been a failure." When she touched his cheek she knew he was dead.

There was no shock. This event had been long foreshadowed and her first thought as she bent to kiss him was that his face had turned young and a little eager, as though, having stayed in one place too long, the old excitement returned once more for his final journey. She sat down in the doorway, her shoulder against its edge, her arms idle in her lap. Her shoulders bent a little, her head dropped.

Coming along the road, Jim Keene saw her in this attitude and recognized her as the girl who had the previous night asked him about the doctor. When he rode before the shanty she looked up and he observed that the fear and strain of that occasion had been replaced by an expression as near bottomless despair as he had ever seen. As much as it was against his manners to dismount before being invited, he stepped from the saddle and moved to the door and saw the dead man inside.

"Your father?"

"Yes."

It was a tone of heartbreak, of a world fallen forever. She wasn't crying. It looked to him as though her feelings were deadlocked, leaving her wholly powerless; once in his own career he had known something distantly similar when, struck in the pit of the stomach, he could not breathe, speak or move. He sat down beside her. "Maybe," he said, in the most sympathetic of voices, "I can help," and took her shoulders and pulled her against his chest.

He felt the quick loosening of her body and then he was listening to the sudden onset of her crying. He said nothing. He sat still, watching color come back to her cheeks. Her hair was a solid black, lustrous in the sunlight; the smell of it was sweet. She was tall for a woman and her shoulders were square and strong, and there was a substance to her body; it was warm and firm in his arms. Her skin was lightly browned by the sun and her lips were broad and on the edge of being full — the lips of a giving woman, but not of a pliant one. He had seen her only once before, but even then she had left an impression with him. The impression had remained.

The weight went suddenly from his arms; she straightened and gave him a full, quick look in which he witnessed a self-willed pride now deliberately shutting out the softer things he had seen.

He stood up with his hat in his hand. A rider showed on the desert, slowly jogging forward on a big horse — a nester riding all arms and feet. The sun was half up in the east, red from late fall's dust. Sagebrush carpeted the desert as far as sight ran. On the southern horizon a blue haze beautifully shimmered. He said: "What can I do for you?"

She had never really noticed him before. Now it was his voice that drew her attention, a voice soft as summer's wind. He was young, his face long and thoughtful and thick-tanned from wind and sun and from health. When he looked out upon the desert his lids came together and she caught the poised and thorough alertness of his attention, as though he lived on small margins of safety and watched those margins with care. But when he turned to her she saw the kindness of his eyes — and the approval in them.

Her deep beliefs were secret and lonely ones, seldom shared. It surprised her to find she was explaining herself to him. "It was always a bright and wonderful world for my father, with nothing unkind in it. But at the last the color of it died out and that was the greatest hurt he ever had. I think that is why I cried — because he had to see anything dark."

"Maybe," said Jim Keene, "it was kind of a desert dark, with the stars all shining and the wind blowing cool from the west. When I take the trail I'd like to start in shadows like that. You can't see heaven when the sun's shining."

He had a voice with idle melody in it; he was thinking about her and trying to be kind. Then she remembered the way he laughed when he had shoved the drunk into Red John's arms. Behind that laughter had been a full knowledge of his act and all that it might mean. He was a strange man.

The rider came steadily up and rounded at the cabin, being Spackman from the homestead two miles east. Spackman said: "Your father better?"

She stood up. "He's dead, Fritz." That was all. It was

a simplicity, Keene thought, that cut through everything. She was through crying and through being afraid.

"I will send the woman over," said Spackman. "I will send to town for Ellenburg. It is necessary for the certificate. We must of course bury him today."

"Yes, Fritz."

"So," said Spackman and turned away. "That's all you want?"

"When you come back," said Aurora Brant, "will you please bring your wagon?"

"Also I will see Cannon. He will make the coffin and Mrs. Cannon will line it as she did for my baby." He looked at Jim Keene, not knowing him; but since there were necessary things to be done he said to Keene, "You will dig," and rode away.

Aurora spoke to Keene: "I wouldn't want to delay you."

He said: "What is a day, or a year?"

He didn't understand the shadow which made its brief appearance on her face. But she was thinking, "So Father would have said."

She had asked that the grave be dug at the corner of the claim which overlooked the river. Keene had finished this chore when he saw her leave the crowd of neighbors at the house and cross the field. She passed him and dropped to the edge of the bluff; and as he came over to her he saw that she had her eyes on the cabin beyond the ford. He sat down beside her and rolled up a cigarette. For a moment her attention turned to him. She touched his hand. "You've been good," she murmured, and then her mind traveled away.

She had twenty dollars, not the two hundred she had told her father; and she was alone. Never again would she watch her father's face grow eager as he thought of moving to some new-promised wonder; never again would she silently, wearily wait for that eagerness to wear away and discontent to return. She had never let him see how much she hated all that, how dreary a life it had been for her. Gay and charming, he had taken pains to teach her many things but he had never known how terrible a lesson in improvidence he had furnished her, how great her hatred was of their hand-to-mouth existence, the friendlessness of poverty, the cheap hotel rooms in strange towns, the humiliation of pawning their possessions to eat, the hours of waiting on dreary roads for a friendly wagon to come by.

It had left in her a passionate resolve to possess something so that she might look the world in the face and be proud again. Never henceforth would she be a shadow drifting along the earth; she would take root and grow. No more gaiety, no more high-hearted gambling with tomorrow, no more bright and gallant dawns fading into empty sunsets. She would stay in one place, she would have one spot on earth which belonged to her. That was her fixed resolve; that was the hunger of her heart.

She wouldn't write her mother's people, for that was

the old story of improvidence again, another version of asking for a free ride and a free meal. She would stay here. She had decided that months ago when she realized her father could not live out the summer. She wasn't a homestead woman and she couldn't handle a plow like Mrs. Spackman but, looking across the river to the cabin, she knew there was another way to survive. She would have a roof of her own and be strong. She would ask nothing and she would work.

Keene said: "They're coming," and pulled her up. She stood by the grave with Keene, watching the slow and heavy homestead men come across the field with her father's coffin. The crowd made a small ring around the grave and Elijah Patterson, who had once been a preacher in the East, stood at the grave's head and made his talk. All the neighbors had come, impelled by that feeling of help which was so strong among the homesteaders. She noticed too that Cleve Stewart, who owned the Chain and Ball outfit, stood by his horse in the background. He was the only cattleman among them; she remembered that.

Elijah Patterson had finished, and there was nothing left now but to fill in the grave; the homestead men were waiting for her to leave before they began that chore. She delayed a moment, every memory of her father so clear, so painfully alive and dear; and then she said good-by to him and felt the strangeness of being alone.

Keene turned her away. They walked back across the

field to the tar-paper shanty. The homesteaders drifted behind. Spackman came up. "I brought the wagon."

"Will you help me load?"

Spackman went into the house with some of the other men; they came out with Aurora Brant's possessions and lifted them to the wagon — a stove, a bed, a trunk, a crate of dishes, and a board table with its soap-box chairs. Keene noticed a rider follow from the grave — a solid man with a square, outthrust chin. He was around thirty, with the cattle trade stamped on him. He stood before Aurora Brant, saying: "I'm sorry, Aurora." He glanced at the things in the wagon and Keene noticed disappointment cross the bulldog face. The man looked tough and he had the shoulders of a fighter, but there was something different behind his eyes — something perceiving and soft. "You're not moving?"

"Yes, Cleve."

"Come up to Chain and stay a few weeks," said Cleve Stewart.

The homesteaders stood in the background, listening. They stayed away from the cattleman, watching him and not trusting him, not easy in his presence. Once he looked beyond Aurora to them; and his eyes were reserved and cool.

"I'll not be going far away," said Aurora. She paused and watched him carefully. "Only across the ford to that cabin."

Spackman, rising to the wagon seat, had gotten as far as the wheel hub. He dropped back to the ground.

"What's that?" Mrs. Cannon said, sharp and alarmed. "Aurora, don't you do that!"

Fear came out of these people like a smell. Keene, now watching Cleve Stewart, noticed how grave his face became as he shook his head. "You can't do that, Aurora."

She said: "Would the cattlemen kill a woman, Cleve?"

An embarrassed blush crossed his face; he dipped his chin toward the ground. Keene looked across the river at the cabin and though he didn't know the story he had seen enough in Prairie City to make an accurate guess. There never was any change in this old hatred between cattle and plow. He admired Aurora Brant for the way she stood in the clear and sunless evening, for her simplicity, for the will that shone out of her, for the changelessness of her purpose.

Cleve Stewart said: "The cabin's on the wrong side of the river, Aurora. It is on Broken Bit grass. I can't help you."

"I didn't ask for help, Cleve."

"Even if I could," said Stewart, struggling with his conscience, "I wouldn't. I'm a ranch owner. I've got to protect my grass. I'd have to stick with them when they protect their grass."

"Not your grass," said Aurora quietly. "It never was yours or theirs. It belongs to the government. It is open to whoever files on it."

Cleve Stewart started to speak, but he looked beyond Aurora to the homesteaders and Keene saw the man slowly shut his mind against them. These two worlds of cattle and plow had no meeting ground. There could never be truce or tolerance between them. There could never be anything but a fight for survival. All he said was: "I'm sorry, Aurora."

Spackman spoke uncertainly: "I don't know about me drivin' over there."

Keene said: "All right, I'll drive the wagon over."

Stewart gave Keene an affronted look. He recognized Keene's type at once — one horseman instantly identifying another. He said: "You're no nester, friend."

Spackman made up his mind. "To hell with those cowmen. I'll do it."

"Spackman," called his wife, "you be careful! You got enough trouble."

But Spackman was a fighter. "We'll see," he said, and whipped the team toward the ford.

"I'm sorry," said Stewart. Tipping his hat to Aurora, he rode away.

The stove had been set up in the yard, pending a thorough cleaning of the log house; and Keene and Aurora had eaten. Now it was a full star-shining dark with the river rustling on the gravel ford and somewhere a coyote crying and wind moving cool and soundless over the earth.

Keene said: "You'll need a man to set up that stove. You'll need a man for a lot of things. How will you plow, how will you build a fence?" After a thoughtful pause he added, "How will you stick?"

She had learned his name only a moment before and used it now. "I'll stick, Jim. I'll never move. Wait and see." Then she brought her glance to his face. "But you'll not be here to see."

He stood by his horse, a thick rawboned shadow in the darkness. He was a man hard to know, he was different than any man she had met. He was smiling and his voice had a soft, swinging tone. "Good luck."

"You've been kind," she murmured, watching him rise to the saddle. He removed his hat and he ceased to smile. He had touched her life and now he was moving on. She found herself saying, "What will you be doing?"

"Just riding — just looking."

"Jim," she said with a vehemence that surprised her, "never do that! You'll grow old, you'll find nothing, you'll die disappointed."

"What else can a man do?"

"Good luck," she said, and watched him disappear in the shadows.

Coyotes were crying all through the ridges at either side of the valley. She listened to Keene's horse tap a slow beat from the earth and heard the sound die. Loneliness flowed in the shadows; there were no homestead lights visible from this low side of the river, no friendliness shining through the night. She turned into the cabin and undressed and lay on the bed, hearing the steady rustle of the water. She thought of her father and of his voice, so eager and cheerful, and his smile which had taken the sting from all his shortcomings. Sadness weighted her down; the sudden solitariness of her life was new and hard to bear. But despite that she was sure of her future. This cabin where a man had died was her home. His name had been Garratt and that would be the name of the settlement. She knew exactly what she would do; she drifted into sleep.

She was roused by the sound of horses scuffing near the cabin and the murmur of voices. Something struck against the iron stove and a man cursed and the stove rang loud in the night and seemed to fall from its legs. "Blackie," said a man, "that's a horse over there. Take it along."

She flung on her robe and slid across the cabin's rough floor in her bare feet and opened the door. She saw two riders on foot in the foreground and two other men farther away. She called out: "Who are you?"

One of the men called: "A woman!"

"Sister," said a voice, "you get the hell out of here tomorrow. We're takin' the horse. You'll find it in three-four days, somewhere out in the valley."

"Blackie," said one of the farther-stationed riders, "whut's movin' over there beyond you?"

Blackie grunted as he turned. "Where?"

A gunshot made its dry, flat breach in the night. Aurora pulled back from the door, seeing the short spurt of that weapon's muzzle. Blackie ran into the deeper shadows; the other three men were suddenly fighting their horses. Blackie yelled, "Wait!" The gun spoke again, a bullet scuffed the earth. Blackie's horse reared high in the darkness and ran off, leaving him afoot. Blackie was a thin-bent shadow in the night as he raced toward the other three. The gun steadily searched the yard. She saw Blackie lift himself behind one of the riders. There was an answering fire from these men. Powder smell filled the yard, but the first gun kept on, patient and unhurried, and Blackie yelled in quick pain and then the group rushed northward.

A man rose from the earth, walking forward. When he spoke Aurora recognized Jim Keene's voice. There was amusement in it, as though this had been an expected thing. "You're all right?"

"I thought you had gone."

He was before her. He was near enough for her to see his face. He was smiling and pleased. "You see?" he said. "This is how it will be."

"Tomorrow," she said, "I'll send to town for a gun."

"Tomorrow," he said, "I believe I'll stake out a claim around here. It looks like fun."

"Jim," she said, "you're a man. They'll kill you."

The smile remained. She heard the soft, windy excitement in his voice. "Mighty odd. I've ridden a thousand miles to keep out of trouble and now that I look back it has been a dreary time. I think I'll stand pat. Maybe what I want is here."

"What do you want, Jim?"

He said in a slow, half-puzzled way, "I thought it was peace and quiet. Maybe it isn't that."

III

ON LOST MAN RIDGE

This hour of the morning — it was before five — contained a silence which picked up the crackling of the fire and magnified it into minor explosions; the clank of the stove lid rolled on and on across the valley. To either edge of the valley the pine ridges, Lost Man Ridge in the east and Skull Ridge to the west, stood purple-black in a sunless, glass-clear light. Night's thin chill clung to the earth. Jim Keene, she noticed, had camped a quarter mile up the creek. As soon as the coffee boiled she called to him.

He came up on his horse, his hair wet from a swim in the creek. He had a tremendous vitality. There was no morning sourness in him, no sleepy irritability. The swim had brightened the blood glow of his cheeks, the smell of coffee and bacon made him smile.

Perhaps it was the coffee and bacon; she wasn't entirely certain of that, for he watched her with the same awareness and approval she had noticed the previous day. She was attractive in his eyes. Those eyes made pictures of her which seemed to please him as he sat down to eat breakfast.

"You slept well?"

"When I realized you were not far away," she admitted, "I slept like a log. Today I'm going to town. Among other things, I'll get a gun."

"I'll be around," he pointed out.

"I can't always be depending on you." Then, because she was more curious and more hopeful than it was wise to be, she asked a point-blank question. "What keeps you here?"

He smiled. His eyes had a long-reaching expression in them; even as he studied her he was seeing things beyond her. His face was alert and a small swift air of excitement brushed fugitively across it. "What makes a man travel," he said in his soft voice, "what makes him stop?" He changed the subject. "I'll be around while you're gone. The boys might figure to burn the cabin."

"I'd build another one," she answered at once. "I'm going to stay. Do you see what I see here?"

"Nice valley and fine grass. It is better land than across the river. But that will help you none. You can't farm alone."

"Here's the road from Prairie City. There's the road running along the edge of the river from Wells to Argonaut. Everything meets here where they cross. That's the way towns are made."

"But nothing stops here," he pointed out. "The cattle outfits will see to that."

"Maybe," she murmured. "But they can't shoot a woman." She rose and washed the dishes. Afterwards she saddled her horse for a trip to town. Idle against the house corner, he noticed on her face a mild expression of stubbornness, as though she foresaw trouble and was prepared for it. It turned her into a cool self-contained woman who wanted her own way and meant to have it. Sunlight burst over Lost Man Ridge, changing valley grass from gray to amber gold in one dramatic transition; the coolness of night evaporated. He watched her pull up her shoulders, the way her body changed curves when she settled on the saddle. Her lips were red and when she looked down at him an expression formed on them and went away. Her lips, he had discovered, were the first to show her thoughts; and now they didn't match the resolution of her face. She was two different persons.

She started from the yard. Beyond the house she swung the horse to look back at him and in her glance then was a woman's inevitable contradiction — a worry for him and a pleased awareness of his presence. She said: "You shouldn't be here, Jim, but I'm glad you are."

She crossed the ford and let the horse have its morning run; thereafter she settled to an alternate run and walk through the streaming sunlight, through late fall's golden haze. The sagebrush flats ran on and on, broken by the dotted shapes of homestead houses. In the air was the dry, tickling pungence of cured grass and sage and the oncoming smell of winter. It was a morning that, like all desert mornings, held a tonic freshness, buoying her and making her believe anything was possible. At this precise moment she needed desperately to believe that.

Yet when she reached Prairie City and racked the horse in front of Worsham and Ross most of the confidence was gone. She faced the store's doorway, watching Worsham wait on a customer, and for a moment the purpose which had brought her here almost died. All that held it was the memory of those long years in which her father had run away from every decision and every showdown. She thought in half panic: "This can't be in me. I must never run, never give up. I've got to start now. I've got to go forward. I've got to." Worsham's customer came out of the store. Aurora went in.

It was easier to talk to him when he was alone and his pleasant manner helped. He said: "I heard about your dad. I'm sorry."

She said: "I wanted to talk to you."

She saw the immediate change, the withdrawal of sympathy and the onset of reserve. A thousand requests from impoverished homesteaders had given him a protective intuition. She could see his mind reaching for the old, ready answer. "Been a hard year," he offered. "Times bad for all of us."

"I have moved over to the Garratt place, across the Silver Bow ford."

"I'd heard."

"So soon?"

His answer was dry. "That kind of news travels fast."

His hand moved along the counter, the signal of his desire to be about his work. It was difficult for her to go on and his manner took all the conviction from her voice. "It is a long ride for the homesteaders into town for supplies. They'd be better customers if they had a store near them. I'd like to start one at the ford. I thought you might be interesting in stocking it on credit for me. A fifty-fifty partnership."

He said: "Why move across the river to start it?"

She drew a cross on the table with her finger. "Here's the road up the valley. Here's the road running along the river. They meet at Garratt's cabin. All travelers meet there."

The skeptic dryness increased. "What travelers?"

"Not long from now," she said, "the valley will be full of homesteads. People will be using those roads."

"Not while Broken Bit's there they won't."

"You're not interested?"

"No," said Worsham.

She went into the sunlight and moved along the walk without conscious direction. Her mouth was dry and she thought quickly back over the talk and remembered all the things she had forgotten to say. Her fear of failure increased and she was self-conscious enough in this new role to believe the town had its eyes on her. This, she realized, was why her father had always run away. He had been too sensitive to endure rebuff.

She arrived at the corner of the bank building and stopped and now found herself looking fixedly at the

small bank window. Tim Sullivan, who ran the Cattleman's Palace, came from the bank with a canvas sack
of silver coins; he tipped his hat and she said mechan-
ically, "Good morning," and for a moment his bright
eyes studied her. Then he went on.

She thought: "I must not be afraid," and went into the
bank. She had met the banker only once during the year
she had lived on the Silver Bow, and had been impressed
by his kindness. He was kind now. He stood behind the
counter and listened to her and she didn't see Worsham's
cold, withdrawing expression on his face. He waited until
she had said everything she wanted to say, but when she
had finished she learned that men had many ways of
listening and of saying no.

"You don't know business very well, Miss Brant," he
told her. "Broken Bit is my big customer. What would it
say if I loaned money to you?"

"Isn't there room for everybody on the desert?"

"If I helped you Grat DePard would be here before
sundown." His voice was sympathetic; it cushioned his
refusal. "What would be your security?"

"Nothing."

"You see? After all, it isn't my money — it's the de-
positors'." He smiled the sting away as he had learned
to do long ago in his business. Then he added with a touch
of fatherliness: "This is a lonesome country for a woman.
There are a hundred good single men here — in town or
on the desert. Have you thought of that?"

"No," she said, "but thank you," and left the bank at

the same moment Jesse Morspeare came from Worsham's store and moved toward her. She knew, from his half-satisfied stare, that he had discovered her errand. He went by her into the bank, the weight of his body brushing slightly against her shoulder. Presently she heard him grumbling at the banker. She wasn't afraid any more but a kind of iron band closed around her head as she tried to think of other sources, other means; her mind kept circling and coming back, finding nothing. Dust puffed up from the traveling hoofs of a passing rider; a swamper slowly swept refuse through the saloon's doorway and even at this distance the stale smell of whisky and old tobacco smoke was a rank emanation. Above the saloon four windows showed half-drawn curtains. A woman looked from one of these, at Aurora, still-caught by her curiosity or her envy. Aurora lowered her eyes. Tim Sullivan stood in a patch of sunlight by the saloon wall, a cloud of cigar smoke covering his face. Aurora knew he was watching her. It was near noon and hunger turned her toward the hotel. Moving along the walk, she held her shoulders up, her chin up. She looked straight ahead and held her lips together. She went into the hotel's empty dining room.

She sat with both hands in her lap, remembering the banker's hint of marriage. There were few things a woman could do for herself in a man's world. She had heard that many times, but now she knew what it meant. She could marry, she could live on the bounty of relations or she could do as the woman above the saloon did. She moved the pewter caster around and around with the tip of her finger. Her eyes were gray against the inshining sunlight; she was outwardly composed but her mind kept pounding at the barriers and found no weak spot. The waitress brought on the meal, family style, and steps beat along the room. Looking up, she saw Tim Sullivan paused near her.

His voice was extremely courteous. "My respects to you concernin' your father," but a moment later the waitress went back to the kitchen and then Sullivan's bright Irish eyes showed a worldly, amused wisdom. "You got no help."

"No."

"And the news is out, like news always is, and Grat will be havin' his private laugh."

"Is that the reason?"

" 'Tis Grat's town, is it not, and his desert?"

"Sit down."

He showed a small surprise; his eyes sobered. "That was a kind heart speakin'. But I'll stand." He was a stubby man with soft hands, with an Irishman's rich complexion and a saloon man's thorough knowledge of the sins of men tucked in the knowing corners of his face. It was a politician's face. Behind its affability lay an opportunist's acceptance of the world as he found it. But in Sullivan, as in every Irishman, was one hot streak of ancient dissent which occasionally had its way. He said now, softly, for no other ears than Aurora Brant's: "Now I like to see spunk and it is born in me to love a fight and see a great man fall. You should not have asked Worsham, or the bank. Do you not know that money is a timid thing? Men who have it fear the world, and themselves even. Have you seen the week's paper?"

He had the paper folded in his pocket. He brought it out and placed it on the table before her, still folded. He said: "I should not open it, were I you, till you had the evenin' heavy on your hands at home."

She put her hand on it and knew its inner folds contained something. She saw the edge of greenbacks. She looked up at him in astonishment and found his eyes dancing with the pleasure of his own intrigue. She said: "I've nothing to give you."

"And did I ask it?" he retorted. "On my poker tables there is a little slot in the center, down which a man drops a white chip each deal. That is for the house. If a man plays long enough, no matter how much he may win, the house will have it all at last. I am comfortable. But comfort is poor diet for an Irishman. Didn't I tell you I love a fighter?"

She was so long silent that he at last said with some concern: "It comes from a saloon man. It is the money of appetite. But you'd not refuse it for that?"

"No," she said gently, "I am thinking of how long you may have to wait before I repay you."

"Ah, that," he said, and dropped his voice until the

words only rubbed in his throat. "This will be our private affair. And do your buying not here but at Argonaut. Now you must find a man who will drive a wagon for you."

"I will find one."

"No," he said, "it will not be like that. By tomorrow Grat will have word around and 'twill be worth a man's life to touch a horse for your sake." He looked at the floor, taking her troubles to him and seeing things to worry about which she couldn't see. The waitress came out of the kitchen. Tim Sullivan spoke in his heartiest voice, "I knew you'd like to see a paper from your old home town," and left the dining room.

She was no longer hungry but a sense of economy forced her to eat the meal. As soon as she had finished she returned to the street and went into Caples' hardware store, buying a secondhand Winchester and a box of cartridges. It was past one o'clock when she left Prairie.

Jesse Morspeare came up to the bar and faced Sullivan. "That girl's after money. Get any from you?"

Sullivan laughed in his face. "Now what would a nice lady be doin' askin' favors from the notorious Sullivan?" He moved a bottle from the back bar, placed it before the big man, and suavely changed the thought in Jesse Morspeare's unwieldy mind. "You've got an imposin' bulk for a star, Jesse."

That part of Sullivan which was pure cynic despised the gratitude which the buttered compliment produced;

the softer side of Sullivan pitied what he saw. "You think so?" asked Morspeare, hungry to hear more. "Yeah?"

"Sure," said Sullivan. "As sheriff you'll stand like a rock."

"I'll win," said Morspeare. "Grat's roundin' up the votes. I'll get the cattle bunch solid." He was a slow and dull-witted creature who had nothing but great physical strength; that and an abject respect for Grat DePard. When Jesse got to be sheriff, Sullivan reasoned, he would be Grat's faithful dog. He had smashed the homesteader Spackman to the dust not because he had any particular grudge against Spackman, but to demonstrate his loyalty to cattle; and never for a moment had he realized the brutality of that act. A clever man like Grat would hold him by the nose and lead him without difficulty. Without that guidance Jesse would be a loose and terrible animal.

Jesse turned from the bar. "I got to tell Grat whut she's after." The swamper came through the doorway the same moment Jesse reached it. Jesse's elbow lifted slyly and caught the swamper in the stomach, slamming him against the doorsill. Jesse grinned at the swamper and went out. A dismal spasm ran across the swamper's face; he laced his hands over his belly and a sucking gust of air rushed into his wide-open mouth. He moved his head at Sullivan, pale and helpless. Sullivan's teeth bit into his cigar; he didn't speak until his voice could be soft. "Never mind, Tonk. That little trick will kill him one of these days."

Keene watched Aurora disappear beyond the opposite rim of the river bluff, attracted by the shape she made in the sun, in the golden haze of dust. These were the things, though he didn't know it, his senses forever awaited in eagerness — sounds and blends of fragrance and scenes which took fugitive shape and left their unforgettable impressions: the single moment when a campfire flame formed a perfect taper against the heart of night; the echo of one word spoken by a woman from the depths of her soul; the cold and immaculate deadliness of a diamond-back coiled at the instant of striking; the thread of some strange smell in the spring wind which, caught briefly and by accident, broke every old thread of a man's career and set him off on strange roads. These were the fragments of a greater mystery, the revealed pieces of an unrevealed puzzle whose answer he sought — yet knew not that he sought it. All the cold ashes of his campfires made an unerring line of search. Some duty, some labor, some love. Somewhere —

He took the ax and shovel from Aurora Brant's piled possessions and rode out upon Cloud Valley, aiming at Lost Man Ridge a mile east. He crossed a shallow sparkling oxbow bend of the creek, passed through knee-high meadow grass turned amber by the sun and softly furrowed by the wind. At the foot of the ridge he paused to scan the dark edge of timber above him. A crow flapped heavily from a treetop and Keene's glance whipped to that area in the timber, a never-dead suspicion clawing its way to the surface. But the crow fled without making its harsh warning cry and presently his alertness relaxed. The ridge carried him up a hundred feet so that he saw the long course of the valley and the figure of a single rider moving along the road in the direction of the ford.

In the timber he hunted up a few thin pines and cut and trimmed them. During the rest of the morning he dragged them to Aurora's cabin to furnish a temporary supply of wood. Meanwhile as he rode he decided upon the location of a cabin site for himself. His preference was for a small baylike recess in the ridge which made a shelter from the winds, but if it gave him shelter it was also a trap in time of trouble, permitting a marksman to come to the near edge of the pines and wait for a shot. Therefore he chose a spot by the oxbow bend of the creek in the middle of the valley, half a mile north of Aurora Brant's.

He cooked his coffee and fried his bacon and ate beside the creek. He marked out a small room on the ground — with an adjoining lean-to extension for his horse — and fell to cutting strips of sod two feet square. By the middle of the afternoon, working steadily along, he had the walls of the soddy begun. Riding had toughened him but this kind of labor pulled at muscles he seldom used and brought the fresh salt sweat to his cheeks. All his life he had handled horses and cattle, looking down upon a homesteader's endless chores with a horseman's disdain. Now here he was grubbing at the earth in the manner of the homesteader. He straightened and laughed outright and then he ceased to laugh. Why was he staying?

Maybe, he thought hopefully, it was natural for a man to grow weary of riding and to rest awhile. But he remembered Jesse Morspeare using his huge hands to club Spackman into the dust and he remembered Aurora Brant facing the cattle outfits alone — and he knew he was lying to himself. These homesteaders were humble people wishing for peace, knowing nothing about the ways of the gun. They were the lambs in the field to DePard and Morspeare and Red John. This was why he stayed.

He was again silently laughing at a man who, deliberately riding away from trouble, paused deliberately to invite other trouble. In his amusement was a regret at the passage of an illusion — the illusion that he could change himself; in it too were the relief and the certainty which come to one who, long idle, returns to his old and familiar trade.

A rider emerged from the timber on the western ridge, quartering into the valley. Keene moved over to the corner of the soddy and belted on his gun, and returned to his shovel; presently he saw it was a girl riding with that rhythm which comes only to those born and weaned on a saddle. She rounded before him and spoke in bluntest manner. "This year you dig out the grass and next year it will be weeds."

He propped himself against the shovel. Sweat ran down his cheek hollows; his cotton shirt clung to his long chest and when he smiled at her wrinkles cut a fine-netted pattern around the edge of his eyes. She appraised him in a single, surprised inspection.

"You're no homesteader. That shovel looks as funny in your hands as a woman's bonnet would on your head."

He said: "Now that's speaking straight out."

"You're a rider. Stick with your own kind. If you want a job come up to my father's ranch. The Crews outfit — Rafter T. Stop making a fool of yourself with a shovel. Don't you know a cowhand is a miserable man off a horse? I'm Portia Crews. You want the job?"

"No," he said.

Her eyelids crept nearer. She looked down with a slanting, inquisitive glance and broke the horse from its impatient fiddling with one competent twist of the reins. She had yellow hair and an oval face on which sunlight pleasantly fell. There was a faint high-handedness in her manner, a freedom and an authority. Yet she was an attractive girl who could change her temper whenever she wished; having come here to give him hell, she recognized one of her own kind and was full of interest and friendly motive.

"I heard you were a little bit tough," she reflected. "Thought I'd find out. Red John told me. You're the fellow who tossed Snap in Red John's lap last night. Red John didn't care for that. He's a bad man to make an enemy of."

"So I gathered."

She listened to him with her head aside. Her eyes

were hazel. They opened fully on him to let out a woman's centered personal interest. "I guess you would gather that. You're one of these quick ones. You do a lot of figuring. You're figuring me now. What's your name?"

"Jim Keene."

"Jim," she said, "what's all this — a bet you made when you were drunk? You know this is no good. Every time you dig up a shovel of that ground you feel silly. Can you feature yourself milking a cow or walking peg-legged behind a plow? No, you can't."

He said, idly: "I'm saddle-sore and I'm tired of the sight of my shadow."

"Ah," she said. "Then you haven't been drunk lately. Maybe it's what you need. I know your kind." Her voice dropped softly on him. "Running off from something. From trouble." Her question was light and quick and insistent. "A woman?"

He shook his head.

"You're probably a smooth liar," she observed, holding his attention with her glance. She hadn't smiled at him yet but her eyes lightened as she read him; color ran across her face and her hands moved on the saddle-horn. She had a firm-rounded body filled with a vitality that produced its physical reaction in him. There was an unconscious daring to her personality, a frank aliveness. When she spoke again he had the impression she had made her judgment of him and would never change it. "You can't stay here. Grat will kill you."

"The gentleman has horns? Fur on his knees?"

Listening to his voice, Portia Crews liked the music it made and the little edge of irony it held. For the first time during the meeting she took her eyes from him. She thought: He's no fool. He's used his gun. He knows about those things. He's dangerous — he's kind. Which is he the most of? How does he like his women — what does he do with them?

She had her glance on the cabin down the creek and then she remembered something and brought her attention back to Keene.

"I hear that homestead girl has moved to the cabin."

"Last night."

Portia Crews murmured, "So," in a long, speculating breath and searched his face for a sign. She saw only a poker expression which told her nothing, and reined her horse about. But she turned to add as a casual afterthought: "If you ride up our way the door's open."

"Thanks," he said, and watched her fade across the grassland at a steady run. Everything she did was done without delay. He rolled a smoke and found himself weary of piling sod. He abandoned the job and rode over to the trees to cut a ridgepole and rafters. It was four o'clock then and Aurora Brant had not yet returned. When he reached the top of the ridge he saw a single rider advancing across the Silver Bow flats toward the ford, and believed it to be her. Sunlight, low in the west, threw long reddening waves of light across the sagelands. All the horizons were filled with a powder haze.

IV

DESERT AUTOCRAT

DURING the middle of the afternoon Grat DePard came down to the Black Bluff ford, twelve miles east of Aurora Brant's place, with four hundred steers intended for the railroad stock pens in Prairie. Red John and a crew of five did the moving, but DePard went along to be sure they were not pushing the beef too fast, thereby reducing the marketable poundage. For Grat DePard was an owner who ran his outfit with a hard fist and permitted no variation from his instructions.

In those hills he was the largest owner and the greatest power. Rough and illiterate as he was, some bitter brand of ambition drove him through alternate tempers; he could be cunning and soft, he could rise to a tremendous rage. In every respect he was the desert autocrat insisting upon his rights and his authority, suspicious always, a grasper of pennies and a watcher of potato parings in his kitchen, a schemer of great schemes, a respector of one thing only — power. He was a sagebrush Prussian general on his horse, planning his own distant ends.

Jesse Morspeare, riding down the Silver Bow, found him here and gave him the news.

"Money?" said DePard. "What for?"

"She wants to set up a store in Garratt's old cabin,"

said Jesse Morspeare, and held himself respectfully still, anxiously wanting to be important in Grat De-Pard's eyes.

DePard rode to the ford, talked a moment with the crew, and came back with Red John. He said: "We'll go see that woman," and turned his horse. The three rode westward along the rim of the river.

Morspeare said: "Think I'll win, Grat?"

"I'll take care of that."

"Lot of homesteaders against us."

Grat DePard looked at Morspeare. "Be a good idea if you'd keep your damned dumb hands off those people until the election's over."

"You mean Spackman?" asked Morspeare anxiously. "I was only tryin' to show the ranch boys I was on their side."

"They knew that already. You go back to town and keep your feet where they won't hurt anybody."

Morspeare obediently swung away. Red John grinned. "You'd do just as well to run an ape for sheriff. Jesse ain't bright."

"I'll furnish the thinking."

Short of sundown they splashed across the shallow ford and came upon the yard of the Garratt cabin. Aurora had arrived home a few minutes before and was inside; when she came out and thus unexpectedly faced them she had an instant of shock which brought her to a sudden halt at the doorway. Immediately she thought of the rifle she had bought in town. It lay unloaded on the table behind her.

Red John first compelled her attention by the attack of an unmistakably acquisitive glance which went along her body with a complete interest. He was a full-blooded man, thoroughly sure of himself and never doubtful of his mastery. She saw the bright hunting glint flare in his eyes and at once turned her face to Grat DePard.

DePard spoke in a way that was like the personal pronouncement of law. He was so certain that he didn't even bother to threaten her. "You'll get no money and you'll start no store, neither on this side of the river nor on the other. As for homesteading, you're plainly not able to do it. Even if you were able, I wouldn't permit you to break this sod. This is my graze. You knew that when you moved over. Maybe you believed I'd let you stay, you bein' a woman. I'm a businessman first and a gentleman second. You move back where you came from. Better if you left the country altogether."

"Is this your land, Mr. DePard?"

"My land."

From the corner of her eyes she noticed Jim Keene coming across the valley at a steady run. "You are mistaken," she said. "This is government land. You know that."

DePard waved it aside. "Let's not talk about it. You've been in this country long enough to know law is one thing and possession another. I've got possession. Law or no law, I won't let homesteaders break up my graze. If I did I'd be out of business. You're a practical woman. You fight for your rights. So do I. If you were in my place you'd be doing the same thing I'm doing. I admire your courage, but you ain't staying."

Keene came into the yard. He stopped his pony and leaned back on the saddle and she noticed the same expression on his face she had seen in Prairie the previous night — the alert interest breaking through idle composure. His arrival produced a change in the yard at once. Grat DePard threw a swift glance at him and afterwards ignored him. But Red John was no longer self-contented; he swung his horse to face Keene and he placed a close watch on him, his own muscles obviously tightened for anything that might come. His assurance, Aurora thought, seemed to have been jarred, and for some reason he hated Keene at once.

She spoke to DePard. "Would you shoot a woman, Mr. DePard — as you did Garratt?"

Red's glance moved at her. His eyes widened, he stirred his shoulders.

"I can skin cats in a lot of ways," said DePard. "Think about that."

"Would you have your men shoot me?" she insisted.

Irritation came to DePard's voice. "Never mind the questions. There'll be no shooting, but you'll go."

She wondered at Keene's continuing silence. He sat on the horse and seemed to be lost in pleasant memories. Smoke curled around his eyes and his hands were folded on the saddlehorn. She turned into the house and got the Winchester and came to the doorway again.

Red John said, "Now, now," and liked the sudden turn of the scene not at all. He wheeled his horse to face Aurora and threw a questioning look at DePard. The situation had gotten out of control for Red John; he was up against the unknown factor of a woman with a gun. DePard straightened, immediately pulling his muscles tight.

"Have you ever had a woman shoot at you, Mr. De-Pard?" asked Aurora.

DePard shrugged his shoulders. "I thought you were a practical girl. Maybe I better point out you can't stand in that door with a gun twenty-four hours a day."

"You're accustomed to having other men do your dirty chores," she observed. "But if they touch me or anything that is mine I'll know that you ordered it. You've taught me a trick. You ride through this country a good deal — through the hills at night. You can't always be watching the brush, can you?"

"Don't talk like that to me, girl," said DePard, wounded to the pith of his vanity. "Try that and I'll put you in jail. There's law to cover that."

"What law?" she asked him, so gently. "We are practical people. That is what you said. The law will do you no good if you're shot from ambush."

DePard said nothing more. Wrenching his horse around he beckoned at Red and raced away with the foreman behind him.

Keene said: "Fine — fine."

She was weak, her courage was gone. "They'll leave me alone, Jim," she murmured and desperately tried to believe it.

He said: "Can you shoot?"

"Yes."

"You've made your bluff. Never back up on it. If I'm not around and a Broken Bit man passes within fifty feet of this cabin throw a bullet at him. I never saw a man yet who liked that." He had kept his eyes on the departing pair and now saw them stop a short distance down the valley. Presently Red John came back, made a wide sweep of the house and crossed the ford to the Silver Bow flats. Grat DePard continued up the valley. Keene turned his horse and moved out on the heels of the Broken Bit owner.

Grat DePard had said to Red John: "Go back to the flats. You tell those homesteaders if they give that girl any help of any kind they'll suffer for it. Tell them I don't want to catch any of them on this side of the river at any time."

Red John went away. Grat DePard moved up the valley, his temper simmering in him, his mind quick and crafty. He didn't look back but he knew Keene was following him. He had deliberately ignored Keene during the talk with Aurora Brant. Recognizing Keene's type at first glance, he had not been quite able to gauge his possibilities, and therefore had let him alone; for De-Pard, autocratic as he was, never quarreled with a man until he knew the strength of the man and never picked a fight until he had chosen his own ground. When he reached the beginnings of Keene's dugout and realized that Keene was still coming, he turned his horse and waited.

When Keene came up the first thing DePard said was: "This yours?"

"Mine. Any comments?"

DePard permitted himself no hard words then for he saw he faced a bad moment. Keene gave him a glance that startled him to the bottom of his belly, it was so openly in search of trouble. This wasn't the same man at all. DePard said guardedly:

"What are you hot about, friend?"

Keene said: "You damned mongrel — you're yellow."

DePard spoke through his close lips. "In that, friend, you are mistaken." His left hand held the reins above the horn, never moving; his right hand was carefully on the pommel; and thus he held himself together, riding out this terrible moment. He knew his own ability as a fighter but he could only guess about this other man's skill; and his guess, when he made it, bothered him considerably. Keene's readiness came right at his teeth; the man wanted to fight. So, unsure of his chances, DePard made his own silent play for survival.

Keene circled his pony completely around DePard. DePard remained rigid, not venturing to look back. The sun was down and grayness ran in sheets across the flats, and in this grayness DePard's face was strained and dark. Keene faced him again. Keene said: "You've got that girl worried. Don't bother her again."

DePard made no move until Keene gave him a nod; and then he rode northward, sitting rigid on the saddle and making no extra motion with his hands until the back of his neck loosened. Then he reached for a cigar and looked at his fingers when he lighted the match. He was sweating but his hands were steady. He drew a great breath of smoke into his lungs, relishing the bite of that smoke; and he had his moment of triumph in realizing that his ability to be humble had saved him from disaster.

What puzzled him was Keene's quick change of temper. In the store yard Keene had rested silent on his saddle; during the next few minutes he had changed to a fellow plainly ready to kill. Remembering that recent scene, DePard felt the backlash of its possibilities. For a fact, something very close to death had jumped straight out of the twilight at him.

"Mighty proud," reflected DePard. "And mighty foolish unless he had a scheme in his bonnet. What'd he do it for?"

The memory of his own part in the scene, strangely, did not humiliate him. For DePard was a man who, despising the human race in general, held an enormous respect for courage when he saw it. To DePard a man was top dog or he wasn't; the top dog showed his teeth and the bottom dog ran away. Whatever was good belonged to the top dog if he could take it. It occurred to him now that he had met a man pretty much like himself, a fellow who knew his own strength and had no scruples about using it. That kind was pretty rare; also that kind, in competition with his own ambitions, made the valley too small. "He's here for something," thought DePard, "and I'll find out. Two of us is too many unless we're on the same side of the fence. Now there's a thought." Riding up Cloud Valley, Grat DePard made his plans.

Red John rode into the Spackman yard. "Spackman," he called, "come here," and enjoyed the cracking fear he saw on Spackman's face when the latter came to the door. It was growing into dark at the moment and Spackman made a fine silhouette against the house light. Red John said: "Keep away from that girl and give her no help. And don't cross that river. You don't want trouble, do you?" He left the yard without listening to Spackman's answer.

Seeing Spackman's bravery waver amused Red John, who had no liking for homesteaders. He dropped his message at Cobb's and at Lacey's, at Cannon's. Cannon and Cannon's wife and children were in the soft dusk of the yard, and Jennie came to the kitchen doorway. For the first time this night Red John put on a friendly air; he dropped his hint in a neighborly fashion — as though it were a favor he asked. Jennie's face showed him a smothered excitement and he let his glance cling to her, passing a message over the distance. When he left the yard he thought he had seen an answer. All women liked to be hunted and differed only in the way they wished to be caught. This was a girl that liked mystery; that was the way she wanted to be caught, Red John guessed. Swinging down the prairie he paused at Hoeffer's shanty and completed his errand at the Comrie place. Heading back to the ford he followed the river bluff, this bringing him near the Cannon place again. Dusk had changed to night and presently he saw the shape of Jennie Cannon in the silver shadows. She had caught his message and she had answered. He got down from the horse.

Her face was white and vague in the darkness; she remained still, waiting for him to break the silence. He knew she had deliberately put herself where he might find her.

He said: "You see, Jennie, I don't have horns."

"I guess you've known a lot of women. I heard that."

She was just a homestead girl but she wanted to try her luck on a man who knew women. She wanted to see if she had the pull other women had; she wanted to sharpen her skill on him. Most women were like that.

"I like pretty girls," he said. "You're the prettiest."

"You're just saying that," she retorted. But the compliment did something to her voice. Red John, who had experience at this, touched her carefully on the shoulder and waited to see if she drew back. She didn't draw back and that was enough for him to know. He pulled her forward and kissed her. She gave him no encouragement, but she didn't fight him; she was experimenting with him and with herself — half cold and half warm. Red John stepped away. He had started this with an amused confidence; but she had gotten into him and had set him afire. His voice revealed the rough, hot agitation he felt. "Listen, Jennie, you're sweet."

She laughed at him. She was cooler than he; she was surer. "Is that how you say it to the others?" she murmured. He reached for her again, unsatisfied with half a capture, outraged by her laughter and her assurance. She faded from him, running toward the house, her amusement softly drifting back.

Red John stepped to the saddle, liking this episode not at all. Somehow, she had beaten him at the game, and she had gotten under his skin. She knew it, he thought irritably; her laughter said so. He broke into a steady run, tantalized by the door she had left half open and thinking already of the next meeting. He'd come back. She knew that too. A girl like Jennie liked to play with fire, but pretty soon she got burned. Every dealing he had had with women told him so.

A rider crossed before him, bound toward the Cannon house, and in the shadows Red John made out young Joe Spackman, who was Jennie's steady man. Red John thought in sour amusement: "That's one kiss he won't get."

The valley was a dull bed of silver under the night; out of it came the soft ruffle of wind-stirred grasses. In the sky from rim to rim stars made their cloudy glitter. Keene stood in the yard, hearing a rider splash across the ford and make a wide circle of the cabin; he heard the rider go northward at a steady, dying run. That, he guessed, would be Red John returning to Broken Bit. And because every move in this game was familiar to him, Keene knew what Red John had been doing across the river.

Aurora Brant came to the doorway of the cabin, framed against the light. She had already explained her trip to Prairie City to him — and now added: "I stopped by Spackman's on the way home this afternoon. He's agreed to freight the store stock from Argonaut."

"You're pretty against the light. Pretty — but a target."

She stepped from the doorway and put her shoulders to the cabin wall. "You know so many things like that. It is the sort of an education that should have made you very hard. But you aren't." Then she turned the subject. "I'll never understand what was in Sullivan's mind when he offered me that money. It was a kindness I never expected."

"He saw you walking on the street. Next thing he knew the idea came to him — and he did it. That's the way it happens to a man."

"He had no reason for it."

"Reason means nothing. It is just what comes to a man. When it comes, he's got to do it."

She said: "You haven't said much about my store, Jim. I think you feel I'm not wise."

"You want to do it, don't you?"

"Yes."

"Then that's excuse enough. You don't have to figure if you're wise. It makes no difference."

"No, Jim. I need to know where I'm going — and why."

He said gently: "Look up at the stars. Where are they going?"

The ford's gravel telegraphed the passage of another rider. Keene's cigarette dropped to the ground and struck with a bright bombing of sparks; he was wholly still, seizing every sound and making the story. It was a heavy horse, a homesteader's plow horse. He thought of Red John and this girl's pilgrimage to town, which was common news by now, and he built his guess on the pattern of that. "It will be Spackman," he said, "telling you he can't haul your freight."

It was Spackman. The big Hollander drifted into the yard and swayed on the broad back of his horse. He said: "Aurora, the wife says I don't go. DePard sent that Red John around with threats. If we help you it is to be trouble. I gave you my promise and I'll keep it if you want. But maybe — "

"No, Fritz," said Aurora, "I don't want you to get in trouble."

"I have stood against DePard," said Spackman slowly. "I will stand again. But the old woman — "

"Fritz," said Keene, "would you lend me your team and wagon?"

"That is not too much," said Spackman at once. "That I would do."

"I'll be past your place in half an hour."

"So," said Spackman and went away.

Aurora said: "How did you know he would come and tell me that?"

When he stepped forward she saw the old silent laughter in him, the quick flare of pleased humor. Challenge had come out of the night and he had seized it. This one thing she knew about him — he never passed a challenge by. "Nothing," he said, "ever changes much. I know this game. I guess it is all I do know. I'll pick up Spackman's team and go on to Argonaut. Be back the third day."

She went into the house and came out with Sullivan's money, never thinking that she had met this man only the night before. It was thoroughly natural for her to give him the money. "The wholesale house in Argonaut," she said, "will know what I ought to have." But even then she was thinking, not of the store, but of him. "Why are you doing it, Jim? It would be so much better if you just kept on riding."

"Same as Sullivan. One of those things."

She said: "I watched you stop DePard. I think you must have said terrible things to him. He stood perfectly still when you rode around him. Why quarrel with him when he has so much brutal power?"

"The first thing to know," he told her, "is what kind of a man you've got against you — if he bluffs, if he comes straight at you or slides around the back side, if he's got a weak spot. That's what I wanted to know."

"Be careful, won't you?"

"So long."

"So long, Jim," she murmured, and watched him step to his pony and swing out of the yard. She listened to him cross the ford, she heard the last sound die. Not until then did she realize how completely she had come to depend on him. For now the silence around her was thick and strange and full of menace. She went into the cabin, barring the door.

V

FIRST BLOOD

CLEVE STEWART crossed the upper valley and came upon the ascending grassy chute which was Broken Bit's front entrance. At the head of the chute, in a bowl-shaped break of Lost Man Ridge, DePard had his ranch. Pines surrounded it and the rough foot slopes of Thunderhead Range touched the north edge of its yard. From this hundred-foot elevation Cloud Valley was a long amber plain upon which fall's haze beautifully lay.

Stewart found DePard on a top bar of a corral watching Blackie Naves break a mustard-colored pony; and DePard, who never found another man's work wholly satisfactory, shouted at Naves: "Don't scar him up like that with your spurs! Dammit, I want a salable horse!" He saw Stewart and came off the corral bar. "Want me to tell you something?" he said. "You ride too much. Who's doin' any work when you leave your outfit? You're too easy and your crew soldiers on you to beat hell."

Stewart flushed. He said: "I'll run my outfit," and showed stubbornness in the long throw of his chin. "What are you doing about that girl?"

"I told her to get off. She was a fool and threatened to bushwack me. We'll see — we'll see."

"Listen," said Stewart, "I don't want any rough stuff. I'll talk to her."

"Talk to her then," said DePard. "It won't do you any good. She's borrowed some courage from a man down there. From that rider — that Keene."

"Let the girl alone."

"Cleve," observed DePard cynically, "you're soft. If that girl stays there she'll draw other damned fools across the river, which is the end of the valley for cattle. I won't have it. As soon as I get Morspeare into office I'm going to scare hell out of those nesters across the Silver Bow. I grazed there once and I'll graze there again. You can't let 'em get thicker over there, for pretty soon they'll stampede over here."

"Pretty tough," commented Stewart.

"Nesters?" said DePard. "Hell, they can't fight. Cut their wire and throw a few bullets around the shanties at night and their women will pack up. They'll pull out."

"Might run into a fighter," suggested Stewart.

DePard was thinking of Keene when he answered, "I'll take care of that, too."

Stewart was troubled. Since he was a cattleman he understood DePard's point of view. But the thought of crossing the Silver Bow and driving out homesteaders was hard on his conscience. DePard saw Stewart's moody hesitation, and assessed it with his sharp voice. "You think you're an educated man, but if you ain't able to fight for your rights what the hell's the good of an education? Those homesteaders come in like grasshoppers.

They don't say nothin'; they just chew the grass. Chew and ruin. They act humble but they keep comin'. That's the way they fight. It ain't my way. I don't give ground and don't draw the line on the way I fight. I'll do whatever I got to do to keep what's mine. When I don't like a thing I buck it and I bust it. I've always found a way and I always will. That's why I'm big."

Stewart said: "There's more to the world than that."

"You tell me what," grunted DePard.

Stewart swung to his horse, thinking of one other thing. "And keep that damned foreman of yours away from her. I'll kill him if he tries his hands on her."

DePard studied Stewart with a half-contempt. "There you go, askin' for help. Take care of your own private affairs. You always struck me as a man a little too light on the power. Now here's something you want and you tell me to keep Red away. Hell, man, you keep him away yourself. It's your woman, ain't it?"

Stewart climbed from the horse with his solid fists doubled. "Don't say that to me, Grat."

Grat DePard was unimpressed by the threat. He had formed his judgment of Stewart long ago after a long period of sly observation and he saw nothing now to change his belief that Stewart lacked the killing instinct. Lacking it, he was not a man Grat DePard, who bowed only to strength, could respect.

"All right," said DePard. "But you take care of Red yourself. That's not my fight."

Stewart left Broken Bit and traveled steadily down

the valley, feeling the sting of Grat DePard's words. He was proud of his education and his perceptions. It was his point of arrogance — this believed superiority of intellect. What hurt most now was to admit that Grat DePard, who had no standards, no civilized qualities, no schooling of any sort, still could look into him and read him. If Grat could do this, what judgments and reservations did other men in the valley hold concerning him? Did they see weakness in him? Was he what De-Pard had said, an impotent man afraid to make up his mind, afraid to fight?

Behind that square face lay an extreme sensitiveness; the toughness of the man was nothing but appearance — an accident of bone growth. He had long suspected that about himself and now he tortured himself with doubts of his own courage.

He arrived at the store yard to see Aurora come from the river with a bucket of water. He said at once: "That's not the sort of work you should be doing."

"What should I be doing, Cleve?"

"You should be married to a man who could do everything for you. You shouldn't be here at all. On this desert alone. Exposed to the tough men that ride by — open to the kind of gossip that people make up about a single girl. You're too much of a woman. You make a man feel strange. Just like passing a pot of gold and not being able to take it. You can't possibly stay here. You can't buck DePard. I can't stand thinking of the risk hanging over you. You don't know the kind of a man

you're up against. Come to my place, Aurora. I've asked
you that before. It's a damned big house and you'd fill
it out for a lonely man."

"Once," she told him, "I thought of that. The night
before Dad died I sat on the steps of the shack and wondered what I'd do. Then I thought of you and I knew
I'd be secure and that you'd always be kind."

He was stirred tremendously. He said, so quick and
so eager: "Why not? Why not, Aurora?"

"Because I've got to make my own security. It means
everything to know I can do something without asking
help."

He said: "If it is because you don't love me, that's all
right. I never asked that. I'd be glad to have what I'd
get."

She spoke in complete candor. "It would be that way
if I married you, Cleve. A bargain between us, and no
love. I don't trust love very much. I know how it should
be but I never really see it. Half of the women in this
world marry without it and some of the others lie to
themselves when they think they have it. I don't like
that. I'd rather not have any of it than to have a miserable little bit to dole out here and there over a whole
life."

"Why don't we make that bargain, Aurora?"

She smiled at him. She was hiding something from
him in her smile; there was a part of her he couldn't
reach. "I've got to try this first, Cleve. And then — "
and she turned away so that he couldn't catch her expres-

sion — "maybe that rare thing will happen and I'll really be in love. If it doesn't I'll make a bargain with you. I can't forever stay single and I can't always wait for something that might never come."

"I don't understand."

"I hate things halfway, Cleve. It has to be all of one thing or all of another."

He turned to the thing worrying him. "You can't stay here."

She faced him with an expression half soft and half stubborn and then he knew he couldn't reason with her. She had a fixity of purpose which greatly puzzled him; it seemed to mean the whole world to her. She was young and in her own fashion she had beauty. Yet she held it back and would let no man have it. He said as much, and got her answer. "If you had led my life, Cleve, you'd know why I won't leave here. I've got to stay here. I will stay."

He remembered Keene and spoke in an altered voice: "Where's that tall fellow — the rider? Did he go on?"

For a moment she seemed to be choosing her answer; he caught that delay and was stabbed by the oldest of emotions. The fineness went from the day and he felt his road blocked and he hated the man who had blocked it. When she answered he recognized the caution in her voice. "He's gone to town."

"You shouldn't have him so near," he told her.

She discovered his feelings at a glance and murmured, "Why, Cleve." He was angry. Blood crawled along the sides of his neck; he tipped his hat and moved away at a fast gallop.

She stood idle in the yard, considering his jealousy; it was a mirror in which she saw herself. She had a close, self-revealing thought and pushed it hurriedly along because she didn't want to let it say: "I think of him — of Jim — rather often." It was disturbing to realize that she felt his presence in the yard; he had left a good deal of himself behind. She recalled his smile and tried to change her thoughts by saying aloud, "I should get another bucket of water." But the image of Keene remained; it penetrated her coolness and crossed the fence she had so definitely built around her inner life.

She filled the water tub and chopped the wood in the yard; she cleaned the cabin top and bottom. At night she stood in the yard's shadows, listening to the drum of a rider somewhere on the flats. Across the river a lantern swung down to the ford and presently went away. Long after she had gone to bed a group of riders slashed across the ford and circled by. One of them let out a yell.

Next morning she baked six loaves of bread instead of the two which would have been enough for her own use. This, she realized, was her tacit admission that she expected Keene to be around. Near noon she saw a rider moving down the valley and presently identified a woman on sidesaddle. In a little while Portia Crews ran her horse into the yard.

Aurora had met the girl a few times during the past year, with always the inevitable homestead-cattle feeling between them; and it surprised Aurora now to find Portia inclined to friendliness. Portia dropped from the horse at Aurora's invitation and began the talk with her customary energy. "I hear you plan to stick here. News does get around. I'd wish you luck but that wouldn't do any good. The truth is Grat DePard's a mean son-of-a-gun and your coming here doesn't please him. Of course he'll run you out. That's really what I wanted to tell you."

"How?"

"I don't know. But he'll find a way. He's sly and he's brutal. Remember Garratt?" Then she said: "By the way, where's that man who was around here?"

"In town."

"I thought maybe he'd drifted," observed Portia. She maintained a nonchalant attitude but her eyes briskly gathered whatever shreds of reaction were to be seen on Aurora's face. Aurora realized that. They were two women facing each other with their pleasant surfaces, both fully aware of what the other thought. Portia was a handsome girl, made spectacular by her swift energy and her startling candor. At first her bluntness and the note of her impetuous will overshadowed her other gifts; but presently when she fell into moments of silence Aurora caught the underlying character of the girl — the hidden sweetness and, more clearly, a certain wistful longing. In repose she had a beautiful face, wide of lip, swift to respond to emotion in its every line. Her body was firm and strong-outlined and would capture a man's attention at once. Her hair, so yellow-gold, threw its warmth against her eyes.

Aurora's fresh-baked bread lay cooling on a bench in front of the cabin, its fragrance filling the yard. Portia wrinkled her nose at it. "Makes me hungry."

"Like some?"

"No-o," said Portia, "but thanks." She counted the loaves mentally and cast another glance at Aurora. "That will last one person a long while."

"But not very long for two people," said Aurora. She knew that question or that suspicion was already in Portia's thoughts; therefore she came out with the truth.

Portia abandoned whatever pretense of indifference she may have had. She faced Aurora Brant directly. "You know it would be better for him if he left here."

"I've told him that."

"But he wouldn't go," murmured Portia in half a question, half an answer. "I knew that." She added a phrase that revealed her completely to Aurora, not only in the words she used but in the relieved and hopeful tone with which they were spoken. "I'm glad."

She swung to the saddle, so obviously thinking of Keene; and because her face was a sensitive mirror of her heart, Aurora noticed the relief and the hope darken into distress. "But how can he ever hope to fight De-Pard? You know that's coming, don't you? You know DePard's only waiting to get that fool Morspeare into the sheriff's office. It will be threats, then it will be burn and kill. It will be anything he has to do. You know that?"

"Yes," said Aurora.

Portia shook her head, and rode away.

Keene drove Spackman's heavy-loaded wagon into the yard at dusk that evening. He got down and stamped the stiffness out of his legs, and stood before Aurora, the old soft smile on his face. Habit made him reach for his cigarette papers; he held his head down over the forming cigarette a long while. When he lifted his glance she saw a strong feeling whip across his features and then it was hard for her to say the casual "Hello" she had planned. The two-day absence had done something. The truth was he had thought of her during the trip and she had had him strongly in her mind. That awareness of each other touched them with its restraint. She was glad to have him back; he seemed to fall into a certain place in her heart, to fill an emptiness.

She said: "Supper's ready."

"I'm ready to eat it."

He left the load of merchandise in Spackman's wagon overnight; and therefore kept Spackman's team. Next morning he said: "Where'll you put this stuff?"

"The cabin will have to be the store."

"You'll have a better store than that by noon," he told her and rode away to the ridge. Presently he returned with two long slim poles in tow.

She said: "What for, Jim?" but he only grinned at her. He harnessed Spackman's team, hooked on the saplings to the doubletree and drove over the ford. It was seven o'clock when he left. By nine she had unloaded all the lighter boxes from the wagon and could do no more. At ten Blackie Naves of Broken Bit crossed the ford, coming from town, and circled the house. He stopped out on the prairie a moment to observe the yard and the wagon in it, and then ran up the valley. Near eleven she heard Keene at the ford and walked from the house to meet him.

He had gone to her old tar-paper shanty, had slid the saplings under it to provide runners; and here he was, hauling the shanty to her.

She said, "I never thought of that!"

He was pleased by her astonishment. "You want a town, Aurora? I'll drag it off the desert for you house by house."

He maneuvered the tar-paper shanty beside the log cabin, wall touching wall, and unhitched Spackman's team. "During the week I'll break down the horse shed and haul over the lumber," he told her and fell to unloading the wagon. He had a casual, steady way of working. Near noon he took back Spackman's team and wagon; when he returned Aurora had dinner ready. Knowing his hunger, she had gone into the store supplies to make a good meal.

"You want to be careful about eating up your groceries, Aurora."

"I feed my men well."

That afternoon she cleaned out the transported shanty and helped him carry in the supplies. In the twilight following supper he lay full length in the yard, long silent and at ease. A rider circled the house at a distance and Aurora, seated in the cooling darkness near Keene, saw the glow of his cigarette fade as he listened to that rider's passage of the river. In all things, she thought, he was acutely attentive, taking in little rumors and stray shreds of sign, and seeing stories before they happened. His life had sharpened that gift. She knew nothing of that life, but its tumult was part of his character, its close and hard risks were visible in his talk, in his way of turning still, in every reaction.

His silence left her alone but because at this hour her doubts always rose and made her small and lonesome, she wanted to creep inside that silence and be sheltered by its comfort. It was hard to be a woman alone, to hold herself always to the cold resolve of self-sufficiency. There were moments when the real part of Aurora, warm and needing warmth, passionately protested this rigid suppression. And so she said:

"What do you think of, Jim?"

"We'll use those packing boxes to make shelves. Next time I'm in town I'd better get some big pickle barrels to put at the side of the store to hold a water supply in case of fire. I'll cut a door through the cabin to connect with the store. Better get the horse shed built next. It won't be long until the rain comes. Snow soon after."

"Does this really interest you that much?"

He was flat on his back, long and boneless, soaking in the night's comfort. He had the ability to seize whatever goodness the current moment offered, to enjoy it before it vanished. "I never helped build a town before," he said. "That's mighty odd, for me. I like the idea."

"But when all this is over," she pointed out, "you'll tire of it. The novelty will be gone. Then what is it for you?"

"More hills to cross. Big world."

The light of the cigarette sparkled against his eyes. He rose to an elbow. His face showed its clear interest in her and for that moment she was inside the circle of his thinking. He had one quality that warned her — the ancient, foot-loose independence of a man. If she ever permitted herself to like him too well she knew she would be bound to his restlessness as she had been to her father's errant impulses. Never again, she told herself, would she play that part. Yet he was a man watching her out of man's eyes, with a man's strong call; the smell of him was the smell of sweat and tobacco and leather. These smells shot home.

She said: "Do you know what it is you really want?"

"No."

"Will you know it when it comes?"

He turned the question slowly in his mind, shaping the phrase that would match his conviction. He made a motion with his arm. "There'll be no doubt. It will be — " he paused to think of it — "like the bolt of a gun sliding into the breech. Funny way to put it. But when you hear that click, when you feel the bolt close down, it's as close to a perfect fit, as near a perfect answer, as there is." He sat up. "You happy here?"

"I never think too much about happiness. I want to be here. This is something I must do. If I don't do it I'll never be able to look myself in the face."

"Like Sullivan. He had to give you that money. Like me. I've got to hunt. Even like DePard. He's got to obey what pushes him." He squeezed the cigarette's brightness between his fingers. "Something pushes everybody. Nobody knows what's really in the other fellow's system. Now you were never meant to be what you're trying to be."

"What am I — what am I trying to be?"

"You're trying to buck the world alone for some reason. But a woman is fire and need, half filled and wanting to be filled. You're afraid of that and you make a battle out of it."

She rose, watching him lift himself from the ground. All along the earth the crickets were filling this night with the bell-like rasp of their intermittent singing. Fall's haze hung on, blending the odors of fire and dry earth and the hinted smell of storm to come. Somewhere a sound or a motion or a presence arrested him; he turned his head.

She said: "There's no need to camp on the ground, Jim. Sleep in the storehouse."

By the delay of his answer she guessed he had already

considered that. He turned his face to her. Between them, flung there by the thoughts they both had, was again that man-and-woman awareness, and its reserve. "No," he said. "It won't rain tonight."

Out of the darkness came the ropy, thinned echo of a distant shot. She wasn't sure of its origin but Keene wheeled at once, facing the river, and then he said more to himself than to her: "I shouldn't have borrowed Spackman's wagon." He ran over the yard, seized his saddle gear and hurried on to the pony picketed in the grass; a moment later he had crossed the river.

As soon as he reached the flats, he turned south, guided on by the outshine of Spackman's lights a mile away. A rider crossed that beam of light, cutting a brief black nick in it; the rider raced by at a distance. All Spackman's dogs were hallooing when Keene came into the yard. He called his own name to protect himself, seeing Spackman's oldest boy bracketed foolishly against the house light with a gun in his hand. Mrs. Spackman was on her knees, half crying and half comforting Spackman, who lay on his side and groaned his misery. Settling beside Spackman, Keene saw something that cut him to the very bone and afterwards poured a scalding anger through him: Spackman's younger children stood hand to hand near their father, silent and terrified.

Spackman breathed: "I won't die. Who's that, Mama? I can't see."

Keene said: "Keene."

"Ah — you dug Brant's grave. Well, you won't dig

mine. I will live to fight that man. It is my arm — that's all he hit."

Mrs. Spackman cried: "You should not have lent those horses."

"Which man?" asked Keene. "Which one came here?"

"All I saw was a shadow before he shot. It was a shadow like a house."

"Morspeare," said Keene.

VI

THE DESIRES OF WOMEN

By the middle of the week Keene had finished his soddy and lean-to. On Friday he disappeared across the ford and was gone all day. That afternoon Sheriff Ben Borders stopped at the store.

He was really an old man, but age had done nothing to his spirit. He was stiff-backed on the saddle, his eyes had a biting keenness; below a long sharp nose a mustache made its silvered, drooping crescent, to give him an old frontiersman's perfect air. His past reputation as a fighter protected him now. Seldom did he use a gun. He displayed an old-fashioned gallantry in front of Aurora, making a ceremony from the lift of his hat, and he had age's one great gift, a thorough understanding of people and a kindness toward them.

"You have been in the country more than six months, Aurora, and you are eligible to vote next Wednesday. I think you ought to."

"I will. Is it going to be a close election?"

The question made him smile; for he had an old man's memory of these elections, and a perfect knowledge of Grat DePard's methods. "As to that I can't say. Where's that man? Keene, I mean."

"Out on the Silver Bow somewhere."

"Liked him," said the sheriff, and went away.

Cannon came into the yard just after dark. "Aurora, you got kerosene?"

She brought him a can of kerosene, plugged the spout with a potato, and took his money. This was her first sale. Cannon kept to his horse. "This would be a mighty handy store for us, Aurora. But I don't know. Risky to cross the river. You know what DePard's told everybody. See what he did to Spackman. But it ain't a homesteader's business to fight with guns. We got to be patient. Someday we'll win. Don't forget to vote. Where's your man?"

"On the Silver Bow."

Cannon's voice held hope. "I hear he ain't afraid of DePard. You think he can help any? That's the only way — some fellow that can use a gun and ain't afraid. You won't find a homesteader like that. None of them could use a gun against Red John."

When he left the yard Aurora remembered that he had said: "Where's your man?" The Silver Bow people, never devious in their thinking, had already put Keene and herself together. She had supper long ready and now found herself waiting and at last worrying. Why should this be? It was the way of a married woman — this troubled fretfulness, this growing fear. When she heard him come down the grade to the ford she turned into the cabin to set on the supper again.

He had gone away on his saddle horse; he drove into the yard with a pair of wild buckskins hitched to a wagon, his own horse tied behind. He was in a fine temper, as he always was when returning with something unexpected. He dropped from the wagon, still holding the reins. The off buckskin struck out at him with an unshod hoof and for a moment he fought this strange wagon team around the yard; obviously he had fought them all across the desert, for they were sweat from muzzle to tail.

"Found a bargain for hauling wood," he said; and had a bad quarter hour getting them out of harness and on picket. "Mostly," he said, over the supper, "their feelings are hurt. This is the first time they've been in harness." Later, lying in the yard with his cigarette making its fragrance, he added: "You've got to have wood banked around the store. I know what winter is like here. There'll be days you won't be able to open your front door."

She said: "You want security for me, but none for yourself."

"Maybe," he told her, "I'm fixing things for you as I'd fix them for myself — if I were staying in one place."

"And you never will?"

He thought about that a long while. "Probably never will. You've got to vote next week, Aurora. It won't help much. Not much chance of Borders being re-elected. The day Morspeare goes in — "

"That bad, really?"

"Yes."

It took him an hour the following morning to harness and hitch the buckskins to the wagon. For a while all she saw was Keene's shadow weaving and ducking through the cloudy dust ripped up by the violent horses. When he got them hitched he made one jump for the wagon seat and was carried toward the ridge in a wild runaway. Near the base of the ridge the exhausted team settled to a walk; presently Keene vanished in the pines.

She saddled her own pony, carrying water from the ford to fill the extra barrels he had brought. He was back with a load of wood at noon, ate dinner, and returned to the ridge. Shortly thereafter she saw a rider come down the valley at a steady gait and curve over to the ridge, following Keene into the timber; it was Portia Crews. Aurora stood at the cabin corner, watching Portia Crews go into the pines, and as time passed and Portia didn't return a strained, resentful emotion worked through Aurora.

Portia Crews sat on a log in the pine's shade, watching Keene work. He was stripped to the waist. At each swing of the ax the muscles of his back made a sharp V. She had thought him thin, which was because of his height. But he had big shoulders and his arms were solid, unlike those of most range men. "Funny to see a rider do that kind of work. Jim, do you know DePard's left-handed?"

He quit his chopping and she observed how quickly he visualized DePard. "No," he said, "he's right-handed."

"Ah," she murmured, "so you have been studying him. I wondered. Let me tell you something. He's the bad one. He's killed at least one man. Red John is tough, too. Then there's Blackie Naves. He's treacherous. He's the one who'd get behind a tree, half a mile off, and spot you with a rifle. Morspeare's very stupid, but cruel. But don't you ever put your back to Grat. You can't tell about him."

"All right," said Keene and turned to his chopping.

"You're foolish to come to this timber alone. And listen. If you ever have to hide, go straight north on this ridge until you hit the high hills. That's broken country, good to hide in. On your way you'd pass my place." She dropped her voice. "You could always stop there."

"I thought you'd be on the other side of this scrap."

She sat on the log, straight-shouldered and firm of body; she had a soft and open and pretty expression on her cheeks if he cared to see it. Suddenly she spoke in a low voice. "Do you only look at men?"

He swung back to her. "No," he said.

She held her hands quiet on her lap; she lifted her chin, presenting herself squarely to him. She was alert to his expression, anxious to know if she pleased him, ready to smile if he wanted a smile and ready to rise and meet him halfway if he came toward her. She had made up her mind about him. She had seen him and within twenty-four hours she had wanted him. Having no subterfuge in her, this was her way of going about it. She knew her own gifts; she knew she could move a man without saying a word and now she watched him to see what he had in his eyes.

The swinging of the ax in the timber's heat brought

a heavy glow of blood to his cheeks; sweat sparkled on his forehead. His glance held her and she realized that, like any man the world over, the suggestion of half a promise stirred him. There was nothing pale about him; his appetites were sound, his urges very strong. Presently she knew she had done what she wished to do. She had penetrated his indifference. He was aware of her.

She got up from the log, her glance leaving him. For she caught one more truth about Keene: he would not want her to be cheap. Therefore, in the way of a woman, she retreated from her suggested promise and became elusive. Looking swiftly at him, she smiled and turned to her horse. "So long," she said, and rode northward through the timber. It was four or five minutes later that his ax resumed its long, smart ringing. That delay made her smile sweetly.

The election was on a Wednesday. On Tuesday night the adjoining neighbors met at Spackman's house — the Cannons, the Cobbs, the Pattersons, the big Murchison family, Kilrain and his flame-haired wife, and Comrie the Scotch bachelor. The younger children ran in and out of the darkness, their feet scurrying furtively from shadow to shadow, their voices crying and going mysteriously still and suddenly crying again. The women sat in the house, steadily talking. The men lounged in the yard, spoke quietly between long pauses. Young Joe Spackman stood at the corner of the house, a dark and hard-worked boy made alternately miserable and hope-

ful by Jennie Cannon. She was near him. When he grew
still she mocked him with her eyes and lifted him out
of his silence, but when he spoke her attention went
away from him and she seemed to listen into the night.
Young Joe, who was no fool, knew where her mind was
at those times. He said now: "Jennie — don't ever do
that again."

"What, Joe?"

"You know what I'm talkin' about."

Spackman sat on a chair in the yard, nursing his
bullet-torn arm. "Sam Venable said he heard this. Tomorrow when we go in to vote DePard's goin' to send
some men here to cut our fences and drive off stock.
That's what Venable heard."

"A threat to keep us home so we won't vote," murmured Comrie.

"We got all day to vote," pointed out Spackman.
"Half can go in durin' the mornin' while the other half
keep watch. Then switch durin' the afternoon."

Cannon, an old man and a gentle one, murmured:
"What good will that do, Fritz? If they come to your
place or mine — how could we fight?"

"I would. I will."

"See what happened to you. We ain't made to fight
with men that use guns. If they come to tear out my
fence what could I do? I'd let them tear it. When they
go I'd put it up again."

"And they'd tear it again," pointed out Spackman.

"Someday," said Cannon, "there'll be a lot of us here

and Broken Bit won't dare do things like that. It is a matter of patience. Take the trouble that comes and wait for it to pass. I do not want fighting. I do not want my children living in fear of bullets. I do not want them to see death in my yard."

Comrie, who was a thoughtful Scotchman, added his word. "It will not be a question of waitin' till the Silver Bow is full of farmers. Whut you think DePard's puttin' Morspeare into office for? He won't let us wait. He's planning to drive us out."

"That's right," said Spackman. "And then, Cannon, is it fight or go away?"

"It will not come to that," said Cannon, gently refusing to believe. "DePard can't be that hard a man."

"Ah," said Spackman impatiently, "you should not trust like that."

"It is not trust," said Cannon. "It is hope. We got to hope. We can't do anything else."

"There's twenty or thirty of us on these flats," pointed out Comrie. "We could take care of Broken Bit if we all got together."

"No, no," said Cannon, agitated by the thought. "Don't consider it. A man like Red John would slaughter us. Can you draw a gun fast, Comrie? No. Can you fire from a horse and hit anything? No. We have got to wait until we are strong enough to make them mind the law. That will come."

Spackman moved in the chair but said nothing, for Cannon's views were the views of a good many homesteaders. They were humble people with families and they wouldn't hunt for trouble. In a little while the group made its plans to go to town in relays; and the meeting broke up.

The families went away, by team and afoot, the children long-calling to each other through the heavy shadows and across the increasing space; lanterns on the reach ends of the wagons scoured yellow channels of brightness through the black.

Jennie, who had her own pony, followed her father's wagon. Young Joe Spackman got his horse and rode with her. They let the wagon draw ahead; they were alone in the felt-black night, with Jennie laughing at young Joe's seriousness. "What's so sad? You're a funny boy. You take on so."

"Keep with your own kind of people. Nothing good will come for you — fooling around."

She said, cool and scornful: "Been spyin' on me?"

"I saw Red John ride away from you that night. Listen, Jennie, he's no good."

"I don't believe all the stories I hear about him."

"You say that," he cried out, "about a Broken Bit fellow. The same outfit that shot my dad."

"It wasn't Red John that did it. Remember what happened in town. Red John didn't cause any trouble with your mother that night when Morspeare wanted him to take her ax."

Young Joe knew this girl and the knowledge was tragedy to him. "You don't mean anything by it, Jennie,

but you're a flirt. That's wrong. You'll get a name —
and men will grin when they see you."

She flung her anger at him. "Don't bother about me if
you don't want to."

"All right," he answered and stopped his horse.

Jennie Cannon immediately rode back to him. This
boy loved her and that was the sweetest thing she had in
her life. In her graver moments she knew she intended
to marry him. He was right for her. He would be a man
like her father, kind and dependable and a thrifty pro-
vider. But she was seventeen and wanted her moments
of foolishness, her time of being courted by men, of
teasing them and seeing them grow jealous of each other.
She touched young Joe's arm. "Joe, don't be angry. I'm
not bad. A girl's got to have some fun. After we get
married — " and the coquette in her swiftly added —
"if we get married, that will be different. Then people
have to work and there's the children. You know that,
don't you, Joe?"

"No," he said, "I don't. It ain't right and I don't
like it."

"A man's always got to have his own way," she answered in a sighing voice.

Usually he ended these meetings with a kiss. She
waited for him to take it, knowing it would dissolve his
resentment and make him awkward and eagerly anxious
to set the marriage time. Then she could tease him again.
But he said "Good night" and rode away, and she realized she had pushed him too far. She wheeled around

and followed in the wake of her father's wagon. She thought: "I'll see him tomorrow and make it up." The wagon was far ahead and young Joe had disappeared in the dark. She moved her weight on the saddle, turning the horse toward the river bluff. Standing in her own yard earlier during the afternoon she had seen Red John ride along the edge of the bluff and look once in her direction; and that was a signal. He would be there tonight.

She pretended it was the pony who wanted to go to the river, not any desire of her own. The night was soft and warm and her heart beat faster; the knowledge that Red John, who had known many women, had singled her out for attention made a stinging sensation through her body. These secret meetings and these covert signals were for her, for Jennie Cannon, a little homestead girl who had long dreamed of a tall dangerous man waiting for her in the starlight.

He was there, waiting beside his horse. He was smoking a cigarette and when she dismounted he dropped the cigarette and ground it beneath his boot. She caught the smell of smoke on his mouth. He touched her and she saw the strange sparkle of his eyes and the frowning, excited look on his face. His arms were hard and impatient as they pulled her against him.

Red John kissed her, feeling the stillness of her body, neither protesting nor giving. He lifted his head to look at her, made violent by the nearness of what he wanted. His voice was broken, rough-edged. "Jennie, that's not the way to treat a man!" He kissed her again and felt her indifference break. Her arms pulled at him and her mouth had its own pressure.

He was inwardly laughing. She had been trying an experiment on him, just holding away and figuring she could quit whenever she wanted. Now she couldn't; and the rest of this affair was a dead certainty. Women were all alike.

VII

"AND NOW IT BEGINS"

KEENE and Aurora left the store during the middle of Wednesday afternoon and reached Prairie near supper-time, entering a street so jammed with wagons and rigs and saddle ponies that they had to leave their horses in an alley behind the stable. Reaching the walk, they were caught in the solid crowd, unable to move faster than it moved; and at last they pushed their way across the dusty street to the courthouse. This was like a Fourth of July crowd, except that there was no lift and laughter in the people. Keene, sensitive to his surroundings, felt fear and suppressed excitement blow along the street like gusts of dry wind.

They entered the courthouse. Aurora took place in line before the voting room while Keene rested himself against a wall, building a smoke. Ben Borders was at the doorway of the voting room checking from a list in his hand the eligibility of those passing into it. Now and then he shook his head, sending a man out of line. Jesse Morspeare stood beside Borders and watched the sheriff with a dull, constant suspicion. Lifting his glance, he saw one homesteader he knew.

"You get out of here. I saw you come to town last June."

Borders looked at the homesteader. "Charley Knorr,"

he said and studied his list. "No, you're all right, Charley. Eight months here."

Jesse Morspeare stared at Charley Knorr, his eyes showing the hot brutality of his threat. It was Charley Knorr's turn to enter the voting room but nobody pushed him; all these homesteaders knew what was in Knorr's mind as he dropped his strained face from Jesse Morspeare's glance. Ben Borders said at last: "Go on in and vote, Charley."

Knorr shook his head. He lifted his eyes to show the surrounding group the complete humiliation he felt; he stepped from the line, leaving the courthouse with the slow, springless step of a man whose pride had been destroyed. Jesse Morspeare grinned at Ben Borders. Borders was angry. He said: "Cut that out, Jesse."

"Not doin' a thing," retorted Jesse. "Just standing here — which is my right."

Aurora moved to the door. Morspeare said to her, "You sure you want to vote?"

Keene strolled from the wall, at once becoming the target of Jesse Morspeare's eyes. The big man, Keene noticed, showed an off-guard uncertainty, a crafty change. He moved his hands slowly down across his hips and held them motionless, trying to make out Keene's intentions. Aurora had stepped into the voting room. Keene removed the cigarette from his mouth; he held it between his fingers and he let his fingers drop, the hot tip of the cigarette falling against Morspeare's hand. Morspeare jerked away; he stepped back. Keene laughed at him. He was close to Morspeare but he stepped closer, and fresh blood turned his face ruddy. He had the big man's mind dead-centered and unable to move; this was something Morspeare couldn't grasp, this deliberate affront. Keene crowded him suddenly. He stepped on Morspeare's foot and moved back, circling Morspeare. He stopped; he threw the cigarette in Morspeare's face and waited for the big man's answer. Morspeare dodged with his head. The cigarette dropped against a fold of his coat and the smell of the burning coat began to penetrate the hall. Morspeare swept the cigarette away with his huge hand. He was against the wall, hating Keene with his close-set eyes, frozen by his uncertainty. Keene stepped slowly backward. The corner of his eyes caught sight of a cuspidor; he reached down and caught the cuspidor by its brass flange and threw it against Morspeare's chest.

It caught Morspeare in the pit of the belly, doubling him over and driving a great grunt out of him. The water of the cuspidor dripped along his clothes; the sound of the cuspidor when it struck the floor was metallic in the hall's complete stillness. Sweat lay like oil on Morspeare's cheeks, the corners of his lips sagged and cut two bitter curves against his skin. He was a great savage dog straining against an invisible leash — the leash of something he didn't understand and therefore feared. He moved his head gently from side to side.

Keene nodded at the back door. The big man looked at the door and snapped his attention back to Keene; in his slow, dim mind was a beast's hatred, and a last surge of cunning. Keene took one more step backward; he put his glance on Morspeare's belly and he drew his right hand slowly upward until the elbow crooked. Morspeare let out a sighing wind and turned to the rear door, dragging his feet heavily on the boards. When he reached it he stepped through rapidly. One sudden plunge carried him from sight.

Borders, standing witness to this scene, drew a hand across his mustache. Keene grinned at him and the two men watched each other, Borders at last nodding. A moment later Aurora came from the voting room and Keene left the courthouse with her.

She didn't say anything until they got into the crowd. She held to his arm, pulling him into the crowd's protection. Then she spoke: "We must leave town right now."

"Supper first."

"Oh, Jim! Don't you know what you've done?"

"Sure," he said, and turned her to the hotel. "I got him out of the courthouse so he wouldn't scare those folks." The strong flush remained on his face and the pleasure was there — the same hard-tempered amusement she had seen before. They moved through the lobby and found a table in the dining room. She started to take a chair facing the dining-room door but Keene's arm guided her to the opposite chair. He took the one facing the door. She was upset enough to be pale. "You quarreled with him — as you quarreled with DePard."

"Sure," he said. He had never, in the time she had known him, spoken a hurried or impolite word to her, but now she heard a coolness that closed her out. He fought his battles alone and wanted no advice. It hurt her to know it. He was a different man. Behind that surface of amusement was the hardest kind of temper. This was the kind of life he best knew.

She said: "All right, Jim."

"Yes," he said, "everything's all right," but he was far away from her, seeing things at this moment she couldn't see.

"When will we know about the election?"

He looked at his watch. "They've started counting now."

The dining room was full. Twilight turned the windows gray and the waitresses went around the room, lighting the lamps. They were half through supper when Cleve Stewart came to the table. He gave Keene the briefest nod, his manner resenting Keene's presence. Aurora said: "Sit down, Cleve." She had a swift moment's glance at Jim Keene and saw the coolness on him.

Stewart took a chair, ignoring Keene. "Going back tonight?"

"Yes."

"My outfit will start home as soon as the election's known. Better go with us."

"We're all right, Cleve."

"No," he said, "I don't think you are. I don't presume to interfere with your private affairs, Keene, but when you pick a fight with Morspeare you get Aurora in trouble. Not thoughtful of you."

Keene said: "Morspeare's your man. You cattlemen want him in office. So why don't you trust him?"

Stewart reddened. "That's my affair."

"For a fact," drawled Keene. "But you opened the subject."

Cleve Stewart sat straight, openly angered. His bull-dog face fell into square lines; his pride was up. Everything about Keene rankled with him. Keene was an outsider, an interloper who had taken the wrong side. Clinging to all his prejudices, Stewart showed his feelings openly. Keene, meanwhile, leaned back in the chair, seemingly disinterested and detached. This was a surface impression only; at the corners of his eyes Aurora noticed the iron pressure of temper.

Cleve Stewart said: "It would be a damned sight better for Aurora if you pulled out alone. You're the man De-Pard will shoot at. Don't put your troubles on her."

Keene's answer drifted like a soft summer's wind. "You're speakin' for DePard?"

Aurora broke in sharply. "Not at this table, please." She rose and left the room. In the lobby — back in a quieter corner of it — she waited for Keene to come up. "Let's stay until we know who wins. I'll wait here."

"All right. I'll be back in a little while."

She watched Keene cross the lobby and push his way to the street; a moment later Cleve Stewart came from the dining room, walking rapidly. He was obviously angry clear down to the bone.

Keene moved by a group of homestead women standing before the hotel and went across the dust toward Worsham's store. Half the town had gathered in front of the courthouse, awaiting the election returns. The Broken Bit outfit had collected near the Cattleman's Palace. Red John leaned against the saloon wall, watching the courthouse. The street now was shadow and lamplight beneath a dark sky and fall's wind came in to catch the agitated dust and carry it onward in slow, thin waves; and in the wind was winter's first chill. Keene was in the dark pool of Worsham's store and he paused here, finding young Joe Spackman near him. Young Joe was rooted to the walk, so intent on whatever he saw that he was unaware of Keene's presence. At that moment Jennie Cannon came out of the crowd near the courthouse and gave Red John one long look and disappeared in the darkness beyond the stable. Red John had a cigarette in his mouth; with a quick gesture he threw the cigarette into the dust and walked past the stable.

Young Joe Spackman spoke a quick, groaning word and whirled on his heels, crashing into Keene. He pushed himself blindly by Keene, hurrying aimlessly down the street. Keene turned, idly walking toward the depot; he was at the corner of the feed-store alley when he heard somebody say "Keene," and turned to find Cleve Stewart advancing at a swift walk.

Stewart came before him, clearly self-pushed to the edge of trouble. Like the bulldog he so resembled, he had set his jaws, he had closed his mind.

"I've got to question your attitude," he broke out.

"You made certain statements I had to ignore while Aurora was around. I'll take you up on those right now."

Keene shrugged his shoulders. "You're tangled up in your own harness, Cleve."

"What right have you got to camp around her place?" demanded Stewart. "The fact is you've got no damned business there. It gives her a bad name. It makes talk. Who knows anything about you? What did you come here for anyhow?"

"My business," observed Keene. "Not yours."

"Oh, no — it's my business."

Keene's answer was dry as the windy-warm night air. "Why?"

"I've known that girl a long time. I feel responsible for her safety. I don't propose to have a stranger come here and get her in trouble."

"Then," asked Keene, "why don't you help her when she wants help?"

"She shouldn't be across the river. You know damned well what DePard's up to."

"What's that got to do with it?" asked Keene.

Stewart cried out: "Good God, don't you understand?"

Keene said: "You're straddling, Cleve. I'd guess you never had much practice in taking the tough side. De-Pard's got you buffaloed and you want to duck trouble by asking Aurora to pull out."

He was unprepared for Cleve Stewart's outraged re-action, not knowing how accurately his words hit Cleve

Stewart's tender spot. Stewart, long uncertain of his own fighting ability and his own toughness, felt blackness close down on him and knew that this was the one moment of his life in which thinking would be fatal. He had to know the quality of his courage, even though it killed him. His jaws clapped together and he caught Keene on the side of the chin with a roundhouse swing. Keene, only half braced for it, fell backward into the alley; and rolled and was up. Stewart ran at him, using his arms in the awkward manner of a man who had never learned to fight.

Keene pulled aside. Stewart's rush carried him past Keene, who caught him in the ribs and slammed him against the nearest building wall. Beyond that thin partition some object crashed to the floor. Stewart threw himself from the wall; in this blinding darkness, Keene saw only the blur of the other man, only the swing of his shoulders. He missed a punch and took one in the chest. He met Stewart in the center of the alley, tied up his arms and jabbed him in the belly, and threw him away. They circled slowly toward the front of the alley, Stewart's wind sawing the silence. Somewhere people were calling; that noise grew along the street. Stewart let out a grunt, pushing himself at Keene again. They stood at arm's breadth, slashing away, arm fouling arm. Keene caught Stewart's next rush on the point of his shoulder. He rolled Stewart off his shoulder, and struck him flush on the chin. Stewart fell like a log. He groaned — and killed the groan as soon as he heard it. They were clear of the alley, in the street again. Voices called more clearly from the courthouse.

Keene said, between the lift and fall of wind: "Don't be a damned fool, Cleve."

The crowd at the courthouse grew thicker and thicker. Talk rose high and quarrelsome. Cleve Stewart pulled himself from the ground. One ragged track of blood lay across his mouth and for a moment he let his head drop, as though to throw himself again at Keene. But this was curious: he lifted his head and all the gray, bitter feeling passed out of him and he was laughing at Keene. It was a relieved and free laughter scouring away malice.

"All right," he said, "you licked me." And again he laughed. "I should have learned how to do this a long time ago. This is the first fist fight I ever had."

He walked forward, his hand extended, and when Keene took his hand Stewart said, "Well, it was none of my business." He ran the flat of a palm across his mouth, staring strangely at the blood there. "I didn't feel you land that blow. Odd." He wanted to say something to Keene, but he could not bring himself to admit the depth of fear that had been in him — the fear of being afraid. Nothing but the bitterest torture of soul had driven him to this fight, nothing but the insufferable agony of a man who had to know about himself at last. Now he was silently saying: "The worst of it is the thinking of it — afterwards there is nothing to be afraid of," and a great load rolled off Cleve Stewart's heart and he was a bigger man than he had ever been.

Keene put an arm on his shoulder, showing Stewart a penetrating kindness. "Fine — fine," he murmured, and that was all they ever said about it. Next moment both of them were turned by the sound of a shot and the long cry of a voice, saying: "Broken Bit!" The crowd fell apart, men running away from the courthouse. Women screamed and raced for the shelter of the hotel. Keene and Stewart, going up the street in long strides, heard another voice cry: "We voted Borders in, by God!"

But the homesteaders kept racing down the street toward their wagons and Broken Bit men were throwing themselves into this stream, fighting toward the head of the street. Keene collided with a homesteader, tripped and went flat down on the dust. Cleve Stewart was by him, shouting: "Trouble up there, Jim!" and gave Keene a hand up, both of them plowing forward. Another woman screamed, so near to Keene that his ears rang. Dust thickened. Through this dust he had one incomplete glimpse of Ben Borders standing on the courthouse steps — tall and lonely and motionless. He saw Borders reach for his gun. That was all he saw, for a wagon and team, swinging down the street at a dangerous run, cut off Keene's vision and made him jump aside; and afterwards the dust shut out everything. Shots beat along the street, those echoes rattling against Prairie's loose windows. A man shouted loud and long and more homesteaders were racing out of town, wagons wheel to wheel. One voice kept shouting: "Broken Bit!"

Keene hugged the wall of Worsham's store, pushing

forward with Cleve Stewart beside him. Tim Sullivan showed up in the dusty, lurid night; his mouth was wide open and a cigar fell out of it. "They shot Ben!" Suddenly Broken Bit was in the saddle, out in the street's middle, and Keene saw DePard wave his arm at his crew. Broken Bit swung through the mass of wagons and rigs. Red John was tall and saturnine in the night and faintly amused. Blackie Naves turned and shot point-black at the head of the street and Red John bent in the saddle and knocked up Naves's arm. Jesse Morspeare cursed at the crowd as he rode, sullen and full of hatred at his defeat. He charged against a wagon and reached out, pulling a homesteader from the wagon's seat. The homesteader fell deep in the tangle, his yell coming wildly up through the dust and the churn of horses; and presently Broken Bit was gone and to Prairie City, now half emptied of its crowd, came a semblance of order. Through the lessening noise Keene heard a small boy's voice crying out forlornly: "Where's my mother?"

Keene ran on toward the courthouse and the group already gathered there. He saw Ben Borders half sitting and half lying on the steps and for an instant he thought the old man merely tired; but as he came up he noticed the stain on Borders' vest. Tim Sullivan pushed the crowd aside and caught Borders at the shoulders, holding him straight. Tim called: "Ellenburg!"

"Tim," said Borders, "I'm a little thirsty."

"Who did it?"

"A short drink of water," said Borders in a voice that

was small and gentle and perfectly unafraid. "Be mighty
dry where I'm going."

"Who was it?" repeated Tim Sullivan.

Borders saw Keene. He raised the back of a hand and
brushed it across his mustache, looking closely at Keene.
There was a freshening of interest in his eyes. "You're
still here?" he murmured. "And stayin'?"

"I'll be staying."

"Pleases me to know it," said the sheriff. His words
were fading and he spoke with a conscious preciseness.
"I want to tell you something. I followed the trail for
many years. When you get to the other side of the hill —
remember this, son — the only thing you'll find there
is just what you brought with you."

He bowed his head and seemed to be thinking deeply.
Sullivan said, "The old man's dead," and sat down on the
steps and held the sheriff.

Somebody behind Keene spoke. "Now where's the
law on the Silver Bow?"

Turning, Keene saw Cannon and a small group of
homesteaders. Aurora stood in the shadows. Ellenburg
came up the street.

"Why," said Tim Sullivan, "there ain't any. If you
want any law, friend, you'll have to make it."

Cannon said sadly: "That's the end of us homesteaders."

Keene swung away. Aurora said: "If you're ready — "
and they walked through the alley to their horses. When
they came out they found Cleve Stewart and half a dozen

of his riders waiting; the whole group left Prairie at once.

Cleve Stewart said: "I'm sorry you had to see that, Aurora. If you're upset, come on to my place."

"No," she said, "I'll stay."

Very little was said during the rest of the ride. Crossing the ford, Cleve Stewart broke a long silence. "DePard didn't think he'd lose. None of us did. The killing, of course, was not accidental."

Keene said: "Who did it?"

"Naves."

"You're sure?"

"Tim Sullivan told me. He saw the shooting." They had stopped at the edge of the yard. Cleve moved his horse in until he had a better view of Keene in the dark. He spoke in a troubled tone. "He was a fine old man — Borders. But if I were you, Jim, I wouldn't entertain any notions regarding Naves. You saw how that outfit works. The lid's off now."

Keene's mind still ran close to the shooting. "Naves — the little one," he mused.

Cleve Stewart looked into the future and had his dark visions and spoke earnestly to Aurora. "Aurora, I hate to harp on this but do you think you ought to stay here?"

"Yes, Cleve."

"Well," said Cleve, "good luck," and rode away with his outfit.

Keene and Aurora rode into the yard and for a little while remained mounted, listening to the steady ringing rasp of the crickets through the silence. Keene rolled a cigarette and lifted it to his mouth and drew out a match. But, watching him closely, Aurora noticed the old, swift caution come to him. There was no warning in the night for her, but for him something happened. He held the match unlighted and his head turned, and then he moved his horse toward the lean-to-stable beyond the cabin. He stopped and she saw him bend forward and presently urge the horse closer to the stable. After that he rode back to Aurora. He lighted the match and cupped it against the cigarette. That glow etched out the bony squareness of his face and the hardening length of his mouth. The light died. Keene said:

"My team's gone."

She felt the quick thrill of fear for she knew, as well as he did, what had happened to those horses. She didn't need to ask. Somehow in the last week's time she had become aware of the dark and wild and treacherous undercurrents of this land. Somehow she had absorbed Keene's point of view. One thing she never forgot: his voice at that moment, its brevity, its softness, its finality.

"And now it begins, Jim?"

"Yes."

"You'll be going after them?"

"In the morning."

VIII

THE LIGHT DIES

HE stood in the yard after breakfast saddled and ready to go, and as he smoked out his morning cigarette he looked along the sweep of the valley, across its amber sunless grass to the clear-black barrier of Lost Man Ridge in the east. Earlier he had scouted the immediate flats, to find the print of pony tracks leading straight at the ridge. He was always a man to have his cool look at the future, Aurora thought. His mind was going on ahead, visualizing how it would be. The pressure of it, and the cool expectancy of it, was on his face.

He swung to the saddle and for a moment his eyes admired her. She showed no fear and she said none of those things that disturbed a man or tried to take him away from the things that had to be done. She had will, she had composure. As she lifted her head to him he saw one quality appear which he had not before seen — a kind of iron resolution which suppressed emotion. He said: "I may be gone a few days."

"I know."

"Remember what I told you about using that gun."

She said: "Do you really have to do this, Jim?"

"Yes."

"Good luck," she murmured.

There was nothing hard about the trail before him; it

led at the ridge in a straight pattern of trampled grass, reached the trees and stamped itself plainly on the dark forest mold. The horse thieves had neither concealed nor wanted to conceal it. They were saying to him, every foot of the way: "This is the way your horses went. Come and find them."

Before he entered the timber he looked back. The store cabin was a dark square against the sun-yellow grass; his own soddy squatted under day's new, strong light; the river made its sparkling bend at the ford. Aurora stood in the yard; he saw her arm lift at him and he answered it and pushed into the timber.

The twilight of the ridge and the coolness of the trapped night air came upon him; the hoofs of his horse sank without sound into the soft mold. One main trail ran northward, veering with the ridge crest and slowly lifting as the elevation of the ridge grew higher. Fifteen miles northward the ridge joined Thunderhead Range. Near that junction Broken Bit had its headquarters.

He had no doubt of his destination. Broken Bit had taken the horses, therefore to Broken Bit he was bound. As he traveled onward at no great haste — and watching all the oncoming alleys of the timber — it occurred to him that this trail was the pattern of his life, leading out of lowlands and sunlight into twisted trails, through shadows in which the old scent of wildness forever lay. He had no illusions about himself. He was glad to be riding, the expectation of trouble was a flame that warmed him — and every old incident of his career now repeated itself. Each man had a life to lead, each man had to play out one part faithfully; this was his part, beyond his power to change or modify.

He was in no hurry and had covered less than ten miles by noon. He came upon a fork of the valley's creek and stopped for a drink. Coolness had gone from the timber; now and then through tree gaps he saw the bright sun shining. Shortly after noon he pushed on, coming to a fork of the trail. The main trail continued north along the spine of Lost Man, containing the print of the horses; a lesser trail curled downgrade toward the east.

They had drawn a line fifteen miles long for him to follow and every foot of the way was an invitation. De-Pard, he thought, was a clever man, for DePard knew he would take up the invitation. Keene smiled at the thought; the old eagerness buoyed him. But at this point he abandoned the direct trail and swung to the left, descending the flank of the hill a mile or more; after that he left the narrow pathway and took to the pines. Ahead of him a bay of brightness showed. Reaching the edge of timber, he looked upon a half-overgrown meadow and the slattern shapes of an abandoned house and barn. Beyond this meadow was a narrow screen of trees; beyond the trees he saw a small shallow valley — with broken country to its east.

He skirted the meadow and turned back toward the crest of Lost Man. A buck mule deer stood up suddenly from the brush and looked at him with a frozen, round-eyed interest and ran away in skimming bounds, leaving the softest of sounds behind. He had not realized until then how close and tight were his nerves. They recoiled, they built tensions in his body. Deep in the lucent eyes of the deer had been the everlasting wildness, the never-ending vigil of nature; in the velvet quiet of these hills a steady danger rubbed against him.

He came to the ridge crest, found the sign of the horses on it again, and quickly retreated into the timber. Through a vista of trees later he saw ranch quarters lying below him near the edge of Cloud Valley; this would be Portia Crews's home. The outer day was still bright but in these woods twilight settled to its first violet shades. He reached an east-west road, scouted it and crossed it. Here the main mass of the Thunderhead Range met him and he rose through denser timber and more rugged contours; high on the mountainside, near four o'clock, he came out to a ledge and discovered De-Pard's ranch below him.

He had circled the ranch. Now from this elevation the country unrolled before him like a map. DePard's long low house and the scatter of outbuildings and corrals lay without pattern at the head of a chute which dropped into Cloud Valley. Timber pressed against the ranch on three sides. The east-west road he had recently crossed came over the ridge and entered the yard; and on that road — a few miles east of the ranch — a file of cattle moved toward the ranch, driven by three riders. He spotted the Crews house sitting in its hidden pocket north of Broken Bit. From this high spot Keene saw

Lost Man Ridge as a dark finger pointing at the distant Silver Bow.

East of the ridge lay a country broken by a hundred short ravines and pockets — a silent and empty and mysterious land, the very sight of which made its imperious demands on his imagination; and such was his incurable love of wild places that he would have turned at once, answering the summons of that broken country, had he been free. He counted five men in the yard below him and through the time space of a cigarette he watched Broken Bit, every detail of the yard biting into his mind — the arrangement of the house doors, the runway between the corrals, the closeness of the pines to the big barn. When he turned down the slope, temporarily within the shelter of the timbered hills, he had put the men of the yard in their exact places and he had estimated it would be another hour before the riders on the east-west road reached the ranch.

The trail dropped in quick switchback loops. Above him the sky made its spectacular evening shift from bright gold to the sunless clarity of evening; and so quiet was the world that the sound of a man's voice in the yard below him, still a quarter mile away, ran up the slope in magnified resonance. When he came off the last turn of the trail he faced the back side of the main house and the blank end of a bunkhouse. A man sat at the base of a corral, hat low on his face. It was the same man, Keene realized, he had thrown at Red John in town.

He lifted his head as Keene entered the yard, and

dropped it again; and it was a long moment — Keene watching him with an undivided interest — before the delayed impact of Keene's presence lifted his head. He was in his thirties, with a face prematurely old and dried-out and sharp-stitched with its line of hard living; he was a passive presence in the dust. Looking down at him, Keene saw the narrowed slot of his eyes. In them was the gray intentness of a man sighting along a gun barrel and waiting the proper moment of discharge. Behind the corral bars were Keene's two buckskin ponies. Keene passed on, cut around the corner of the house and found DePard on the porch.

DePard said: "Took you all day to get here, friend. What you been doing since six o'clock this morning?"

He sat in a rocking chair, his two heavy hands idly dropped on the rocker arms; he had been teetering gently, and now was still. On the surface of his wide and fleshy neck the pulse of his heart broke heavy and slow. He wasn't surprised. He had known Keene would come and on his face was the gray satisfaction of guessing right. "Naves is out there on the main trail, expectin' you."

"I wouldn't be that much of a sucker," drawled Keene.

"No," said DePard, "you wouldn't. But Naves don't rate you as smart as I do." He came as near laughter as his nature permitted. Somewhere in this unscrupulous and powerful man a pleased foresight stirred. "Men are no brighter than they ought to be, friend. Or if they're bright they've got no guts. Those with guts are almost

always damned fools, like Morspeare. I don't often see
a smart man who ain't afraid. When I see him I admire
him. I get lonely sometimes for a talk with my own kind.
Glad you're here. Step down."

"You're wrong," said Keene. "I'm not your kind."

"In that one respect," answered DePard, "you fool
yourself. You have got a kink, which I have observed.
What did you come here for?"

"Horses."

"You never would have lost any horses if you had
minded your own business. You was just ridin' through.
Then you saw a lively game and dealt yourself in." He
put his hands on his solid knees, leaning forward in the
chair. "What'd you do that for, friend?"

"The game," said Keene, "needed a little fresh blood."

"The ridin' got dull and you wanted action," DePard
pointed out. "So you stopped here. But you got a kink,
so you had to make out some sort of a story to please
yourself. You made out that these people were gettin' the
worst of it and needed help. The real reason was you had
a bellyful of bein' good."

The man with the burnt, expressionless face stumbled
around the corner of the house, took one brief look at
Keene, and moved back to the corral; when he sat down
it was at a position which kept Keene before him. DePard
said: "It's all right, Snap." Two other men moved from
the barn and paused. Elsewhere in this yard the fourth
and fifth hands were hidden; he had counted them from
the hill.

"You're foolin' yourself," said DePard. "I never do. I know what I'm after. I go for it and I get it. I never had a bad night's sleep over anything I ever did and I never will. I take what I'm big enough to get. Let the other fellow cry, if he ain't heavy enough to stop me from gettin' it. Now, friend, you're a quick man with a gun and you didn't learn that shootin' the tops off daisies. When you want a little hell you stop and have it and you don't care who foots the bill. What's the difference between us?"

The pattern of this yard was in Keene's head; the old coolness moved in him, the old temper sang through him like wind. The man at the foot of the corral had dropped his hat over his head but Keene saw the basilisk gray of his eyes underneath the brim; he noted the two men near the barn. He said gently: "As for the horses, Grat — "

Grat DePard's answer was amused, it was completely confident. "You ain't answerin', friend. What's a homesteader to you? Nothin'. I know you like a book. You ride high until you see a man that casts a big shadow. And then like every tough one in the world you stop to see if that fellow is as big as you. I'm that fellow, friend, and that's what's in your craw now."

Back of the house a door banged, its sharp clap running sheer and flat across the yard. A triangle began to beat steadily, ringing like a great bell, the echoes rolling on and on through the hills. Twilight moved through the yard, wave after wave. DePard stood up.

"I'm as tough as you," he repeated, "and you're as tough as me. Which makes it kind of interestin'. Light and eat, friend."

Keene had DePard centered before him; he could take his chances with the three men visible in the yard. But somewhere, like a breath of air on the back of his neck, was the threat of the other men he had seen from the heights. This was the thing that held him. He stepped from the saddle and went into the house. He followed DePard to a mess hall, took one swift look around him, and moved to the chair at the foot of the table. One by one the other men walked in. He counted them in his head, waiting until all five should have arrived; that was the moment he had chosen — when all five were together in front of him. But one man never came and he saw DePard's heavy lips creased in half-suppressed amusement. DePard knew what he was thinking. Keene sat back, the drive leaving his muscles. Nothing showed on his face.

A rider came out of the hill trail, whirled before the house, and stamped through it; at the doorway of the dining room he stopped as though a stretched wire had caught him across the chest. This was Naves, shocked still; his little eyes raced from Keene to DePard in swift search.

DePard said: "I said you'd be wrong, Blackie."

There was an empty chair on the far side of the table. The little man moved on, intending to pass Keene's back. Keene looked at him; he had a coffee cup in his hand and he held it half lifted, looking over its brim. Naves flashed one more glance at DePard and turned toward the opposite end of the table. He sat down, saying nothing, and, as the rest of them did, ate his meal in hurried silence.

There was one more man in the yard. That man clung to Keene's mind; it was a weight that tipped the scales gently down, against action. He watched the group finish eating — and the urge to make a play crept into his muscles and turned to a half-formed impulse. But he sat still. That coolness still was on the back of his neck. He relaxed on the chair, heavy and inexpressive, watching the crew go out. DePard remained. DePard rolled a cigarette, his stout, stubby fingers turning and tapering the paper.

"You threw the hook into me the other day," said DePard. "I ought to be tough about that. But I ain't. When I meet a man of your kind I'd like to have him with me. That's why I took your horses, friend. I wanted to talk. There's a job here for you."

"No," said Keene. "I guess not."

"Friend," pointed out DePard, "you could raise a lot of hell. If I didn't think so I wouldn't be foolin' with you. There ain't room for the both of us in the country. Either you ride right on out of here, or you take this job."

Keene said: "Quit singing that same old tune, Grat."

DePard stared at him through the rolling smoke of his cigarette. DePard's skin cast a mahogany shine back against the lamplight; close wrinkles fanned out at the base of his temples. He propped an elbow on the table and sank low in his chair, animal keen in the things he knew. There was a chestiness to him, a broad flare to his nostrils, a stallion's boldness to his eyes. Slouched in the chair, he showed power and an insensitive vitality.

"I admire you," he repeated. "I could trust you as much as any man, which is not much. You got the same ideas I've got, which is to take what you want and do what you want to do and to hell with what the other fellow says. This is my country. I run it. All that talk about law and rights — what good's that if they can't make it stick?"

"When you trouble those people across the Silver Bow you're overplayin' your hand."

"Little fellows," said DePard. "They hide in the grass like crickets and you don't see them until they cover the country. Then they eat you up. They're going out of here, friend."

"You'll lose."

"Me?" said DePard, really surprised. "Oh, no. They'll run." He came heavily back to his main subject. "I like smart men. Don't disappoint me, friend. Don't do something that ain't smart. Hell, here's a whole thousand square miles for you. Go out there and take your piece of it. I'll stand you some cows to start on."

Keene gave the thought a long consideration. It engrossed him, it took his fancy. But he smiled and shook his head. "What would I want with that?"

DePard displayed his first sign of puzzlement. The

hearts of men, according to his philosophy, answered to fear and to profit. These were the major compulsions. He had tried them both on Keene, but this man laughed at him. He was less sure of Keene; he was curious. "What do you want, friend?"

"As to that," answered Keene, "I do not know."

"Don't spend your time lookin' for nothin'. If it ain't something you can see or smell or bite between your teeth, — " he stretched out a solid arm and closed his fingers slowly, — "if it ain't somethin' you can get between your fingers, it ain't nothin'."

"I knew a man once, down the trail," observed Keene. "He owned the town. He walked down the middle of the street and folks stepped aside. He rode high and he cast a pretty big shadow. One day a little fellow — just a little fellow scared of his own skin — walked up to him and said, 'Hello, Bill,' and shot him dead."

"Bill," pointed out Grat, "was a fool for bein' careless." Then he asked in a quick way: "What happened to the other fellow?"

"One of Bill's friends killed him."

"You see?" pointed out Grat DePard, and blew a long breath through his nostrils. "The little fellow was a fool, too. He's dead. What good did it do him?"

"Something you don't see and can't bite. You could reach for it forever and never get it in your hand. How about those horses, Grat?"

DePard stood up. "Naves was right. You're not as

smart as I figured. Your pony's out there where you left it."

The cook moved around the kitchen. That, Keene decided, was the extra man he'd been worrying about. Evening's silence hovered over the ranch, the silence of waiting, the silence of preparation. One thing alone broke it — the cry of a coyote somewhere in the hills. Keene looked down at the table, no longer needing to watch DePard, for he had already seen the involuntary break-through of the man's purpose. He had observed it before in other men, that dark emanation which no pair of eyes and no face could ever conceal. They would let him rise to the saddle; they would never let him ride from the yard.

He said: "Thanks for the meal. You've got a good cook."

"Chinaman."

Keene thought. The extra man was a Chinaman. No danger in him. The kitchen was a way of exit, but it left him without his horse. He moved along the table; he stopped near the doorway which led into the front room. The front room was still unlighted and the mess-hall lamp thrust one bright yellow corridor straight across the living room to the front doorway. To either side of this corridor shadows clung. He fished out his cigarette papers and shook up a smoke. He tapered it, he lighted it and pulled his lips back from his teeth, relishing that first fragrant draw of smoke. Grat DePard stood at the doorway, his faithless, animal-alert mind anticipating every possible play in Keene's head. Knowing his man, Keene started for the doorway. It surprised him when DePard stepped into the living room ahead of him.

Keene said: "Just stop there — and keep your voice down."

DePard's confident answer came back at him. "You damned fool, you're as good as a mile from that horse. Put up the gun."

"Slide your hands into your pockets. We'll walk to the porch. We'll stop a minute. We'll move out to the horse and just walk along."

"And you showin' a gun in your hand, friend?"

"It's still in the holster. Go ahead."

DePard was close to open laughter. "Now you'll see why I like smart men. See how far Blackie Naves lets you walk."

"Go on."

DePard stepped to the porch, with Keene behind him. Keene said: "How far over this ridge to the river, Grat?" In the stillness he heard his own voice carry — and wanted it to carry.

DePard made a half-turn to him. "Nineteen miles."

Keene slid a match along his leg, lighting it. He brought it to his face, holding it steadily against the cigarette. The light reached out to DePard and caught the round, wide-open surfaces of the Broken Bit owner's eyes. Keene watched the dark pupils grow small against the light; he saw the flame of the light dance as tiny pictures in those pupils. The match died and he heard DePard's short strong sigh of growing strain. That same strain made hollow places inside Keene; it dried him up and made all his nerves too sharp, it stung like sweat on his face. Water fell into a near-by trough. The smell of the hills moved steadily down the narrow canyon meadow and the weight of the hills pressed against the meadow. He noticed one shadow erect against the corral.

"Well," he said, and moved toward the head of his horse. DePard dropped down the steps, in front of him. Keene caught up the reins. He had the horse on his left, he had DePard close to his right. Then he said: "Let's call Naves over."

DePard set himself. He meant to resist. Keene pushed a shoulder point gently against DePard and held it there; he felt the steady strike of DePard's heart.

"Blackie," said DePard.

Keene said: "Walk on a piece and I'll tell you about this." He stepped ahead, DePard's feet keeping time. Keene, looking into the shadows, saw only that one still shape against the corral wall. He heard the scuff of boots elsewhere to his left. There was also a man, he presently discovered, hard by the barn. And Naves called out: "What's up?" He was opposite the house, near the pines; and now his boots had quit moving. DePard's head turned and Keene saw satisfaction tighten his mouth. Keene pulled his horse around, aiming between house and corral, thus putting Naves behind him. He passed the silent shape at the corral. He reached the kitchen door, he aimed at the hill trail out of which he had come.

Naves's voice rose again, thin with suspicion. "What's up?" His boots struck the yard, now at a steady run. Keene slapped his hand down against the butt of De-Pard's gun and seized it. DePard moved against him, hands still in his pockets; he felt DePard's muscles tighten. He lifted the gun from DePard's holster, murmuring: "Better take care of that fellow."

"Blackie," called DePard, "what the hell you doin'?"

Naves's boots went scuffing around the far side of the corral; he was circling it to reach the mouth of the hill trail in advance of Keene. DePard yelled "Blackie!" and threw all his weight against Keene. His hands came out of his pockets. Turning, he drove his knee at Keene's stomach. Keene stepped back and, with DePard's head a growing shadow in front of him, brought the barrel of the revolver hard down.

DePard dropped. Another crying voice pursued Keene. "Grat — that you?" Keene ducked under the head of his horse and let go of the reins, running at the corral. He threw a shot back of him and left the corral's protection. The dark mouth of the trail was fifty feet in front and as he ran he saw a little shape suddenly wheel before him and crouch like a cat. Naves had beat him to the mouth of the trail. He jumped aside, the flash and roar of the little man's gun in his face. He threw his shot and heard it tear through that little man; he watched Naves wind half around and drop.

He was in the trail, with the lead of other Broken Bit men whipping the earth at his feet and singing against the trees. The sound of that firing was odd and hollow and increasing. He turned about, sheltered by the trees but still in the trail, catching the steady flash of a gun near the corral. But the hollow sound grew until he knew it was not in the yard. Swinging, he saw blackness rush at him and rear high above him and one stunning, crashing force came down on him and the roar of a great waterfall swelled through his head.

He was down in the dust, bitterly grasping the tail end of consciousness, rolling beneath the feet of horses. One sharp hoof struck him in the head and light burst like an explosion in his brain; and his last thought, struggling with strangled effort through the smell of dust and of his own blood and the knife stab of pain, was a cold conviction of death; and then all light faded and he dropped into a bottomless black.

IX

"YOU ARE NOT COLD"

DURING the latter part of that afternoon Cleve Stewart rode down from Skull Ridge to the store and found Aurora chopping wood. Cleve was genuinely irritated. He took the ax from her. "That's something you never should do." He looked at the woodpile. "There's enough stuff split for a week."

"I have to keep busy."

"Where's Jim?"

"Broken Bit took his horses last night. This morning he went after them."

He took one swing at the wood on the block and came around. "My God, Aurora, he didn't go there alone?"

"Is it that bad?"

Cleve Stewart breathed out his astonishment. "I thought he was far too smart to fall into a trap like that."

She thought back on the morning scene, soberly visualizing Keene. "I think," she murmured, "he knew what he was doing."

"Well, I guess so." Then he added hopefully, "Of course he did. The man's proper element is trouble. I believe he even likes it."

"He said he'd be back in a day or two."

"If he isn't here noon tomorrow," decided Cleve Stewart, "I'll go to Grat's."

Aurora found herself freshly interested in him. He showed the world a stubborn bulldog expression; his face, so square and outthrust, fell into aggressive lines without effort. But she had long ago noticed that his hardness was more apparent than actual. He really had a streak of uncertainty in him and his eyes, the warmest of brown, betrayed him. They were expressive eyes, sensitive to change. In a way he reminded her of her father, who had never been able to face pain or cruelty.

"Why are you so concerned?" she asked. "You don't like him."

He gave her an almost embarrassed glance. "Matter of fact I really do. I got acquainted with him last night."

She said: "I wondered about that. Something happened. You followed him. You had a fight."

"We had a hell of a brawl. To tell you the truth, Aurora, he licked me." He shook his head. "I've heard of situations like that but never expected to participate in one. He licked me and we're friends." He showed her a kind of sheepish reluctance. "A good knock-down-and-drag-out seems to be good for the soul."

"Why, Cleve!"

"I know. Silly of a grown man with some pretensions to an education to get into a brawl. Or is it? Maybe I've been too damned educated."

She said: "Don't apologize for yourself, Cleve. I think I like you better for the change."

"I've always heard," he said dryly, "that women liked a dash of the primitive in their men."

"I'm not so sure," she said.

"It all boils down to that," insisted Cleve Stewart. "One way or another we've all got to fight. It took me a long time to learn that. Your friend taught me something."

"Jim?"

"Well, he's fundamental. He never got tangled up with education. The current runs straight in him, never muddied up with a lot of nonsense. Simplicity, I suppose."

No, she thought, not simple. Direct and high-tempered, loving the fresh, edged sensations of life. But not a simple man. A thousand images boiled in his mind, his restless heart had its complexity.

Stewart moved back to his horse. From the saddle he spoke again. "I'll be by at noon. Aurora, do you have to stay here?"

"I've got to stay."

"All right. I worry about you a lot but I'll back you up."

She came beside his pony and laid a hand on his arm. "I like you a lot better," she said. He was quite sensitive and this praise and the touch of her hand got under his skin. He turned out of the yard at once.

He had shown her a tougher fiber than she had believed he possessed. Facing raw force and a kind of life he was really unfitted for, he had made the difficult change. It was a rare kind of courage; in one respect it was a greater courage than that of Keene, who, like a gambler in a familiar game, knew the exact odds against him at all times.

Still it was Keene she thought of during the afternoon. She changed the picket stake of her pony to give it a new range of grass. She watched the sun drop behind the western ridge in a brass flare of light and made her supper in the condensing twilight. Night brought its distinct coldness. She washed the dishes, brought up water from the river and put the horse in the shed. Slipping on a coat, she walked idly into the valley, through a curdled blackness, hoping for the sound of hoofs in the valley, for a view of Keene's oncoming shadow.

Fear oppressed her. She was really nervous. Realizing it, she had a woman's moment of clear intuition. If she ever came to love Keene, this would be what she must expect — these hours of worry and wonder. He would never be different; always he would answer to his natural instincts. Men like Cleve Stewart, less forceful and more analytical, saw themselves with some detachment; they had the power of change, the ability to bend and modify. Keene, natural a man as breathed, could not.

There was neither sound nor sight of him on the valley floor. She returned to the house, took up the lamp and went to the store shanty. Unable to be still, she sorted out the groceries from the boxes. Her mind kept digging at Keene and at herself. It was alarming to realize how her thoughts included him. She wanted no entanglement like that. If a man got into her life it had to be a man like Stewart; a steady and enlightened man who would not tow her from pillar to post, who would respect her burnt-child need of security. All her life she had followed a man who, kind as he was, had been blind to any needs but his own. To this gentle egocentric who was her father she had surrendered her own rights as a person and had concealed her own girlhood dreams because she could not bear to hurt him. That would never happen again. Assaying herself realistically, she knew that someday she would need marriage. But when she married it would be to a man who saw her not only as one to be loved and possessed, but as one who was his equal, to be included in all his thoughts and all his needs; to a man who would delight in watching her grow, to one who would need her strength and thus make her proud of her own value to him. Cleve Stewart would be like that. There were parts of him she could fill out; perhaps she could give him, in return for his love, something as necessary as love — a more complete faith in himself. This, she now realized, was the reason for the troubled thought she had of Jim Keene; there was a part of him she could never share, one self-sufficient chamber that he would never open to anybody.

Always her thoughts drifted back to him, which was a sign of danger. She had to be colder, she had to push her real self farther into the background so that his interested eyes would not see her need of warmth. She quit working on the groceries and took up the lantern, moving out of the storehouse. She faced the door, padlocking it, and turned to the other cabin; and at that moment saw the high shadow standing before her — the shadow and then the face of Red John.

The complete silence of his approach and the shock of his presence went through her like terror. She had never known so complete and paralyzing a fear; she threw herself back against the storehouse wall, the lamp trembling in her hand. By the lamplight she saw the gray dilation of his eyes, the self-assured half smile, the rise of a hunting excitement on his features. She knew why he had come.

"Sorry if I scared you," he murmured. "Would have made a noise comin' in, only I figured you'd use your gun."

She had no power to speak at that instant; her mind was moving too rapidly, she was watching him too closely. She knew why he was here but she could not yet discern how much of a danger he was. She was aware of his reputation and she could see the depth of his boldness. He looked at her now with an insistent, masculine attention, trying to read her weakness. His eyes had no modesty, they credited her with none. About him was a soft and knowing cynicism, as though he believed her to be easy.

"You've got a lot of fire," he said. "When you turned the gun on Grat I admired your spunk. If it was me I'd never try to get you out of here."

If she tried to be reasonable with him it would only give him hope. So she said: "You get out of here."

"I'm not doing anything, am I?"

"I notice you don't come around when there's a man here."

"I'd take my chances on any man. Let me hold that lamp."

"Get on your horse and move along."

"You don't mean that."

"Don't I?" she said. The Winchester stood inside the log cabin's door and she moved toward it. Red John slid over to the door, blocking it. He turned still, watching her, reading her.

"If you want a man's help, pick a man that can do something for you. You've got the wrong one now."

"Go on — get out of here."

"What you so particular about? Keene lives here with you."

She threw the lamp at him, but never quite caught him off balance. He ducked, taking the lamp on the shoulder. Kerosene spilled on him; he knocked the lamp away before the flame exploded on his coat. She pushed at him, trying to get into the cabin. He reached out and caught her shoulders; he shook her and said something in a throaty, hard-breathing way. He pulled her in, his mouth searching her face with a hot anxiety. She hit him on the jaw and her fingernails dug through his skin and she felt him cringe away. His hands ripped at her

dress and she heard it tear away and for a moment she
fought him with a blind and furious hatred — a hatred
intensified by fear — catching his face with her nails
again and again until he had to break clear. She was
exhausted and she had lost her sense of direction. She
flung out her arms and found the door by accident, at
once seizing the gun. But by then he was in the outer
darkness, shouting at her.

"You're not cold, sister. If you were you wouldn't
be keepin' a man around here. Why pretend to be something you ain't?"

She lifted the Winchester and let go. He was on his
horse, moving out from the cabin. She ran after him
and fired a second time at his shadow, and missed; and
then the shadow vanished and there was no use of wasting bullets. She was shaking, she was so weak that the
gun pulled her arms down. Her heart throbbed in her
throat, she couldn't pull enough wind into her lungs.
She turned to the cabin, dully remembering the lamp,
and got on her hands and knees to hunt for it; but the
desire for light went as quickly as it had come, and she
went into the cabin and dropped the bar against the
door.

She sat on the bed, bent over in the darkness. She
rubbed her hands together, feeling grit between them.
She knew that Red John, believing her to be loose,
would come again. He was that kind of man. And then
she thought: "I must not tell Cleve. Cleve would go

after Red John and be killed. Should I tell Jim?" Long afterward, in bed and still shaking from reaction, she tried to answer that question.

Sheltered by the darkness, Jennie stood at the river's bluff and waited until she knew Red John wouldn't come. This was the second night she had waited in cold, fearful hope. Presently she turned and walked slowly toward the house. Once she paused, thinking she heard his horse running through the night, but it was only a homesteader on the southern flats; she went on, hating Red John and hating herself. This prairie night which had always been so beautiful to Jennie thickened around her and wrapped her in its darkness and now she saw no beauty in it. She walked with her head down, heavy-bodied and ashamed. She had pity for herself and nothing but a sick dread of the days to come — and that dread grew so powerful that she thought of the river bluff and its hundred-foot drop. She thought of it with a kind of sleepwalking fascination, and morbidly pictured herself floating dead in the river, her hair floating loose around the marble whiteness of her face. Once as a child she had seen a woman in a coffin, dead of carbolic acid, with that waxen whiteness on her cheeks.

She came into the yard and saw young Joe Spackman's horse there. Joe was in the house with her folks and she thought they were talking about her; the last few days it seemed that everybody had a strange way of looking at her, as though they knew. She stepped through the doorway and dropped her eyes from the strong lamplight. Her mother gave her a quick glance, and she was afraid of her mother now for the first time in her life. Young Joe put his hands in his pockets; he pulled them out. He was ill-at-ease and he was sorry because of the quarrel they'd had. Jennie met his eyes and knew that he was ready to forget their quarrel. But she hated him at that moment. He seemed to see that it was no use for he said, "So long," and left the room.

As soon as he stepped into the yard she was afraid he wouldn't come back. She followed him and found him beside his horse. He had one hand on the saddle but he came around and showed her a fiery, hopeful expression — that one expression which always made her forget he was just young Joe Spackman, slow and steady. She had nothing to say; she had lost her power to tease him and so she stood and waited for him to speak. And then, waiting, she noticed the expression fade. He spoke as a stranger would speak, even his bitter jealousy gone.

"I guess he didn't show up tonight."

"No," she murmured. "He didn't show up, Joe."

"That's too bad," he said, so distant, so civil, so lost to her.

He stared down at the dead set of her face and now she thought he knew; she had to drop her glance from that agony of suspense and reluctant suspicion showing on him. "I guess," she said in the humblest voice, "I've

spoiled things for us. It wouldn't be much for you to
kiss me any more. I mean it wouldn't really mean what
it used to mean. Maybe you better not bother any
more, Joe."

"Guess that's what you want."

"No, Joe. It isn't what I want. I guess that's all I
can say. I used to tease you a lot. I never meant it, Joe.
I never meant to make you feel bad. I'm awfully sorry."

He got on his horse and turned away. She called after
him, "Joe," and he stopped the horse, listening to her
but not looking back. "Joe," she said, "don't hate me.
I hate myself, and that's hard enough."

He rode out of the yard. She heard her mother coming
but she couldn't stop her crying; she cried without making a sound. Her mother said: "You quarrel with Joe?"

"No."

Her mother let out a long sigh and took Jennie's
shoulders and pulled her around. She looked at that
little girl's soft face smeared with its tragedy. Mrs.
Cannon took her girl into her arms. "We will not tell
your father, Jennie."

"You don't hate me, Mama?"

"How could I hate my little girl?"

Coming down the valley as though a band of Sho-
shones were hot on her trail, Portia Crews met Cleve
Stewart at Keene's soddy. Portia said "Whoaa," and
came to a sliding halt before Cleve.

Stewart said: "You'll break your neck some day."

"My friend," observed Portia, "I like things to happen suddenly. What does that serious look indicate?"

"Keene lost two horses day before yesterday and went after them. He's not back yet."

"He'll get them. That man will."

"DePard took the horses."

Portia Crews breathed, "Oh, Cleve," and all her gaiety disappeared. She was a pretty girl in every mood but this one; in this moment of complete soberness she was beautiful. "So he went to DePard's? Why did he do that? He knows what DePard — " She knew the answer before she had finished asking it. "Of course he knows DePard. And he wouldn't beat around the bush. Where are you going?"

"To find out what happened."

She swung with him. They rode up-valley side by side in a half-cold sunlight overcast by a gray-moving haze. They hit a brisk clip and not for a half mile did the inevitable thought occur to her. She turned to Stewart. "Why are you doing this, Cleve? You don't like Keene."

"Well," he said, "I kind of do."

Being a woman she made a quick inference. "Or would it be for the sake of Aurora Brant?"

"Certainly," he said. "But I said I liked Keene."

She watched the upper valley, her eyelashes touching; she was soft and thoughtful. "How strange," she murmured. "Yesterday nobody knew him. Today here we are riding to find him, because we like him. Tomorrow he'll be gone."

"Will he?"

She shrugged her shoulders. "That's the way he is."

Long later in the day, not far from sundown, they turned into the chute which rose to Broken Bit's front yard. She said: "What could you do, Cleve?"

"I don't know."

"After all, you're a cattleman. That's your side of the fence."

"Yours, too."

"No-o, Cleve. My side is wherever I want to be."

Stewart couldn't make his adjustment that easily. He had some trouble explaining himself. "The homesteaders can take care of themselves. But I draw the line on Grat DePard. That's too rough for me."

"You've changed somewhat," she observed, and looked at the nearing ranch with expressive distaste. "That place always gave me the vapors. I never trusted Grat and I never got very close to any of his crew. Sun has a hard time shining on Broken Bit."

As they came into the yard Jesse Morspeare moved around the house to meet them. He stopped in the dust, staring at them out of his small sullen eyes. Since neither of these two had any power he was bound to respect he treated them to his dumb, animal-like silence.

Stewart said: "Where's Grat?"

Morspeare jerked his head at the house.

Portia Crews fired her resentment point-blank at him. "Don't stand there, you big overgrown ox. Tell him we're here."

Morspeare's face revealed that meanness which lay always so near the surface.

"If you was a man — "

"No you wouldn't," broke in Portia Crews. "You wouldn't do a thing unless the man was old or crippled. Well, I'll go get Grat myself." She started to leave the saddle, and noticed watchfulness spring to Morspeare's eyes. It told her something when he moved toward the house, grumbling, "I'll get him."

"Cleve," whispered Portia, "he's here. Jim — "

She was quicker of eye than Cleve Stewart. While he sat still on the saddle, slowly stiffening himself to a scene he dreaded, Portia's glance ran around the yard. She knew Keene's horse and looked for it in the corral. She watched the second-story windows of the house; she listened for voices from the house. One man sat near the barn, so posted as to keep an eye on the road leading into the woods. The rest of the crew was away.

Grat DePard came from the house, Morspeare trudging silently behind him. Grat, Portia noticed, threw an alert glance at her and at Stewart. He didn't say: "Step down." That courtesy was missing. All he said was:

"You're browsing a long way from pasture."

Stewart said: "Keene been here?"

"He was here."

"Here now?"

"No — not here now."

Portia, possessing a woman's profound interest in men's reactions, noted that Stewart was relieved to have it pass off this easily. It had been difficult for him, she realized, to come here; he had obviously dreaded the trip. She liked him for the courage he had shown but she had a quick picture of Keene sitting on that same saddle, and knew how differently Keene would have spoken.

"Where did he go?" asked Stewart.

"Now how do I know?" answered DePard, becoming irritated.

Portia tried to throw him off balance with her question. "Did he get the horses?"

But Grat gave her a gray, smart look. "What horses?"

If she had doubted him before, she now knew he was lying. There was no reason for him to cover up the horses unless he had something else to hide.

His thoughts, always nimble in this sort of thing, marched parallel with her thoughts; he grew rough. "What the hell's the difference to either of you? You turned homesteaders?"

"Wait a minute, Grat," said Stewart.

"No," responded Grat, "I don't wait." He came forward until he stood at the head of Stewart's horse. He took the cheek strap in a hand, staring up. "Quit diddling around, Cleve. You with me or not?"

Cleve set his jaw forward. He showed the tinge of

paleness. His voice skirted uncertainty and drew away from it. "I'm not with you on any rough stuff."

"That's good," said Grat DePard, making his voice loud. "That's fine. You're with me as long as it don't cost anything, but you're not if it does. Damn a man that crawls on his belly. Where's your backbone? You want me to do all the fighting while you sit back reading a book somewhere?"

"Nobody asked you to do any fighting," said Cleve Stewart reasonably.

"You think I'm just standin' still while those people come up the valley and push me out."

"There are other ways," said Stewart. But it was a hollow answer and he knew it to be such and closed his mouth. He was caught between two factions and even yet could not bring himself to make his stand. DePard knew that and pushed his question home.

"For the love of God, Stewart, don't straddle all your life. You with me or not?"

Stewart sighed, long and deep. He spoke in a low voice. "If it's got to be that way, Grat, I'm not with you."

Grat DePard let go the horse's cheek strap; he slapped it across the jaw with the full swinging force of his hand. It went up on its hind feet and around and for a moment it pitched along the yard. Stewart fought it to a stop.

"It's more nerve than I thought you had," commented

DePard. "Now you get the hell out of my yard and don't come back. And don't expect anything from me."

"Portia," said Stewart, "come on."

He started down the incline but Portia called to him. "We'll take the hill trail, Cleve."

"No," contradicted DePard, "you keep going that way. I'm surprised at you, Portia."

"Grat," announced Portia, "I take whatever trail I please." He moved toward her horse. He reached for its bridle. Portia's cheeks were red as dye. She called, "Cut that out," and jabbed her spurs deep in the pony. The horse surged at DePard, knocking him back. Morspeare ran forward and Stewart cried: "No, Portia." Portia followed DePard. She rode him down and slashed him with her crop and kept on going until she was near the hill trail. She turned to face him and saw him with his gun out of his holster. He hadn't pointed it, but she thought his intolerant anger might, in another moment, drive him to it. Cleve trotted up and cut in front of her. He called: "Don't do it, Grat!"

"Portia!" yelled DePard.

"Don't do it, Grat," repeated Stewart.

There was a sudden and tremendous change in DePard. One moment he was out of control; and then he caught himself. "All right, Portia," he breathed, "all right."

"Come on," said Stewart, and herded Portia around. They went single file up the steep trail, the view of Broken Bit's yard fading behind the trees. At the height of the ridge Portia stopped. "I'll take this short cut home, Cleve."

"You think Keene's back there on Broken Bit?"

"I don't know." Then she murmured: "You know something? Grat's really afraid of women. I just noticed that. He doesn't know what to do with them."

He said: "I'm going over the pass and see if he went that way. If he hasn't I'll have to do something about Grat. I don't know what it will be. Something."

"Cleve," she said, "you don't have to."

He shook his head. "Yes, I have to." He looked at her, trying to smile. "Fighting comes hard with me, Portia. But other things are harder sometimes."

"You're a strange one, Cleve. You get me all mixed up trying to follow you."

"That's what an education does to a man," he said.

"I like you, Cleve."

"Thanks," he said, and rode around the bend of the trail.

Portia waited until the sound of his horse died in the pines. Thereafter she moved through the trees, east-ward, riding a half circle around Broken Bit. Close to sunset she came to a ledge on the north side of the ranch, dismounted and crawled forward until she had Broken Bit's yard below her. Here at the same vantage point Jim Keene had used two days before, she waited, not knowing what she would do yet certain that Keene was in DePard's house. She added one dismal qualification: He was there — if alive.

X

DULL AND DARK GIANT

KEENE struggled up through unconsciousness like a swimmer fighting toward air. He moved through whirling indefinite sensations of light and sound and unrelated stabs of feeling. The first tangible thing was pain. It began to take root in his head, in his chest, along his left side, setting up its steady attack. Light was a brilliant flame in front of him; gradually as his sight focused he looked beyond the light and discovered Snap impassively near him. Snap crouched now in the corner of the room; he sat motionless, a cigarette in his lips; his eyes were round and gray and empty.

Keene moved his legs, at once rousing long runners of pain from muscles hard battered by whatever had struck him. He rolled a little and brought a hand over his eyes. Directly above him were the slats of an upper bed; he was in the bunkhouse. Men's voices set up an odd clack in the outer night. He distinguished DePard's voice: "Tuck, you ride for Ellenburg." A few moments later DePard came into the bunkhouse, followed by Red John.

DePard said: "Friend, you took a fall."

He was cool about it. In a way he was even amused; it was a drab amusement, without the grace of pity. That was the kind of fighter he was, Keene realized;

one way or another DePard would get what he wanted,
unhindered by any scruples. And always he was cool.
Looking beyond him, Keene noticed the flicker of triumph in Red John's eyes — the reviving memory of an
old score which remained still unsettled. It was Red
John who came over to the bunk and looked down on
him. "Not so tough now," murmured Broken Bit's foreman. "Just another sucker who made a bad bet. Know
what happened to you?"

"No."

"I rode you down," said Red John. "You went under
the horse, rollin' like a keg." He enjoyed the memory
of it, he relished it. "I heard somethin' break and I
thought it was your neck."

DePard spoke. "Naves is up in the house with a
bullet hole clean through him. Maybe he'll pull out of
that. But maybe he won't. Somethin' for you to think
about, friend. You put the hole there." Then he turned
to the little man crouched on the floor. "He stays in
that bunk, Snap."

Red John's hazel eyes showed a dancing light. "You
don't look so big any more, Keene. You come in this
country like a tall breeze and folks got the idea you
were a terror with rings on your tail. Just a sucker, kid."
His smile stretched wide. "You won't be much help to
that girl." He turned out of the bunkhouse with De-
Pard.

Keene lay on his back, a hand over his eyes. The fear
of increased pain kept him still, yet pain pulsed all

through him, so that he had the sensation of motion. He had never known more brutal misery. Heat burned at him, drying him out. He murmured: "How about a drink of water, Snap?" Snap crouched against the wall, making no answer.

He braced himself against each long wave of pain, like a man meeting a strong surf head-on; the effort wore him out. He tried to think of Broken Bit and his own position here, painstakingly reviewing what had happened and what was yet to happen. That too was a failure. Pain broke through every ordered thought; it reduced Keene to the lowest stage of life — the bottom level of muscle and nerve screaming for ease, with sensations of agony eating at his control. At last, exhausted and hard-racked, he closed his eyes and tried to swing with the recurring pulses, mentally rolling back with each oncoming shock. That one thing helped; and at last — long later — he fell into a half sleep.

He woke and found the light still burning. He thought Snap was still in the room, though he was too tired to turn his head. His senses faded to a kind of half rest, threading in and out of troubled dreams and strange feelings that were not dreams; he heard riders coming into the yard, their voices sharp through the night silence. From the corner of his eyes he saw gray light in the windows. Not long after that he dropped into real sleep.

When he woke again sunlight showed through the bunkhouse window and Snap was gone. Riders crossed

the yard, inbound. He heard DePard speaking. For a
little while Keene lay still, half afraid of what he might
find when he moved. Pain had left him during the night,
to be replaced by a cement-like stiffness. Moving his
arms he felt his muscles draw slowly. There was a great
sore patch along his chest and as he gradually doubled
his knees he felt an instant ache in his thighs. He had
met Red John's horse with his chest and in falling had
turned to the right; most of his soreness was on his left
side. He felt the swollen patch on his left thigh.

He lifted himself with a good deal of effort. He bent
over on the bunk's edge, pulling the warp from his back.
He teetered carefully up and down, strain biting him at
each motion. He put his teeth together; he was too
dried-out to sweat but the effect of sweat worked along
his face like nettles. He heard a man moving toward
the bunkhouse; and he was flat on his back when Snap
came in.

Snap waggled a thumb at him. "Over to the kitchen."

Keene swung from the bunk with a deep grunt. He
stood up and rubbed a hand across his face, his fingers
catching a bump on the side of his chin. He stopped
in the doorway, putting a shoulder point to the casing.
Snap said: "Go on, go on." Keene stepped down from the
bunkhouse sill, grunting again at the drop. He moved
with a short, stringhalted limp. One ankle began to
throb and he walked on his heel to remove the pressure
from it. Horses stood in the yard and men waited in
front of the house for something to happen. Keene went

into the kitchen and sat on a cracker box. He drank three cups of black coffee before he touched his breakfast; and ate with a hunger that had no end.

Snap was sleepy. He stood at the doorway, the long night's guard loosening him. He was irritable. He said, "All right," and waggled his thumb again. Keene moved back across the yard, seeing Red John in the saddle. DePard stood near the foreman's horse, talking to him. Keene watched those two until Snap grumbled, "Cut it out." As soon as he got inside the bunkhouse, Keene rolled on the bunk full length and built a cigarette. He took his long drags on it, watching the smoke break against the slats of the upper bunk. Snap had stopped at the doorway. He watched Keene a moment and disappeared, leaving the door open.

Keene heard riders go out of the yard at a fast run. He finished his smoke and dropped it on the bunkhouse floor. He laced his hands across his belly, his thoughts moving slowly across his chances. He thought of Snap, who was ready to fall asleep; his mind came to a full stop on Snap. Snap was outside but when he came in he would crouch at the base of the far wall, crosslegged and nursing his thoughts, whatever they were, in dry silence. It was twelve feet from this bunk to that wall.

He put Snap aside and reconstructed Broken Bit's yard in his head. It was a ten-yard run from the bunkhouse to the corrals; fifty feet more to the pines. A quick run without a horse. The horse was out of it now.

He was tired again and his thoughts were slower and slower; the night and its misery caught up with him. He had no knowledge of falling asleep.

DePard's voice said: "Friend, you're in trouble."

He opened his eyes. DePard was in the room. Red John stood beside him and Morspeare blocked the doorway with his immense shoulders. Morspeare stood with his head ducked, faithfully staring at DePard. Snap was gone and the sunlight didn't show in the immediate yard. It was late afternoon, Keene realized. He had slept through the day.

He pulled himself from the bunk. He forgot about his ankle and put weight on it fully, and grabbed the upper bunk. He was wide-awake.

"Naves died," said DePard.

Jesse Morspeare, answering the only impulse he knew, stepped tentatively forward and showed a red immediate desire in his eyes — a desire to use his clublike hands. Left to himself he would have killed Keene at that instant. Red John's face held the same gray amusement. He murmured: "Sucker." But DePard was cooler than the other two, less controlled by either hatred or the need of satisfaction. His mind had moved ahead. He was seeing things the others did not see, he had made his own plans. All he said was, "You should have joined me, friend," and left the bunkhouse. The other two followed him.

Keene sat on the edge of the bunk, bent over, his hands gripped together. He stared through the doorway, across the narrow vista of the yard. The Chinese cook came out of the kitchen, sloshed a kettle of water across the dust, and went back. It was edging toward evening then and another set of riders went away. Presently he heard a man run forward. The man appeared in the doorway and looked at him a moment, and slammed the door shut. In a few minutes he caught the voices of Portia Crews and Cleve Stewart.

He heard that talk, the quarrel, and DePard's last phrase. Later, with Stewart and Portia gone from Broken Bit, Keene got up and moved toward the bunkhouse window. He stood away from the window, looking out of it at the farther yard. DePard and Morspeare were by the front porch. Presently Red John stepped from another corner of the house and joined them.

Keene cat-walked around the bunkhouse, his glance seizing every article in it. He moved along the bunks, he ran his hands beneath the straw ticks in hopeful search. He walked in a steady circle, the old feeling beginning to sing. There were one table and one chair in the bunkhouse and a stove in a corner. He lifted the stove lid, hefting it in his hand; he calculated its possibilities and laid it back. He paused by the chair, looking down at the lamp on the table. He gripped the chair's top with his arms, swinging his weight against it. Then he moved the chair to another side of the table, within arm's reach of the bunk he had been using. Slowly circling the room, he noticed one thing he had missed — a mirror tacked to the wall. He faced the mirror and saw a blurred face come back to him. Darkness had begun to settle through the bunkhouse. He moved nearer the mirror, noting the dark-whiskered surface of his cheeks, the heavy red scar gouged along the left jaw. He murmured, "Tight, friend. Tight." The man in the mirror showed a hard-mouthed grin; that man looked bad enough to scare a horse. The supper triangle suddenly made a long ringing racket in the yard. A set of riders came rapidly into home quarters.

DePard sat in the porch rocker, with Red John before him and Morspeare a great dull shape beside him. Red John said: "If Ellenburg tells it around that Naves got shot people will know where Keene is. They'll be lookin' this way."

"Who's goin' to look?"

Red John said: "All right. What you thinkin' about now?"

"Tonight we're cutting every piece of homestead wire on the Silver Bow."

"You leavin' Keene here?"

"Jesse will stay to watch him."

"Sure," said Morspeare. He was a great dull lump in the gathering dark, faithfully watching Grat to find what was required of him. He moved around so that he might catch DePard's expression.

"Just watch him, Jesse," said DePard.

"Sure."

Red John gave out his warning. "Don't fool with that fellow too long."

"No, not too long," said DePard.

"Then there's that Brant girl. She says she's stayin'."

"She had a man to help her. She ain't got him now."

"Suppose," said Red John, "you don't scare 'em by cuttin' their wire?"

DePard looked at his foreman. "You afraid of something, Red?"

"Me?" said Red John and tried to wave it away. "Always got to think of the other fellow's hole card, Grat."

"If I didn't know this game," said DePard, "you think I'd be playin' it?"

"I guess not, Grat."

"They don't know me. Nobody knows me, Red. I never make a move unless I mean it. Sometimes I don't move — and maybe somebody thinks I'm bluffing. I never ran a bluff in my life and I never backed up. Those homesteaders think they can wait me out and eat me up little by little. I know what they're thinkin'. They figure that they've got somebody to do the fightin' they ain't able to do. That's Keene. I hear it said he's the man they're countin' on. If it ain't enough to cut their wire then I know something that will clear up the Silver Bow overnight."

"I don't get it, DePard."

DePard rose from the rocker, absorbed by his speculations. Red John, possessing his weaknesses of flesh and his moments of doubt, had his uneasy intimations of a trouble he could not name or see. What he feared was DePard's inhuman faith in himself.

"Keene's the Dutch courage for those homesteaders," said DePard, "and for the girl. Remember that box-elder tree at the ford, Red? If those people found their Dutch courage swingin' from that tree with his neck crooked they wouldn't stay." He stared straight at Red John. "You don't know me very well, either, Red. I'll do what's got to be done."

Keene heard Broken Bit leave the yard in one long running column. Dust drifted across the yard and softly sifted through the cracks of the bunkhouse wall. It was completely dark. He fished up a match to light the lamp on the table and then a new thought arrested him and he held the burning match in his hand, turning the thought around his head until the flame scorched his fingers. He dropped the match. Somebody moved over the yard slowly and opened the door.

Morspeare said: "Go get your supper."

Keene moved through the door, with Morspeare stepping backward and aside. The man was a massive beast in whose small, cloudy brain stray thoughts and impulses moved toward blind ends. The whole night had changed; something had happened and now Morspeare was watching him like a huge rhino uncertainly waiting for the impulse to drop his head and charge.

Keene sat down to the kitchen table. Hungry as he was he ate but little and took a long time at it, steadily searching his mind for the answer to Morspeare's presence. He heard nothing from the yard. It lay wholly silent, squeezed by the blackness of the surrounding hills.

Morspeare said: "Come on."

Keene moved into the yard again. Morspeare backed away and once more came to a stand in the shadows. Keene stopped. "I need a smoke, Jesse," he explained and carefuly reached for his tobacco. He rolled up the cigarette, looking to either side of him and seeing no more Broken Bit men. He lighted the smoke. "I been in that damned bunkhouse all day. Let me walk around the corral."

Morspeare nursed his ponderous silence. Water dripped steadily into the corral trough. Wind, freshly risen from the east, ruffled the tree tops. Morspeare said at last: "All right."

Keene passed the bunkhouse and got into the deeper shadows clinging to the corral. A horse laid its muzzle against the corral posts, emitted a trumpeting blast of wind and ran away. Keene moved to the right, limping on his left heel, keeping the circle of the corral's side near his left shoulder. Morspeare's boots heavily scuffed the earth behind him. Morspeare coughed.

Half around the corral, Keene picked up the blocky shadow of the barn at the edge of the yard and suddenly was convinced that he was alone with Morspeare

— and the cook. Everybody else had gone. Continuing, he faced the house again, seeing only one pony before the porch. That would be Morspeare's.

He had been moving slowly on but now he stopped, the sharpest of sensations tearing along his nerves. He was for that instant frozen in his tracks, not knowing why. The shock had come first; now the reason for the shock followed — Morspeare had quit moving. Morspeare was back in the shadows, still as a dead man. Keene had the cigarette in his mouth. He lifted his arm and expelled a breath of smoke and made his careful pivot.

Morspeare stood fifteen feet away with his revolver lifted and pointed straight on Keene's chest.

The arrival of the bullet waited only on the final pressure of a half-crooked finger. Morspeare, that great and dark-minded animal, had run true to form. Pulled by sullen loyalty and by his own unlighted savageness, he had tramped around the corral in vague anger, to be finally caught by one powerful thought, to be made deadly by it. The thought was plain. Morspeare, brooding upon his wrongs and those of his master, to whom he owed a doglike faith, had decided to shoot Keene in his tracks, and then explain it, perhaps, by saying Keene had tried to break away.

The impulse to throw himself aside trembled along Keene's legs. He had to set himself against it; he had to freeze himself in his tracks. He said: "Afraid?"

Morspeare let the gun muzzle dip. His voice burst

through the night. "Me? I ain't afraid of nothin' that walks."

"The hell you're not. What's that gun up there for?"

Morspeare slid the gun into its holster. He said: "You go on back to the bunkhouse."

Keene wheeled about, cutting away from the corral wall. He moved on, one shoulder lifted by a strain that would not leave. But he knew now, from what Morspeare had intended to do, that the yard was empty. He went into the bunkhouse. He sat on the bunk's edge, watching Morspeare move through the door. The big man lifted the lamp and stepped back to the wall, placing his vast shoulders to it. He was still nursing Keene's talk in his slow mind, working it over and over; his lips came apart and he stood this way, nothing restraining the overbearing greed of his strength but some thin tether of uncertainty he now was obviously trying to break.

"Why the hell should I be afraid of you?" he wanted to know.

"Maybe you just wanted to shoot a hole in the dark."

"If I had my way — "

"Sure. You'd shoot me in the back and tell DePard I tried to run."

"How'd you know that?" asked Morspeare in a puzzled tone.

Keene pulled out his tobacco and creased a paper between his fingers. He shook tobacco into the paper, caught the pouch string between his teeth and let it dangle while he rolled the smoke.

"How'd you know that?" insisted Morspeare, the oddness of it clinging to his mind.

Keene replaced the tobacco sack in his pocket. He sat with the cigarette in his mouth, crouched on the bunk's edge and looking straight at the lamp. His eyelids moved nearer. He saw the square doorway's black mouth, he saw the lamp, he saw Morspeare. Morspeare was near enough the doorway to block it with one roll of his body and for an instant Keene debated some phrase or act which might move the big man deeper into the bunkhouse, away from the door. But in Morspeare strange streaks of cunning leavened his ignorance and it was too much of a risk to arouse that cunning. Keene let his hands dangle over his legs; pressure got into his legs, awaking half-settled aches and pulling at sore muscle masses. This was as near the time as he would ever get; thinking that, he watched yellow light pour through the opening kitchen door across the yard. The Chinaman came out, threw a pail of water on the dust, and returned to the kitchen, leaving the door open. Morspeare turned his head to watch the Chinaman, one great cord in his neck standing sharp and straight from ear base to throat point. Then, realizing this error, he whipped his glance back to Keene.

"You answer me," he grumbled, "or I'll bust you."

Keene rose from the bunk. He stood stooped at the

table, bringing his face toward the top of the lamp chimney to light the cigarette. He brought up the lamp and held it that way until the cigarette caught fire; and kept on lifting the lamp until it was at his shoulder. He flung it into the far corner of the room and made a jump for the door.

He had forgotten his sprained left ankle and he had incorrectly judged the quickness of Morspeare in action. The weight of his jump collected on that bad ankle; it gave way and threw him to the floor — and the next moment Morspeare's body blocked the door from side to side.

The lamp broke against the wall and kerosene smell filled the room, and the guttering blue glare of the wick suddenly flared into full fire leaping at the stain of kerosene on the pine wall. Flat on the floor, Keene heard Morspeare's shout, he saw both Morspeare's feet come forward. Keene rolled. He seized the legs of the table and flung it over as Morspeare made his jump. Tripped at the knees by the table, the big man crashed down.

Keene threshed through the tangle of table legs, rolling and rising. Morspeare was on his feet. He was across the room in one tremendous rush, his great hands reaching for Keene. He missed the side-dodging Keene and shook the bunkhouse as he struck the wall. He was away from the wall, his head down, driving at Keene again. Keene wheeled, ducking low under Morspeare's reaching hand. He jumped the capsized table, seized the chair, and whipped himself around. Fire licked along the wall, the pine boards began to crack. One runner of flame raced under a bunk and caught hold of a straw tick. Heat swelled in the room and smoke flowed across it. Keene had the chair half lifted and Morspeare was a great animal coming at him once more in a terrible, cursing haste, so bereft of thought that he had forgotten his gun, so filled and swamped by his one great greed that no outside thought touched him; he was a battering, insensitive wall of flesh. Keene caught him with the chair, driving the point of a leg against his mouth and through his teeth. Morspeare let out a huge, savage cry and reached for the chair. He caught one rung and splintered it in his fingers. Keene dodged behind him; and then Morspeare was around and charging again, turned mad, his arms outreached for the chair. Keene felt the fire breathe at his legs. He brought the chair full down on Morspeare's head; he saw it fall apart around the big man's shoulders. Morspeare stopped in the middle of the room, blind and stunned; he reached up with his hands to draw them oddly down over his head.

Keene's legs came against the stove, reminding him of the iron lid. He reached for the lid and missed it, but his hands caught the stove's front grating and he broke it from its hinges, carrying the whole stove from its legs. Morspeare jumped again. Keene brought the iron grating from behind in one circling upward loop and hit him across the side of the head. The weight of Morspeare went against him and took him down. Fighting free, he smelled the scorch of his own hair. He rolled Morspeare back and climbed around him on his hands and legs. In the middle of the room he faced about, expecting the big man to be at him again. Morspeare lay still, his arms touched by flames.

Smoke stung Keene's lungs. Still on his hands and knees, he caught Morspeare by the legs and dragged him toward the door. He stood up and got the big fellow by the coat collar, rolling him into the yard.

The Chinaman was at the kitchen doorway. He was crying in a high jangled voice and beating the supper triangle. Keene yelled at him, whereupon the Chinaman jumped inside the kitchen and slammed the door.

Keene turned Morspeare over and over. He reached down and unbuckled Morspeare's gun belt and strapped it on — and ran at the kitchen door. He knocked it open, to find the Chinaman standing in the middle of the room with a long knife pointed straight ahead of him. Keene said:

"You watch him."

He ran out of the kitchen, hugging the house wall until he was certain no other man remained on Broken Bit. He reached Morspeare's horse and stepped to the saddle. The bunkhouse doorway and its window were red-white with flame; sparks circled slowly from the chimney as he crossed the yard. At the foot of the hill trail he turned the horse to have a last look. He thought: That house is going to catch fire. Flame exploded through the bunkhouse roof; the Chinaman slowly labored Morspeare along the ground toward the north side of the yard. Keene turned into the hill trail — and heard a woman's voice calling:

"Jim."

He saw Portia Crews move from the near-by pines into the outreaching light of the fire. Distant in the hills somewhere, above the snore of the fire, he thought he heard a shot. Portia Crews rode in against him; she was a tall, bending shape in the saddle. Her hand reached out and her broad lips expressively moved as she touched his face. All this light made her hair yellower than he remembered it; it softened her smile. "Jim!"

He sat loose in the saddle, his leg troubling him and a revived pain hammering his chest. He heard another shot, this time unmistakably definite, and then saw two riders rush into the yard from the hills across the way.

Portia said: "Come on, Jim! I saw DePard take part of his crew into the valley. But there's more of Broken Bit scattered around here. Follow me!"

"Circle around to the valley — "

"Don't say anything, Jim! Follow me!"

Looking at her he saw genuine fear on her face; behind its strength and its willfulness and its beauty he saw fear. Energy slipped rapidly out of him, the old salt sting of temper went away. He said: "All right," and obediently turned, following her up the hill into the darkness and into the bite of a rising east wind.

She called softly back: "Keep close to me, Jim. I saw four Broken Bit men up here near sundown."

XI

IN THE CANYON

KEENE had followed Portia along the black and winding mountainside trail for a steady ten minutes when he called a halt, impelled by a warning that was nothing more than a sense of having trusted chance too far. There was no other reason for stopping; yet this impalpable threat of uncertainty which somehow made everything wrong was the oldest and surest of his guides. He said: "Wait," and drew off the trail. She pushed her horse after him and the two of them turned thoroughly still, hearing the steady breathing of the ponies and, above them, the strengthening sweep of wind in the pine tops. From this height they saw the glare of the burning ranch. The bunkhouse was a dark-traced skeleton in a yellow ball of flame; the main house roof had begun to burn. The Broken Bit yard was day-bright and now they saw men running in and out of the house.

"We're going the wrong way, Portia. I want to get back to the valley."

She said as an apparent side thought: "I met Dr. Ellenburg on the trail yesterday. He was coming back from Broken Bit. What happened to Naves?"

"He's dead."

She pointed at the fire below them. "And then that.

DePard will never let you spend another day at the ford."

He thought of DePard riding out at twilight and he thought of Aurora at the ford, and the feeling of things turning wrong nagged at him. He sat quiet, watching the roof of the main house explode into one tremendous cone of flame. He counted five men down there. Three of them rode over the yard and disappeared on the trail he had so recently taken. "They're following," said Portia. "From now on they'll never quit following. Don't you see that?"

"We could make a wide circle and follow the ridge back to the Silver Bow," said Keene, thinking aloud. "Wonder where DePard went?"

She knew what troubled him and what pulled him toward the ford so strongly. "That's the first place they'll look for you, Jim."

"Where?"

"At the ford."

"Sure," he said. "They'll go straight there."

She realized she had said the wrong thing. Now he would never rest until he got back to Aurora Brant. That was a bitter thought for her and brought her close to the worst fear she had — the fear that perhaps he loved the homestead girl. Of that she was still unsure and therefore had her own hopes. But she realized more clearly than he did how small a chance of survival he had if he returned to the ford. DePard would storm through these hills night and day to find Keene; he would lie in wait by the ford, he would watch every trail. And so Portia, wanting him to be safe, lied.

"That girl," she said in an offhand manner, "is all right. Cleve Stewart took her up to his place yesterday afternoon."

By his quick lift of head she knew it took something from his conscience; she pressed her talk softly against him. "We're wasting time, Jim. Those fellows are coming up this trail. There's another bunch holding beef in a meadow just south of here, not far away. And De-Pard will be back pretty soon. We've got to get off this mountain. I know this country. I know where to go."

"All right."

He followed her again. The trail moved upward in bending, unseen curves and reached a minor crest and kept to it for a mile or more. Up here the night wind was thin and sharp; winter moved over the land this night, sweeping out the last summer's warmth. He heard its crisp singing in the trees. Portia murmured back at him, "Down," and took another trail. They dropped through layers of darkness, came to a pine flat and a road lying east and west. Keene moved abreast Portia Crews, traveling at a steady run along the road. They had left the wind behind and now only the steady rhythm of the horses disturbed the night. But he bent on the saddle, listening, and suddenly said: "Off the road," and charged into the trees, Portia behind. He stopped in the timber. Portia whispered, "What?"

Sound murmured forward and grew into a beating

rhythm of three or four riders moving westward toward Broken Bit in haste. Keene saw their shapes vaguely and impermanently against the night and heard one voice speak. He sat still, aware of Portia's hand resting on his arm. It was a light and steady pressure — a soft, fugitive offer of her presence. One voice in the distance came briskly back. "Smell that dust!" And then the party had stopped and was still. Presently the same voice called into the night: "Broken Bit!"

Another voice harked thin and brief through the silence. "Shut up, Len."

"Somebody ridin' around here."

Silence closed down, with that group attentively paused on the road. Presently one man cruised back. He came abreast Keene and Portia — twenty feet distant — and reined in to again listen. His horse blubbered and flung up its head, the metal of its bit jingling like music. This rider murmured: "Somebody around here."

"Come on, Len."

Portia's fingers clung to the cloth of Keene's sleeve. He heard her sigh. In another moment the riders on the road went away at a long run.

"That was close," said Portia. "We might have bumped into them. Come on."

She didn't immediately return to the road, but found a side trail that circled into Lost Man Ridge. The country grew rougher and sharper-sloped. Within half an hour she was on the main road once more. When she left the road she struck northeast, dropped into a narrow ravine and crossed a creek. Looking overhead, Keene saw the broken edges of hills flung carelessly against the metal sky. They went deeper into this country, through one close defile and another, across narrow pockets, along sheer cliff faces and on up through pines. They had been in the saddle, he judged, better than two hours when they entered a canyon no more than six yards wide, skirted the stony margin of a creek clashing rapidly downgrade, and at last stopped.

"This is it," she said, and stepped from the saddle.

Above him he saw the blankness of perpendicular walls. The creek rattled at his feet. He got stiffly down from the horse, moving forward through ink-black shadows to a kind of rock gallery cut into the canyon wall. He turned from the gallery and walked beside the creek, and presently his exploring hands touched short pines clinging to the steep walls. Stripping off all the branches he could reach, he returned to the gallery. The resin blisters of the branches exploded into sudden light and warmth when he held a match to them.

He said: "Where is this?"

"East of Broken Bit five or six miles. You're in the Short Hills, Jim. If you went south you'd come out at the Silver Bow Canyon, twelve miles from the ford." Her voiced lightened and grew hopeful. She was asking something of him and for a moment he didn't know what it was; she was really eager to have him say some one thing. Then he thought he knew.

"Thanks," he said, "for the help."

"Ah," she answered, and was pleased. She dropped to the ground, near him. "This is a spot I found, riding one time. I said if I ever had to hide this would be the place. They'll be a long time finding you here." Then she slowly added, "Long enough for you to rest and move on."

He dropped to his shoulders, lying on the hard floor of the gallery. Firelight reached back another ten feet and came against the gallery's end; it danced on the rock and dirt ceiling above. Smoke lifted to the ceiling and drifted outward. Fire's heat made a half-barrier against the raw damp cold slowly condensing in the canyon. His ankle ached and the battered muscles of his chest and left side steadily throbbed. What pressed against him now as a dead weight was the letdown following hard action; he was emptied of strength, he had no enthusiasm, no wish to think. Even the necessity of rising to scout more wood for the fire was a dreary chore; he lay there, all passive, unresisting, glad to drop his guard.

Portia said: "What now, Jim?"

"You're sure Aurora went up to Stewart's place?"

"Yes."

"The ford's the first place DePard will go," he reflected. "He'll burn that store. Tough for Aurora. Had her heart set on that spot."

"She can change her heart. Most of us have to do that." She still wanted to know what Keene's own desire was; it grew increasingly important to her. "What next, Jim?"

"A night's sleep."

She said: "'I think I can guess where DePard went tonight. To raise trouble with the nesters. That's been in his mind ever since the nesters came. He'll drive them out, Jim. What's to stop him? Who can stand up against Broken Bit?"

He said: "We'll see."

She sat near him, holding his eyes with her glance. She was a woman with a will, with her own daring. Her lips were broad and softly placed together and firelight flowed over her features and heightened the yellow shining of her hair. At that moment every thought she had was of him; those thoughts reached toward him and touched him intimately. "Don't think of it, Jim. You're a marked man. If you stay in this country you'll never know which trail holds your death. You'll never dare show yourself in the valley. They'll be waiting for that and they'll box you in. Daylight's not much good for you now." Her voice dropped to a quiet low tone. "Not easy for me to say this — but why don't you just ride out, the same way you rode in?"

"No," he said, "I guess not."

"Why stay when it means DePard will kill you sometime, somehow? What is it, Jim? Why?"

"I guess that was settled the night I saw Morspeare slug Spackman, in town. That was a hard thing to watch."

"It happens every day, all over the world."

"A little man against a big one," he reflected. "I saw Spackman's eyes when he got up. A little man looking at something he couldn't lick — being pushed around by something he couldn't fight. Everything he dreamed about, for himself and his kids, down in the dust, busted to pieces. Ashamed of himself in front of his family. That kind of a look in his eyes."

"Is that your fight, Jim? Or is it that you just have to fight, because that's the only thing you like?"

He showed her his first smile; it broke self-deprecatory and gentle across the battered, whisker-dark planes of his face. "How do I know? A man was put in the world to do something. The only thing I can do is fight. Maybe that's it."

She steadied her chin on her hand. "You're odd," she murmured, "and you'll be cold tonight." She got up and went outside and was gone for a long while, returning at last with an armful of pine limbs and pieces of wood drifted up from the creek. She freshened the fire, kneeling before it. She turned perfectly still, her head dropped and her eyes watching him. "I'll be back in the morning with something to eat — and a razor. You look too tough with whiskers. I like my men smooth-cheeked." An unsettled expression went across her eyes and left its increasing disturbance on her face. She was near Keene. She put a hand on his chest and let it lie there; she seemed to be drawn completely into herself, listening to an inner voice, to an inner command. Suddenly she bent down and kissed him, her lips warm and the fragrance of her hair very strong to his senses.

She pulled herself back. "Did it mean anything to you, Jim?"

He looked up at her, his senses sharp-whipped. She saw the lean kink of muscles along his cheek, the repression he threw into them; and she saw the ancient manlike expression in his glance, the gray and heavy and hungry awareness of her presence. He said: "Don't do that again, Portia."

"Ah," she said, half laughing, and pleased with the feeling she had produced. "You'll be miserable tonight. I'd stay — I'd keep the fire for you."

"You start home."

She rose and left the gallery again. She came back with his saddle and blanket. She put the saddle under his head and laid the blanket over him. Her fingers, warm and soft, ran across his mouth. She murmured, "Good night," and then in an altered and apprehensive voice, she added: "Don't leave until I see you again, Jim. You won't, will you?"

"All right," he said, and watched her go.

Nine o'clock that night DePard crossed the Silver Bow at the Black Bluff ford, twelve miles east of Aurora's store, and came upon the first homestead fence. This was the fence of Aleck Comrie — that angular and reserved pipe-smoking Scotch bachelor who held his eccentric theories of farming, one of which was that

the Silver Bow was orchard country. He had ordered
the young trees from Missouri, had planted them along
the river bluff and had put his barbwire around them.
After a summer in a soil whose riches could only be un-
locked by water, half the orchard was dead, but it was
Comrie's contention that the hardy survivors would ad-
just themselves to dry land.

Comrie sat in his doorway and watched DePard's
riders move straight at the yard. He knew then he was
in for trouble but his only reaction was to tap his pipe
against the doorsill and refill it. The group rode up.
DePard said: "You're Comrie?"

"That would be so," admitted Comrie and lighted a
match on his thumbnail. The flare of it slanted along
the angular jaw, the frosty gray eyebrows — along the
winter quiet of his eyes; and went out.

DePard sent his riders into the orchard with a brief,
"All right," himself standing watch in front of Comrie.
Comrie leaned back against the door frame; his lips
made little puckering noises at the pipestem. "We're
cutting that fence, Comrie," said DePard.

"Aye," said Comrie, "it seems like that from here."

"Don't put it up again."

Comrie heard the tight wire snap when cut. He
watched the shadows drift around the orchard; he
watched them collect and move into the yard again, the
job done. DePard said in a sharper voice:

"You hear?"

"My hearin's good," admitted Comrie, the starched,

burred inflections of his voice strong as the smell of heather on a damp day.

"Fine," said DePard.

But Comrie did not wish to be misunderstood and now added distinctly: "I did not say I wud not put it up again."

DePard said: "You put it up again and I'll drag this shanty over the bluff, you in it. Better leave the country, Comrie. I'm running cattle on these flats next spring and I don't want you around."

He whirled away with his riders, leaving the Scotchman solemnly sucking his pipestem. Comrie smoked on until nothing but cold ashes remained; and rose and knocked the pipe against the doorsill. Then he murmured to himself, "I did not say I wud leave the country, either."

DePard rode a crisscross pattern over the desert. There was no wire at Ambler's but he paused to drop his hint. "I wouldn't stay here long, if I were you people." The Brighthand family was away. DePard wrecked the door of the shanty, threw a loop around the stove and dragged it to the yard. He ran into wire again at Elijah Patterson's place and cut it before Patterson's anguished eyes. At the Kilrain shanty he faced an Irishwoman who swore at him steadily as long as he stayed. She had her children behind her, but still she swore. Mrs. Kilrain kept saying: "Kilrain, go get your gun! Don't stand there! Go get your gun!" Kilrain shook his head, knowing better. It was Red John who lassoed the Kilrain rig, towed it on into the prairie and tipped it over.

Far off to the north other homestead lights winked at lonely-spaced intervals. DePard traveled steadily west, visiting those nesters in his path, and as he traveled he grew more impatient with his own mildness until at last, when he reached the Cannon yard, he was a harder man than he had been at Comrie's. It was close to midnight then, with the Cannons silent inside the lightless shack. DePard called impatiently at Cannon, his men meanwhile threshing through the yard. Somebody found an ax and began to break up Cannon's new well frame.

Cannon came to the doorway, a white shape in his nightgown. Mrs. Cannon cried: "Come back in here, Sam," but Cannon stepped into the dust with his bare feet.

"Mr. DePard," he said, "what are you after? Let my place alone."

"You don't want trouble, do you?"

"No," said Cannon, "I want no trouble."

"Then get out of here."

"Mr. DePard," said Cannon, "I'm an old man and I have seen more trouble than you have ever seen. I am not bothering you. I'm a man of peace. This country's big enough for all — "

"No," contradicted DePard, "it ain't. Leave the country, old man, or I'll be here again." He called up his riders and moved out of the yard. Cannon followed him.

Mrs. Cannon kept crying: "Sam, come back here." But Cannon, his nightgown making a gaunt and gray apostle of him, followed DePard and spoke on.

"You are not the law. I have seen men like you before and I have seen them make the same mistake. No man is as great as the law. No man is almighty. What you are doing is wrong. You have no right to destroy and I have no right to destroy."

Broken Bit's riders moved around him. He was caught in the center of the group; he walked rapidly to keep from being stepped on by the horses. He was pushed aside by the horses, and pushed back. He breathed harder, he tried to catch DePard's reins and his voice was the saddened voice of a man seeing evil and pouring his honest goodness against it. He reached for DePard's hand.

"There are men, Mr. DePard, who will take your example. If you destroy, they will destroy and we will all be fighting. That is not the way for men to live."

"Get on," said DePard, and put his boot against Cannon's chest. The pressure forced the old man against Red John's horse, whereupon Red John reached down and shoved Cannon away. Cannon reached again for DePard's arm.

"Don't you see what you're doing, Mr. DePard? The law is your defense as well as mine. You are strong enough now to have your way — "

"Go on, old man."

" — But someday the homesteaders will be strong

and you will want the protection of the law. If you destroy it, Mr. DePard, you are signing your own death warrant."

DePard ripped his gun from its holster and spoke one fiery word and brought the barrel of the gun down on the old man's head. Mrs. Cannon came from the house, screaming: "Sam — Sam, what's the matter?" Broken Bit rushed away and dust shimmered in the dark night and Cannon, wrapped in his apostle's robe, lay dead on the ground.

Red John heard Mrs. Cannon's scream, and Red John was afraid. He pushed his horse beside Grat DePard. "That was a damn-fool thing to do!"

"Tired of listening to him. Next time he'll keep his mouth shut."

"Next time, hell. He's an old fellow. Maybe you killed him."

Spackman's lay to the right, a mile off Broken Bit's trail. DePard drew in, considering the dark distant square of the Spackman shanty. He listened to Red John's irritated, half-worried voice.

"He dropped like a dead man. You exposed yourself on that one, Grat. All these homesteaders know it was us."

"What good does it do 'em?" asked Grat coolly.

"Trouble," grumbled Red John.

"Not for me," answered DePard, confidently. "I'm makin' the trouble, Red. For the other fellow, not for me." He had put the Spackman shanty out of his mind and now turned to the ford. Broken Bit went rattling across the shallowed water, the clack and grind of their passage rolling brittle echoes on ahead. DePard swept wide of the store and then Red John, who had studied his boss for many years, knew that one of his silent observations was true. Grat DePard, totally unafraid of any man on earth, had a spooky aversion to women. Not understanding them, unable to forecast their actions, he lost his sureness when he came to deal with them; and so now he ran around Aurora Brant's, heading into the valley.

Red John said: "Somebody coming."

The outfit reined in, hearing a single horse rush down the valley. DePard said: "Red, drift off a bit," and watched the foreman sink into the dark. He sat still on the saddle, forever suspicious, his mind grasping at possibilities of chance and error. The horseman, following the bend of the creek, came impetuously forward and sighted the blur of the Broken Bit crowd. He was a hundred feet away when he started calling:

"Grat — that you? Grat?"

He swept in, the momentum of the pony carrying him half through the group. "Grat — the ranch is burnin'! The ranch is goin' to hell, Grat!"

Red John rushed in. "What happened?"

"I don't know. But the ranch is burnin'. That Keene hit Jesse on the head and knocked him cold. Then he got away."

Grat DePard swayed in the saddle and in the long

silence he turned slowly old at the thought of his hopes
vanishing in smoke — at the wreckage of the one thing
dear to him; he turned old and dull and he thought of
Keene, and then Keene was the target of every foiled impulse in Grat DePard's body; he became an obsession
that grew greater and greater to DePard until there was
no other thought that meant anything. When he spoke
it was in a dead, outbreathing sigh: "Red."

"Yeah?"

"He'll come back here to the girl. You stay here where
you can watch. When it starts getting daylight, move
back to that east ridge, but keep watchin'. I'm going to
the ranch. I'll be back later." Then he said to the mes-
senger, in faintest hope: "Everything on fire?"

"She's up in smoke, Grat."

"Ah," groaned DePard. "Be sure you keep watchin',
Red. I am going to get that man. I am going to ride him
clear to hell."

He moved on so quickly that he caught the rest of the
group flat-footed. Broken Bit took out after him. Red
John stepped from the saddle and crouched against the
earth, prepared for a lonesome night. He watched the
shadowed bulk of Aurora's cabin, a quarter mile away;
and as he watched he began to think of her with a gradual
excitement.

Young Joe Spackman came into the store yard early
next morning. "DePard raided the flats last night. He
hit old Cannon on the head. Cannon's dead."

Aurora had a clear feeling of tragedy, a heart-pulling compassion for the Cannons; but as she stood in the yard she realized that the events of the past few weeks had built a fatalism around her sympathies. She had lost all sense of security, she had come to expect anything; and nothing — not even this news — shocked her as much as it would have a month before. She said: "I'll go back with you, Joe," and went to saddle her pony.

Before she left the yard she locked up the store and the log cabin. Leaving the store involved a good deal of mental struggle. Everything she had was here at this spot, every material possession and every hope, and she had come to feel that if she left it, no matter for how brief a time, she would lose everything. What decided her was the call of neighborliness. These homesteaders had helped her; it was her turn to help them. On the desert it worked this way. As a sudden afterthought she left a note tacked on the door for Keene, explaining where she had gone, and then rode over the ford with young Joe.

"I heard riders come by last night," she said.

"That was them. They cut wire all the way from Comrie's to here."

"DePard wants to scare us out."

"Why, yes," said young Joe, "I guess he does."

He was nineteen, she remembered; an earnest slow-going boy who would somehow wrest a living from the soil, who would never complain or grow sour with the hard labor that was his lot, who would always care for his responsibilities and hope for good to come. In a way he was typical of the best of these homesteaders in his patience, in his steadfastness. It took young Joe's kind to settle the land. Then he looked at her and said: "They got a lot to answer for — that Broken Bit outfit," and she realized he had changed since she had last seen him. He had matured, he had lost his boyishness.

They rode into the yard and found fifteen or more of the Silver Bow men gathered there. Comrie, who had Old World manners, stood up from his seat on the well curb and removed his hat — an angular, frosty-browed man with the bluest of eyes. She smiled at him and went into the house. Homestead women sat around the small living room, dutifully lending their presence to Mrs. Cannon. Mrs. Cannon appeared unconscious of them; she swayed steadily back and forth in a rocker, her hands idle on her lap.

"Can I do anything?" asked Aurora.

"I do guess everything's bein' done for me," said Mrs. Cannon, but she added, "Aurora, you should come back across the river. You shouldn't stay there. Nobody can help you, and God knows we'll all need help enough. What did Cannon ever do to them? DePard did it. I saw him do it. Don't you stay over there alone any more."

This room was too crowded. Aurora moved on to the kitchen where Mrs. Spackman and Mrs. Kilrain were doing the day's cooking. She talked with them a moment and continued on out to the back yard, to find Jennie standing alone. "Jennie," she said, "I think young Joe's looking for you."

"Oh no, not me," said Jennie.

That lost and desolate answer puzzled Aurora, for she knew how close those two had been. Jennie met Aurora's glance and seemed to shrink away. "I have been a bad girl, and now my daddy is dead."

Aurora reached forward and pulled Jennie around. "Jennie," she murmured, shocked and hurt by that blank lifelessness she saw. Jennie Cannon stood obediently still, her eyes on the ground.

"I would like to die," she said, precise and colorless. "But it is too late for that now, isn't it? My mother — "

"Jennie!"

Jennie slipped away from Aurora's arms and walked farther out from the yard, her hands folded across her breasts; she walked on and on into the sagebrush obviously not aware of her surroundings.

Aurora turned around the house and found that another homesteader, Cal Murchison, had arrived with news. "Broken Bit was burned last night."

That news stirred the homesteaders and brought half the women from the house. Spackman said: "How'd it happen?"

"Why," said Murchison, "there was a fight, accordin' to what I hear. That man Keene went up there and I guess they treated him pretty rough. He was there when DePard came down here. Jesse Morspeare was watchin' him and they had a fight. The place burned."

They were all looking at Aurora. Spackman said: "You know about that, Aurora?"

"No." The news chilled her. She waited for Murchison to go on talking and when he didn't add anything she asked: "What happened to him?"

"I don't know."

Her voice was high in her own ears. "Didn't you hear anything more?"

Spackman said thoughtfully: "I kind of hoped maybe he would do something."

Aurora had her moment of irritation, born of worry. "Hasn't he done something?"

"Yes," said Spackman. "Something. But DePard is still against us." He made a half apology to her. "What should I want him to do? It is our trouble, not his. But it is natural, I guess, to lean on a good man. He was. Yet now — "

She said: "What are you going to do?"

Her voice was still sharp. Spackman rubbed his chin. He reached for his pipe and nursed it in thought. She saw Kilrain look across the yard at his wife, and look away. None of the other men had any desire to speak. Theirs was the indecision of men who, though they would fight as individuals in ways with which they were familiar, could not see themselves armed and riding together against DePard. It went against everything they knew.

Brighthand's wife called: "I'll tell you what we're doing. We're leaving."

Mrs. Kilrain said, scornfully: "Ah. What a shameful thing to say!"

Brighthand retorted: "What's to be ashamed of? Next time DePard comes back he'll shoot at the houses. I ain't proud enough to stand around and see one of my kids get hurt. There's a lot of land left where a man don't have to take those chances."

Aurora looked at Spackman, knowing him to be more of a fighter. But now Spackman nursed his pipe in silence. Elijah Patterson said: "What a shame. No law, no sheriff. Nothing but a man that can do what he pleases."

"Can he now?" said Kilrain.

"Well, he has."

"Sure — he caught us by surprise. But there's a next time. Or will we be hidin' in the root cellar?"

"Can't be ridin' back and forth all winter, like an army. There's farmin' or there's fightin'. Can't do both."

"Do one thing first," pointed out Kilrain. "There'll be plenty of time for farmin' after."

"You think you can face a bunch of gunmen?" asked George Lacey.

"As for that," said Kilrain, "I'll pick me own spot. When a man's too heavy for me fists I use a board. There's ways, Lacey. There's ways."

"We're leavin'," repeated Brighthand.

The hardness of their position was on them all. They sat in desperate reflection of their injustices, but they were family men and that responsibility was heavy. All this was going through them, swaying them and influencing them. Comrie said:

"Aurora, you've got to leave that place. It is the worst spot of all."

"Yes," said Spackman, "that's right. You want I should take my team and move you?"

She walked to her pony, stepped to the saddle. "No," she said. "I'm not leaving."

Comrie cast a sly glance at Spackman; he looked around at the other men, and at Aurora again. "You're not afraid, Aurora?"

"I can be afraid," she said. "But I'll stay there." She started from the yard, but turned back. She had something more to say. "If this man can scare you out here, some other man will scare you out somewhere else. If you're going to run, you'll always be running. This is your land, isn't it? These are your houses and fences. All the work is yours — a year out of your lives. Where will you go that's better? What will you say to your children when they want to know why you don't stay?" She pointed across the river, toward the hills and toward Broken Bit. "Do you know why that man dares to raid the flats? Because he believes homesteaders have no courage. He believes they'll run when he frightens them. And after you're gone he'll laugh at you and know he's right. Just remember that. He'll be laughing at you."

She went out of the yard at a run. She hadn't been angry in the beginning but she was now because she was thinking of Keene, who had ridden straight at Broken

Bit, one man against the outfit. She remembered the cut of his shoulders against the sunshine and, riding toward the ford, she had her dark and rising worry. Where was he now?

Comrie looked around the crowd. He said in a soft, pressing way: "The girl has got the spunk. Now, for me, I will mend my fence and I will stay. And if we could find that Keene and he would show us how to do it properly, for there is a proper method in fighting and a wrong one, I would do more. I would follow him."

Spackman said: "An idea there, Aleck. Yes, an idea."

Mrs. Kilrain said: "Ye should all be ashamed, waitin' here like geese. If ye want that man Keene go and find him. And maybe he's needin' help now, wherever he is."

Elijah Patterson said: "Those are big hills. Who knows where to look?"

Indecision swayed the group again. Spackman rose, motioning to his wife and young Joe. "We will see about that," he said, and went to his rig. He got in the rig and waited for his wife to take her seat and drove away. Young Joe followed on his horse.

Young Joe let the rig get ahead of him. He rode at a slow walk, his eyes on the ground and his heart eaten by the despair of vanished dreams. By turns he was a boy, hating Jennie Cannon for her unfaithfulness and for the agony she had given him; and by turns he was a man, catching a faint intimation of a gentler wisdom. There was need of something in him but he could not understand the need. The thought of Red John rode with him and it was that thought which, gouging deeper and deeper into his soul, hardened him out of his boyhood.

His father was in the shed putting away the buggy horse when young Joe arrived. Spackman said: "Something is not right with you. Is it the girl Jennie?"

"Maybe."

Spackman considered his son, who was half a head taller and twenty pounds heavier. "A boy makes nice things in his head and they are just so. But a man knows things are not just so." He pulled out his pipe and, with his eyes on it, he added: "Mistakes are mistakes. The hot blood makes many. The cold blood makes none." He had filled his pipe and he had lighted it. He had a gray square-cut beard on a ruddy, round beaming face. He was a Hollander who loved his comfort, who had his convictions and his tolerance. He said at last: "It comes to me you are a man now," and left the shed.

XII

THE QUARREL

PORTIA returned to Keene's hideout before daylight, bringing him food, a frying pan and a coffeepot. She brought him also one of her father's razors and a cake of soap. "You're beginning to look like an outlaw with those whiskers," she remarked, and cooked breakfast while he shaved. It pleased her to see how much satisfaction he got from the meal; he was a sound man with no fat on him and his energy compelled an appetite. In everything he was robust and forward, even in the way he had looked at her the night before, when she had kissed him. Watching him roll his after-meal smoke, she realized she was trying in every way she knew to make herself a part of his life. It troubled her to think of what might happen to him if he stayed in the country, but it was unbearably hard to think of his leaving. The truth was, and this she had decided in the long night hours, she would go with him when he left, if he asked. If he did not ask —

He said: "You're a help, Portia."

She was hungry for whatever kindness he could offer. Not that kindness was enough, but perhaps behind the kindness there was something else which could be encouraged. She lay back on the gallery floor, beside the fire. Day had not yet penetrated the heavy, crystal mists lying in the narrow canyon and a chill dampness clung to everything so that the fire was a comfort. Keene, having shaved, looked fresh again. He had slept away his fatigue and his body once more was controlled by restlessness. For her own part she was half asleep, having spent most of the night riding to and from the hideout.

She said: "I guess I've got to get out of here before it is light. I don't want to give away your hideout. What are you going to do?"

"Don't know yet."

She sat up. "You might ride over the hill and keep going."

"No," he said.

She got to her feet, finding it hard to go. Everything moved off into nothing; she couldn't look ahead. "I'll see you again, Jim?" She wanted to ask him to stay in this hideout, but she knew his mind was already alive with his plans. He was the kind of man who would hate a woman's interference. He was thoroughly independent and she loved him for it, yet it was hard not to have him need her.

"Yes," he said.

"Be careful, won't you?" she asked him. Later, because she could not check her feelings, she added something she really wished she could have held back. "You know, Jim, it would be tough for me if anything happened to you."

She went to her horse and got on the saddle. He followed her and took her hand. She saw the cheerful glint of his eyes, the half-rash confidence in him. He had a heavy, strong hand and its pressure passed physically through her. "I'll see you tonight or tomorrow. Don't come back here, though. I'm moving out."

"Where?"

He shrugged his shoulders. "Just moving around. That's the way this thing goes. You'd better go to bed. You're just able to keep your eyes open."

"All right," she said obediently, and had a thought then that made her secretly embarrassed at herself. She let her hand remain within his solid grasp, wistfully wishing this moment could be more than it was and wondering if there ever could be more for her. Then he pulled his arm away and she rode down the creek.

In the space of the last two nights Indian summer had gone and winter was here; day broke late somewhere above the cold overcast of fog. When she came near the mouth of the canyon the dark fog still covered her but she cut quickly into a right-angle ravine, crossed it and turned from defile to defile, deliberately confusing her trail.

Reaching Lost Man Ridge later, she detoured to the edge of Broken Bit's home quarters and came upon a yard which held no sign of activity. DePard was out on Keene's trail and never would leave that trail. Better than most people she knew DePard's capacity for hatred, his thirst for breaking down opposition. Observing the charred and still-smoking ruins of the ranch house —

only the barn remaining — she knew that this one thing would drag up all his killing instincts.

She cut back toward her own house, alert to trouble in the half daylight of the timber. At home she went upstairs and pulled a quilt over her and slept soundly until the middle of the afternoon. Her father was somewhere in the hills and most of the crew was gone; but, eating a quick lunch in the kitchen, she heard the story of De-Pard's raid on the homesteaders from the cook. The news had traveled fast. At once she saddled a fresh horse and started for Cleve Stewart's ranch; she found him in the middle of the valley.

He had been beyond the pass, he told her, and had found nothing and now was headed for Aurora's. "She ought to know something about him."

"Ah, Cleve," she said, "I'm the one you should ask," and told him where she had been.

"What's he going to do now?"

"I don't know."

He shook his head. "He'll never get out of this alive. I wish I knew what I could do to help him."

"I guess we both wish that, Cleve. I guess I wish it more than you." Then she added the news of the Silver Bow raid. Cleve Stewart's instant reaction was to throw his horse into a gallop. "I've got to get Aurora out of that store. DePard will watch it. He'll expect Keene to go there."

"I told Keene you'd already taken Aurora to your place," she confessed. When he looked at her in surprise, she added defensively: "I know it was a lie. But that's why I said it. I didn't want him to come back into the valley."

They ran down the valley underneath a cold, silver-misted sunlight. Stewart, she thought, was one of those men who had never been born to be tough. He had too much sentiment in him, too much honesty; he wore his feelings on his sleeve. Even though he tried to play the hard game of the country he lacked that iron core and that temper which, in self-defense, could be as thoroughly cruel. Those qualities belonged to Keene and though in some respects Keene was less fine a character than Stewart, neither as truly civilized nor as gently con-siderate, he was far more the whole and natural man. In this world of dust and action and raw force he fitted perfectly. She drew one more sharp distinction between those two. Always Cleve Stewart would possess under-standing and would defer to a woman's wishes. Keene would take what he wanted, but his smile and his strong man-quality would always justify him in a woman's eyes.

She said: "You like her a lot, don't you, Cleve?"

"Yes," he said. "A lot."

"I wish you luck," she sighed. In another few mo-ments they were in Aurora's yard.

Aurora had seen them coming and now stood waiting in the yard. Portia, prying into this girl's every reaction, saw her black worry, her shadowed fear. Still, it was odd to Portia that with all this strain on her Aurora could stand so composed and keep her voice so calm.

"Do you know anything about him? I heard about the fire and the fight. But do you know — "

"He's over in the Short Hills," said Portia, close to being blunt. "I found a hideout for him. I took him breakfast this morning. He's all right."

Aurora's eyes clung to Portia; they were gray and they held everything she felt away from Portia and Stewart. She showed no relief, she showed nothing. All she said was, "I'm glad." It was a coldness or a repression Portia could not, from her own warm heart, possibly understand. It built up her resentment; from that moment onward she disliked Aurora Brant.

Cleve said: "Now, Aurora, you've got to leave here. You've got to move to my place. You know what's happened across the river."

"I know," said Aurora. Portia, absorbing every shred of sentiment on the other girl's cheeks, saw the arrival of stubbornness. "But I'm not leaving," Aurora added.

Stewart spoke with concerned irritation. "I can't protect you here."

"That's all right, Cleve."

Portia, who had a will and a tongue of her own, used them now. "You're not the only one on this desert. If somebody comes here and hurts you, then Cleve's got to take care of you. Don't make it hard on him."

"I'm not asking any favors," answered Aurora. She dropped her eyes and her voice faded to a drawn murmur: "If you knew — No, I'll stay. I'm sorry, Cleve."

"Look," said Portia. "This is the first place Jim will

ride for. Because you're here. DePard knows that and he'll watch this place. You better go with Cleve."

Aurora gave Portia a half-angered look. "Why didn't you say so? If that's the way it is, I'll go. But how can you tell Jim I'm not here? How can you tell him to stay away?"

"I can find him."

Cleve Stewart blurted out, "I thought you already told Jim that Aurora was at my place, Portia."

Portia murmured, "Oh, you fool, Cleve." She faced Aurora. "Now you won't go."

"No," said Aurora coolly, "it isn't necessary now."

Stewart realized his error too late. He flung up his arms and turned off. "All right," he said, "if you won't, you won't. Come on, Portia."

Aurora called after the other girl. "Would you mind staying a minute?"

Portia swung around. "That," she said with some degree of venom, "is exactly what I'd like to do. Go on, Cleve. I'll see you later."

Cleve cast one puzzled backward glance at the two women and struck out toward Skull Ridge. Portia stepped from her horse. She moved around it, ready for a quarrel and half disposed to make one.

"Why did you tell Jim that?" asked Aurora.

"To keep him from riding down here and getting shot. Don't you know DePard will comb this country clean until he gets Jim? You don't know DePard. You don't know him at all. Remember, he killed Garratt, who lived here last. I'd bet a hat he's got somebody over on the ridge watching us now."

Aurora said, briefly polite: "Thoughtful of you to warn Jim. But what made you think he'd be so anxious to get back here? After all, I think he would see the trap and not walk into it."

"The smartest of men are betrayed by their weaknesses."

"What does that mean?" murmured Aurora.

"He'd come back to you."

"Is that a weakness?"

"Why," said Portia, "love is everything and anything. To Cleve Stewart it would be a strength, making him do things he'd never otherwise have the courage to do. But to Jim it would be a weakness because, knowing better, he would still come here."

"We are not talking about love," said Aurora, softly speaking across a distance growing greater and greater between them.

Portia watched this girl whose reserve was like a wall. Her own impetuous and outgiving nature was increasingly challenged by Aurora Brant's consistent refusal to reveal what she really felt. To Portia the rules of conduct were very plain. If she felt a thing she spoke of it; needing a thing, she sought it. If she could not capture what she wanted she would surrender to it and possess it anyhow. Therefore Aurora Brant's unwillingness to display emotion was to Portia Crews the mirror of a cold nature. Keene deserved a better woman than that.

"He worried about you," she said. "It was the first thing he wanted to know — if you were safe. You mean something to him. A man never stops halfway. If Keene wants you a little he'll soon want you a lot."

"Where is he now?"

"I don't know. He's gone from the hideout by now." Then, wanting to break Aurora Brant's reserve, she added: "I brought him his breakfast. I cooked it for him."

She saw that it went home. Aurora Brant held herself straight. Her pride, her willful self-containment, grew more obvious. All she said was: "It is nice to know he wasn't badly hurt."

"He ought to leave the country entirely," pointed out Portia.

"Yes, that's what he ought to do."

"If you loved him and he wanted you to ride away with him, would you go?"

"We were not talking of love," repeated Aurora.

"Would you?"

"Why should you keep on talking of that?"

"I'd go, if he asked," said Portia.

She had not expected this to rouse Aurora. It was only something she had to say. But the dark girl's broad lips forgot their pressed-in firmness and her eyes showed the release of a temper long confined. A real feeling showed through her; it quickened her words. "If you can give up everything you believe in and everything you have ever wanted to follow a man wherever he wants to go — and if that man's star is his star and never yours — go ahead. I can't. A man should find contentment in a woman. She should be enough to hold him still. If she isn't enough, all talk of love is foolish."

"A man like Jim Keene has his ways. You can't change them."

"And I have mine and will not change."

"Then," said Portia in a swift break of voice, "why don't you let him go?"

An expression of astonishment showed on Aurora's face. "I'm not holding him."

"Yes you are!" cried Portia. "A woman can smile at a man and make him believe anything. You want him but you won't give up your own wishes. You look at him and he sees a promise there, and that holds him. But you never mean to keep it. If you're so proud of yourself, don't cheat by letting him expect something you don't intend to give. If he's not worth following then you're not worth having."

"Is that all?" said Aurora.

"You want a hired hand for a husband," retorted Portia. "A man to fill the woodbox and haul water and sleep in the barn. You're afraid to be human — and you don't deserve a man." She turned to her horse and stepped to the saddle. Her cheeks were richly red, she was angry clear through. Anger heightened the restless, gambling spirit she lived by; it made her beautiful.

Aurora said: "I wish you luck, Portia."

"Luck for what?"

"For what you so clearly want," said Aurora, and watched Portia Crews leave the yard at a sudden run. She kept her eyes on the ranch girl until the latter had rejoined Cleve Stewart in the valley. The two of them quartered toward Skull Ridge and at last disappeared.

Aurora moved slowly across the yard. She picked up an empty bucket and carried it to the washstand in front of the store; she stood by the stand, her energy taken out of her by Portia Crews's flaming honesty. The little world she had so painfully built up since her father's death, the small hopes she had nourished, the scattered pieces of courage she had collected, all lay strewn around her. Portia had done that.

For Portia was right. It was courage she lacked. Perhaps she had smiled at Keene and permitted him to be encouraged. She moved into the log cabin and faced the wall. She touched her forehead to the wall and felt tears run warmly down her face. Portia Crews thought her cold. How could Portia know what really was in her heart — the terrible dread of again living from pillar to post, the emptiness of owning nothing and having no help? How could Portia, whose life had been pleasant and prosperous, realize the depth of her longing for one secure spot on the earth? Portia was a girl who had always taken what she wanted from life. How could Portia ever feel the loneliness of being a shadow behind a man, as she had been with her father — suppressing every desire to his will? Aurora cried slowly and steadily, making almost no sound. Nobody would ever know that, behind her coldness, many dreams lived in starved hope, that she had her own desperate wish for love. This was her greatest problem and her greatest fear, this inner war between the warmth of her heart which wanted so much and could give so much, and the burnt-child need to be a person with a place in life. She was not really cold. The coldness was her defense — so that she would never surrender her own fresh-won dignity as a self-sustaining individual.

She took a towel from the wall, dried her face, and walked around the yard. Suddenly the sun, all day obscured by a sparkling argent mist, dropped over the western ridge. Darkness moved in. She cooked her dinner and ate it without appetite and was again uneasy, thinking of Keene and worried about him. There was nothing for her to do and not much to plan for as long as the desert remained a battleground.

The temptation was strong on her to ride to Spackman's. She was that unbearably lonely. But by now the reaction set in from her crying and she pulled herself together, rebuilding her resolution. She would not cry again, she would never ask for help; and when she saw Keene she would not mislead him with her smile or with her words. When this affair was done, and if he were alive, the old spirit would make him restless and he would move down the trail. She would not follow.

There was the high, sighing sound of a developing east wind in the sky. On the wings of the wind came a fine, chill rain. Suddenly all around her the smell of wet dust rose, cloying and wet-pungent after the long summer's dry spell. The prairie was lost in a smothering darkness and she had to grope her way across the cabin to the lamp. She lighted the lamp and filled the stove. The fire was a comfort, the beat of the rain on the cabin broke the terrible suspense of the desert silence. She thought of Keene riding through this dismal weather, she felt the coldness of it for him.

She remembered she had not brought her washing in from the line by the shed. Taking up a coat, she threw it over her head and opened the door. She closed the door behind her and for a moment was motionless, adjusting herself to the intense darkness of the night. Turning, she moved forward — into the sudden closing arms of a man.

She screamed out her shock, hearing the man grit his teeth. He said, — and it was DePard's voice, — "My God, woman, cut that out!" She fought him, kicking his legs with her feet and twisting in his grip. She could not get free. DePard called: "Get her horse, Red. Get her gun from the house."

She threw her weight against him and carried him across the yard. He tripped himself on the chopping block and went down, pulling her with him. "Len," he yelled, "come help me! She's wilder'n hell!"

She struck his face with her head time and again; she threw her knees into his stomach. A man ran out of the blackness and seized her around the waist and throat and hauled her upright. She was half strangled by the pressure of his arm. DePard spoke at her with an irritated reasonableness:

"Stop it — stop it. You're safe enough. Not doing a thing to you — not going to. Just moving you out of here. Red — got that horse?"

Red John moved up with the horse. She saw his face come toward her, long and inexpressive. DePard called: "Len — upset the chair and table in there. Make it look like she had a fight. Keene will see that when he comes along. What I want is for him to follow us." Then he said to Aurora: "He'll hunt for you, won't he, sister? He likes you that much, don't he?"

She didn't answer. Rain came beating down against her face and a man's arms held her tight-caught. It was Red John who drawled: "Sure he'll follow."

"That's what I want," said DePard coolly. "Now, sister, you want to take anything? You got a heavy coat?"

There were five or six shadows moving around the yard. Another man came up, grumbling: "She dropped this," and handed her coat to DePard.

She said: "Where do you want me to go?"

"Don't bother yourself about it. We'll take you. It's a line cabin up on Lost Man. Look now. Get on the horse and don't fight. What's the use of that? I'm not doing a thing — don't plan on it at all. You'll be there a day or a couple days and then you can ride away. That's the whole thing. You going to get on the horse?"

"All right."

"Let her go, Snap."

The wind came down from the sky in one boisterous, chilling sweep; great balls of tumbleweed were rolling shadows in the yard. The darkness was a solid wall all around. When Snap's arms dropped away she had one wild impulse to run but other riders came in and surrounded her and she realized they were waiting for just such a thing. She took the coat from DePard and slid into it. She breathed, "All right," and went to her pony, climbing to the saddle. DePard said again: "I'm telling you — you're as safe with me as if you was in church."

She pulled the coat collar around her neck, wishing for a hat. Water began to drip through her hair and the wind, striking that wetness, set up a quick cold ache in her head. Broken Bit's men had mounted. DePard moved beside her; they rode out of the yard, heading east. She heard him say in his close, satisfied voice: "You're the honey which draws the bear, sister."

They crossed the flat and rose to the timber. She was in a darkness that had no outer limit, Broken Bit riding a trail that wound and lifted and seemed to swing north. She tried to keep her sense of direction sharpened but presently it was as if she had been whirled around in a lightless chamber, the four quarters of the world blurring. Above her the wind cried in the branch tops and occasionally a pine limb snapped like a gunshot and dropped near at hand. She heard a voice say: "Early for snow, but it'll come tonight."

It was perhaps an hour later when they made a last turn and stopped. DePard said: "Get down," and took her arm. A door hinge squeaked and, under DePard's guidance, she stepped into the cold, close air of a cabin. She stood still, hearing men move around her. DePard spoke through the darkness to one of those men. "Get the fire going. You stay with the girl. I'll be back by early morning. Keene won't pick up the trail until then — but keep your eyes peeled."

He went out and presently Aurora heard horses move away and the dying murmur of voices. When those sounds fell off there was nothing left but the gusty rattle of rain on the cabin roof and the steady slash of wind in the trees. For a moment she thought she was alone, and then she heard a man's boots scuff around the room and stop. A match bloomed in the back, traveling down toward a table and a lantern on it. She watched that man's hands close around the lantern; she saw the pack of cards on the table, the cribbage board and an empty tobacco can. Light swelled from the lantern wick and afterwards she saw Red John.

He stood by the table, tall and redheaded and silently watching her. The florid coloring of his face deepened and his glance clung to her with a thoroughly interested expression. Long welts ran diagonally across one cheek — the imprint of her fingers — and when he saw that she noticed them he brought up his hand, half covering the scratches, and a recurring excitement made its smoky fire in his eyes. Wind poured through the open doorway. He moved around her, kicking the door shut with his boot. He said: "Starting to sleet already. I'll get that fire goin'."

XIII

HEART OF NIGHT

YOUNG Joe Spackman that night reached the end of his painful thoughts and knew there would never be any rest for him until he met Red John. He was at supper when this occurred to him. He finished his meal and left the table and the room. Night had come to the Silver Bow and rain moved out of the crystal mists, turning from fine dew to solid buckshot pellets driven slantwise by the rising wind. He saddled his horse and got his Winchester from the porch rack; and was in the saddle when his father came to the shed.

His father was in some respects a stranger to Joe — as every man is to his son — and young Joe remained silent, not knowing how to explain his intentions. But he needed no explanations. Old Spackman had followed his boy's misery through the week and perfectly read his mind. It was, for the elder, a hard moment. This was his only son, still immature in many ways and now riding into actual danger. Yet if he kept the boy back it would be as bad, for then young Joe would always have the sense of his own failure in his mind. So Spackman only said: "Riding?"

"Yes," said young Joe.

"Ride careful then."

"All right," said young Joe and went away. Wind beat out of the south and east. At the pitch-dark ford he heard the slash of the rain on the river's surface and the slap of small wind-driven waves against the bank. He took his way over the ford very carefully, using Aurora Brant's cabin light as a beacon. He was not more than two hundred feet from the store when he heard her scream.

His first impulse was to race in, but young as he was Joe Spackman had absorbed much of the sly sharp reasoning of the country, much of the instinctive caution. So he moved quietly forward and saw the vague shapes in the yard and — arriving at the back of the store — he heard men talking. Stationed here he guessed what was happening and suppressed the impulse to use his gun; it was impossible to do that with Aurora in the center of the men. Afterwards he saw all of the group move away to the east; and when they had disappeared young Joe set out after them, maintaining his distance.

Sheltered by the noisy beat of the rain and by the darkness, he followed them toward Lost Man Ridge and up the side of the ridge into timber. Now he moved closer, no longer seeing the shadows they made but following the one main trail and still catching the rumor of their travel. A man's voice drifted back faintly, the wind boiled through the trees, and the trail seemed to bend and fall downhill. Knowing nothing of the ridge, he let his horse have its way until he realized the sound of Broken Bit was gone. He kicked the horse into a faster pace. At the end of ten minutes he knew he had lost them completely.

Perhaps if he waited for daylight he might pick up the Broken Bit trail, though that meant more skill in following tracks than he possessed. He might cross the valley to Stewart's ranch. But Stewart was a cattleman and young Joe distrusted him. There was, then, one other thing left. Turning about, he retraced his path to the flats and headed for the ford. He knew his own people best. He would tell them that Aurora was gone — and they would help. He would ride to Comrie's first and work back until he reached his father. At this moment the rain was hardening into sleet.

After Portia Crews left the hideout Keene moved to the edge of the creek, watching daylight crawl into the canyon's narrow-black slash. In the upper gorge, to his right, he heard the steady rumble of a waterfall and realized there was no exit in that direction. This spot was a trap. Moreover the smoke of his fire drifted upward and put a scent in the air which some traveling Broken Bit man would sooner or later catch.

He saddled the pony, watching its warm breath turn to steam in the raw air. He crouched by the fire, soaking in the heat against the cold ride to come; and at last mounted and followed the creek downgrade. As soon as he left the canyon behind he turned back against the ridge and climbed toward its crest, through brush discharging its wetness against him and beneath the clinging blackness of timber. Beyond the timber he came out upon an open summit and from this point caught incomplete glimpses of the land around him.

Sunlight still seemed to shine upon the Silver Bow, twenty miles southward. Elsewhere and all through these hills stormy clouds steadily moved and a misting rain began to close in like silver-gray wool. Below him the broken ravines had turned to rivers of pale fog. To the north stood the main mountain chain; to the west lay Broken Bit somewhere. In that direction he made out the Broken Bit wagon road and now saw three riders moving along it, small-figured by the darkness and the distance.

He slid into the brush, descending the ridge until he struck a trail that seemed not to have been recently used. This he used, aiming at the Thunderheads before him, his purpose now being to reach the highest possible ground and put pursuit below him. DePard would have his riders out in this sullen day, blocking trails and watching all the gaps.

This was Morspeare's horse, and Morspeare's slicker was rolled behind the cantle. He untied the slicker and worked into it. Rain made crystal bubbles against it; rain dripped off his hat. Wind grew wilder, pushing great slate-colored clouds over the main mountain peaks from the southeast; those clouds boiled against the mountain peaks and broke apart, rain turning steady and solid. Cold bore against Keene, whipping bright red color into his cheeks. Steam rose rankly from the pony. He watched the trail with a centered, nerved-up attention; he raked the side coverts of the timber. Around the middle of the morning he came upon the Broken Bit road and stopped a long while to watch it; and then ran across rapidly.

The massive shoulder of the Thunderheads faced him, too rough and abrupt to be traveled except by the existing trails. He reached a trail and saw upon it the clear-cut prints of a horse's hoofs, so recently made that rain had not yet dulled the crisp edges. That traveler was not more than ten minutes ahead of him, somewhere beyond the short and constantly turning bends.

At each bend, Keene hugged the inner edge and drifted cautiously around. Pines crowded him right and left and in the deeper heart of the hills was a rain-glittering semidarkness. Five hundred feet upward he shoved himself into the brush and looked down upon the Broken Bit road; and saw a pair of riders coming out of the east, along the road. They went on rapidly toward DePard's ranch and were soon lost to sight, but it occurred to Keene then that his own recent passage of that road would have been spotted by any Broken Bit man posted on the higher hill points.

He turned into the trail again, rapidly climbing, more and more alert to the side timber. Beyond another bend he saw a long straightaway climb before him; coming to the summit of this straightaway he reached a hillside meadow covered by gray, waving grass. There was a cabin in the meadow; to the far side of the meadow the mountain slope rose again.

The trail ran across the meadow. Keene refused it, turned right and skirted the meadow. The timber sheltered him until he reached the meadow's far end. At that point he faced a short alley of grass lying between him and yonder trees; this was no more than ten feet wide and Keene went immediately across.

As he did so Jesse Morspeare, doggedly stationed at the far edge of the meadow, caught that one fugitive glimpse of him. Morspeare reached for his Winchester and flung it to his shoulder. Before he got his sites leveled on Keene the latter was out of sight. Morspeare lowered the gun across his saddle. He wiped the back of a wet hand against a wet face, swearing at himself; and he sat still, his slow mind picturing the country into which Keene had faded, the trails Keene would have to follow, and at last he moved westward as fast as the timber would permit him. Reaching a trail he went along it at a gallop, traveling abreast Keene and intending to get ahead of him.

It was nearing noon. This bench continued west, the higher peaks to Keene's left, the lower canyon in which lay Broken Bit to his right. Wherever trails crossed he made a wide circle through the trees, stopped to watch the timber around him, and went across the trail at a fast trot. Above him the sky was a silver-and-black overcast out of which a thickening rain continued to fall, not far from sleet. The day's edge grew rougher and sharper and wind slashed through the pines, drowning out lesser sounds. Beyond noon Keene sighted Broken Bit below him. Now descending the slope to a pine thicket he left his horse, crawled forward to a screen of brush and made a peephole in it.

There were only the barn, a corral, and the blackened square of the burned houses in the Broken Bit yard. A cookstove sat in the open area, smoke wheeling crazily around the Chinaman who stolidly crouched by it. Four riders showed themselves at the barn door; one more rider came in from the timber a little later, ate dinner and rode out again. Cramped and uncomfortable and made hungry by the sight of men eating, Keene waited out the gray, fitful day. Beyond four o'clock DePard arrived with five of his crew.

They clustered around the stove while they ate. Afterwards DePard moved his arms in a slow circle, pointing at the hills. Red John came up, talking to DePard, and presently Keene saw men mount and ride separately into the timber. DePard, with Red John and four other Broken Bit hands, swung down the gap toward the open valley. They reached the valley floor and turned to the south, growing vague in the rain mists.

Crouched in the dripping brush, Keene was thinking of what next should be done. Since early morning he had known how the ending to all this would be. Hunted by DePard, he had himself turned hunter. It was the old game again — its pattern thoroughly familiar to him. He proposed to keep DePard in sight, to feint and run through the timber and show himself when necessary, thereby shifting pursuit until at last he had pulled De-

Pard apart from the rest of the Broken Bit outfit. Somewhere and sometime in these hills he would catch DePard on even terms. That was the way the play went. Cool and without illusions, he foresaw that meeting — and had foreseen it since his first meeting with DePard. The course of his life ran like this; he was this kind of man, born to trouble. Peace for him, he reflected, was a dream of gold, beautiful and unreachable; for he knew himself at last. Wherever he saw women crying and little men troubled, there he would be. Some fire in him always flared hot at the sight of cruelty.

He rose to stamp out the stiffness of his legs. The trail from Broken Bit was twenty yards distant in the timber and now he heard a pair of riders come upgrade, their horses grunting at the climb and one man grumbling. In a little while the wind carried these sounds away. Keene stood by his horse, watching the premature shadows of night shift through the trees. He was thinking close and swift of DePard's latest journeying, trying to fathom its reason. In the direction DePard now traveled would be the homesteaders on the Silver Bow and Aurora's store. And, he also remembered, Cleve Stewart's ranch was across that valley in Skull Ridge. DePard would be thinking of one of those places.

DePard's group, meanwhile, had vanished beyond the rain mists. It was still too light to follow DePard directly; but by backtracking to the head of the valley he could cross the pass and reach timber again and sweep down on the west edge of the valley under the cover of darkness, parallel to DePard. It was important to keep on DePard's trail. Climbing to the saddle, he turned upgrade through the trees and around five o'clock came to the pass.

He was at the edge of the pass trough, sheltered by timber and looking down at the hundred-yard open strip. Somewhere, along one edge or another of the pass, Broken Bit men would be watching; it was one place they could reasonably expect him to show himself. Yet now the sleetlike rain and the heavier clouds had brought along a false night and the trees across the pass were nothing more than a dark blur; if men were watching they could not see far. With that in mind he touched a spur to his horse and drove it out of the timber.

The slope carried him down to the floor of the pass and now for the first time he felt the tension of his long day; it pulled at his nerves and made him look behind with the full expectancy of seeing riders break out of the darkness after him. But he saw nothing and, squaring himself in the saddle, he ran up the farther incline and rushed into the trees.

There was some kind of path before him and this he used for a short distance until the falling darkness made travel too slow; swinging to the right he came out of the timber at the head of the valley and saw full night close down. When he dropped into the valley one round soft snowflake struck his cheek. He was at a steady run, with the shadow of the Skull Ridge close at his left elbow, and presently he recognized a road in the darkness and turned on it, entering the ridge. Half a mile along that road he picked up the lights of a ranch house — Stewart's, he believed — and drifted into the yard. Dogs came out of the yard in full cry and presently a door opened and he saw Stewart blocked against the light. Stewart said: "Who's that?"

"Get out of that light," said Keene, and dropped from the horse.

"My God, Keene — come in here!"

Keene passed through the doorway and heard Stewart slam it behind him. He had been cold since morning and now the warmth of the room began to burn on his ears and cheek points. The light struck him full in the face, its brightness blinding him. He heard the gathering storm shoulder against the house.

Stewart said: "You're all right?"

"Sure. Where's Aurora?"

He waited for an answer. Not hearing it he turned about and discovered the odd look on Stewart's face. Stewart said with the greatest reluctance, "Down at the store."

Big Jesse Morspeare stood at the east edge of the pass, patiently waiting. He had his eyes turned toward the summit of the pass and so it was not until Keene was half across the clearing that Jesse caught that motion in the corner of his eyes. Jesse flung up his gun and made another try at the elusive target; and there was one touch-and-go moment when he thought he had Keene in the sights. But the distance was bad and the light simply faded from the earth and then Keene was gone. Big Jesse laid the gun over his sadlde, once more figuring ahead of Keene. "I was right about him comin' here," he thought. "I think I'll be right next time, too."

He shoved out from the timber and entered the pass. Instead of going into the farther trees he moved southward toward the valley. When he came to its floor he settled to an alternate run and walk.

Keene said: "Didn't you bring her here?"

"No," answered Stewart, "she wouldn't come."

Keene stood in the middle of the room, water dripping along his slicker and puddling at his feet. The thawing warmth made a red flame on his cheeks; the violent flash of temper brightened his eyes. "By God, Stewart," he said, "I thought you had better sense."

"Wait a minute," interposed Stewart, astonished by this kind of talk. "She wouldn't come."

"That makes no difference. You know what's happening. You know she's got no business being out there alone."

"I told her that. She wouldn't come."

"Cleve," rapped out Keene, "you should have brought her."

"Oh now," said Cleve Stewart, nettled by the other man's manner, "I couldn't drag her away against her will."

"Couldn't you? Why the hell couldn't you?"

"Well," said Stewart, "I guess that's the difference between you and me."

"Maybe it is," said Keene and turned about to find Portia Crews standing in the kitchen doorway.

"Yes," she said, "I lied to you, Jim. Otherwise you would have gone straight to the store. DePard expected you to do it."

"Fine," he murmured. "You left her where DePard would find her. He's on his way there now."

Stewart said in a kind of groaning misery: "You sure of that, Jim?"

"I saw them."

Portia turned into the kitchen. Stewart said: "We got to get down there, Jim. I'm going to the bunkhouse and talk to the crew." He left the house.

Keene went into the kitchen and stood at the warm range while Portia poured coffee from a big pot simmering at the back of the stove. She handed him the cup, her eyes blackened by her thoughts. "Now," she murmured, "you really hate me."

"No," he said, "but you should have thought."

"I did, Jim. I did. I thought of you."

"You should have thought of her."

She said: "That's never the way. A man thinks of a woman. A woman always thinks of a man. Nothing will happen to her. You're the one DePard wants to kill." She turned from him and looked into the kitchen cupboards. She found a platter of cold meat and got bread out of a box. "I think you must be hungry."

He made a meal from the bread and meat; and burnt his tongue on the coffee. It took the chill out of him. Portia saw his haste, his impatience — and knew what was in his head. He had a slanting, angular wickedness on his face. His anger stayed and his worry increased. She murmured: "You could break almost anybody's heart. I wish you didn't hate me."

"I don't, Portia."

"Ah, you might just as well." She made an expressive gesture of resignation with her hands. In the room's lamplight her lips were soft, her face showed its child-like sadness. "I could never be very cold. Perhaps it would be better for me if I were. I'm pretty easy to read, aren't I?"

He said: "You're a hard woman to know."

"Me?" she answered in astonishment. "Why, Jim — look at me! What do you see?"

Stewart came into the kitchen from the yard; and now he was angry and helpless. "I'm going to fire that crew tomorrow. They won't go along. That," he added bitterly, "is what a man gets for being considerate. They think I'm soft and they tell me to go to hell. They won't buck DePard. I'm going with you, Jim. Let's move."

He caught up his heavy coat from a chair in the front room and went into the driving dark. Keene moved to the front room, Portia Crews behind him. He saw an extra Winchester in the room's gunrack and reached for it; he was at the door when Portia's voice turned him.

She said: "What do you want me to do, Jim?"

"Stay here," he said. "Don't cross the valley tonight. There's a real storm coming up."

She came to him and reached out to button his slicker. She showed one brief flash of hope. "Would it worry you if I were out there? Would it really?"

"Yes," he said, "it would."

"Ah," she sighed and was pleased, with the shine of wetness in her eyes. "Then you should know why I lied — because I'm worried when you are out there. Why should I be hard for you to know? All you need to do — " She stopped the explanation. She held it back and shrugged her shoulders. "Well, be careful. I'll see you soon."

She stood in the blast of wind and wet snow coming through the doorway, watching the shadows of the two men dissolve in the blackness; and closed the door. Wind cut a shrill sound at the eaves of the house, wind shouldered heavily at the walls. She moved idly around the room, restless because alone and cast down immeasurably by Keene's departure. She said aloud. "It would have done no good to have told him what I felt. If I could only be cold, if I could only be indifferent, and make him come after me and break his heart. He wants nothing easy. But how can I be that way?"

She stopped in the room's center, listening into the steady, increasing pound of the storm. Great wet flakes spattered against the windows and slid slowly down; and in a little while, unable to be alone, she put on her coat and went out to the shed for her horse. She turned down the road, came upon the valley and headed westward across the three-mile flat to her own house in Lost Man. The full sweep of the wind was against her, the thickening smother of snow. She felt her horse drifting from the wind's pressure and now and again turned it into the weather. Ordinarily she would have seen the lights of her house over the valley but tonight there was no visibility at all. She had no fear; she had lived here all her life and had never known fear of anything. Traveling steadily onward, she was swallowed by the night.

Keene said: "Get out in the middle of the valley and catch the creek. We'll follow it down."

Stewart called: "Go slow, Jim. If DePard's in front of us — "

"Go on — go on. We're late."

Swinging across the valley, they reached the creek and put their backs to the bitter drive of the storm. Snow packed against Keene's collar and the heat of his body melted it and water ran along his shoulders and down his arms. The horses, boosted by the wind, ran at a steady gait. An hour from Stewart's ranch Cleve said something that was ripped away by the wind; he lifted his voice to a half cry: "Should see a light pretty soon."

"Not in this," said Keene.

"Wait!" howled Cleve and hauled in. Keene ran beyond him before stopping and when he turned back he saw nothing in the mealy flitter of snow. It was that black, that solid. He held his horse broadside to the wind until Stewart bumped into him. They swung together, Keene discovering the faint glint of light ahead. He bent on the saddle, speaking close to Stewart's ears. "Circle to the left."

They had the light for a definite guide. They swung around the light until the corner of Aurora's shed cut it off. They wheeled back a few feet and caught the light again, and drifted slowly to the shed. Keene said: "Wait," and got down.

He moved into the shed, expecting to find Aurora's pony — and discovered it gone. He moved out of the shed, crawling along the store wall. Light sparkled through the snow-fogged window of the main cabin. Keene stood beyond that outthrown fan of light, distrusting it. He retreated farther from it, walking deeper into the yard. Twenty feet from the window he tried to catch a view through it, unsuccessfully. He circled the yard and closed again on the cabin. Tight against the wall, he put his ear to the logs; and then, turned impatient, he reached for the latch and lifted it.

Wind threw back the door. He had one half view of the room before the lamp blew out. He yelled: "Cleve!" when he stepped into the room. He ran against an upturned table, against a fallen chair. Stewart ran in, slamming the door. "What's up?"

Keene scratched a match on the floor and found the lamp, and lighted it. He made one complete wheeling turn of the room. The table and chair had been tipped over, but the thing his mind closely played on was the location of the lamp. It had been placed on an empty soapbox in the corner. Somebody had taken it from the table — where it normally would have been — and put it on the soapbox before the table was tipped. The bed was smooth. The stove held only a little heat. He pulled back a stove lid and saw the gleam of a single coal in the ashes.

He swung from the stove and Stewart observed then how changed this man was. He had never seen this consuming fire before in Keene; he had never seen that complete destructiveness. "There you are," said Keene, his talk gritting into the noisy night. "God damn a man — !" He whipped a hand across the lamp chimney, killing the light. He was across to the door in a long jump, throwing the door open. "We get out of here," he said, and moved into the darkness. Stewart found him on the edge of the log wall. "It may be a trick," said Keene.

Stewart moved away from Keene, hearing the other man's swift challenge. "Where you going?"

"Over to Spackman's. She might be there. Wait for me."

Keene paced through the yard's blackness again. He pushed against the arriving wind; he bent his shoulders to it. A hundred feet or more from the cabin — which was now lost in the blur of the storm — he cut to the right and crisscrossed the yard. He came against the woodpile and skirted it. Back at the cabin he made another wide-angled slant into the desert, circled the store entirely and reached the shed. None of these trips told him anything except that the yard was empty. He stood in the shed a good fifteen minutes before returning to the cabin. Lighting the lamp he made a thorough search of the cabin and found nothing informative. Nor was there anything in the storeroom when he passed into it from the main cabin. Out in the yard again, he heard Cleve hail him from the deeper darkness. Cleve arrived on the run.

"Joe Spackman came here tonight. He heard Aurora scream. There was a bunch of men. They took her toward Lost Man. Joe followed. He got too far away from them and took the wrong trail. He went back and told his dad. They're getting up a bunch of the homesteaders now."

Keene said: "What's up in those trees? Any place to stop?"

Stewart searched his memory. "A line cabin would be nearest. Then there's Bowley's abandoned house. Nothing else until you get to what's left of the old army post, twelve miles into the Short Hills."

Keene went to his horse and came back to Stewart. "Try the cabin first."

When they turned southeast the night was solid with a slant-driven snow that rattled against Keene's slicker like buckshot and bitterly stung his cheek flesh. The wind swept down the long fifteen-mile slot of the valley with a pressure hard to beat against. The horses yawed from it, they had to be constantly turned into it. Ten minutes away from the store Keene called:

"More to the right."

"No," shouted Stewart, "the mouth of the trail ought to be right ahead."

Keene swung the course, shoving Stewart's horse southward. It was a faith in his own sense of direction which made him do it; in this blind night that sense was as clear a guide as the bright north star. He remembered, too, that the east ridge fed a low spur into the valley quite near the trail, and when the pony lifted beneath him he knew he was on the edge of that spur. Stewart complained: "We're south of it!" Keene moved on, feeling the ridge move against him, hearing the racket of the wind in the nearing timber. He went steadily upslope and gave his horse its head; this was Jesse Morspeare's horse and familiar with the country. In another minute's time Keene had passed into the trail, the enormous pressure of the wind sheered off by the trees.

"All right," admitted Stewart. "You guessed it. There's a fork in this trail about a half a mile on. Take the right."

The wind was a wild, smashing racket in the pine tops. Branches tore away and dropped down. Keene kept a slight rein pressure on the left side of the horse's neck, so that it would swing to the right when it reached the fork of the trail. Sometime later he realized he was being carried due south and knew the horse had passed the fork.

Stewart called: "That cabin's on the left. Mile beyond the split in the trail."

Keene had come up this trail once before, on the way to DePard's. He remembered the cabin and the small clearing in which it sat — a low log cabin with a door and no window. He traveled at a walk through a kind of blackness that had weight; it was a tangible substance he pushed his shoulders through. The wind came at him in contradictory crosscurrents, blizzard-cold. Stewart called up from the rear, the words not penetrating Keene's mind; for he was thinking now of Aurora with a nerve-breaking anxiety and his thoughts brought her before him as a bright picture in the dark — the curve of her lips, the adopted willfulness which held her shoulders up, the pride of her eyes burning like a steady candle flame in a still room. Sometimes he had caught the hint of warmth and loneliness, of a generosity waiting for a man; sometimes she had looked at him across the wall of an unbreakable resolution.

Alone of all people, Aurora Brant had brought to him the only real doubt he had ever had — the doubt of his own future. Her quiet, long-dreaming glance made a mirror for him and in that mirror he saw himself and was disturbed by what he saw, the restlessness that drove him, the love of excitement, the wish to ride on and on, the search that kept him in motion and seemed to have no end. When all this was over he would ride away as he had always done; but this time he would be leaving something behind. It had never happened before. Even now some of the fun had gone.

Wind steadied against him, blowing through one fixed channel in the hills; he caught the smell of smoke in the turbulent air. He had reached a clearing; now, paused on the trail, he saw the faint hulk of a cabin in the solid night. Stewart was beside him, whispering: "Somebody in there. Smell smoke."

"Wait," said Keene, and slid from the horse.

He moved toward the cabin, his feet sinking through a surface of half snow and half slush. He was at the wall, with his head against it as he listened for inner sounds, but all he caught was the sing of the wind against the trees. He moved around the house, looking for horses. He came back to the front of the line cabin. Stewart was near the door.

"I'm going in there, Jim."

Keene said: "Stick against the wall." He ran his hand down the door surface until he caught the latch. He lifted it and kicked open the door. He was inside, wheeling back to a wall. He said: "Aurora," and put his shoulders against the wall and waited, his revolver drawn and half lifted.

All he heard was the gusty wind against the cabin, the rattle of the stovepipe. One eye of fire showed in the stove, fanned bright by the fresh air scouring through the doorway. The room was warm. He held his gun up against the darkness, he stood stiff as iron, listening until he could no longer wait. He slid a hand into his pocket and brought out a match. He ripped the match across the wall and watched its light flare through an empty cabin.

Cleve came in on the jump. Keene said: "Go outside and keep your eyes peeled. Something wrong here." Cleve Stewart retreated, pulling the door shut. Keene lighted another match and found the lantern. The lantern globe was still warm when he touched it, the smell of coal oil was strong. He swung the lantern slowly around, noting the puddled water on the floor — from somebody's feet. A double-deck bunk frame stood in one corner of the room, both bunks covered by straw ticks; there was nothing on the ticks. Turning back, he looked at the table again and saw a woman's handkerchief.

For a moment longer his glance swept this room from wall to wall, from corner to corner. Then he killed the lantern. Cleve Stewart opened the door.

"She's been here," said Keene. "She left a handkerchief."

Stewart's strain poured out as a long, ragged sigh. "You know, Jim, they only had one reason for taking her. To pull you into a trap. This must have been the trap. Then they changed their minds. What'd they do that for?"

"Something's wrong."

"Maybe they went on to Broken Bit."

"Too far to go on a night like this."

"Lige Bowley's old house then. Or the abandoned military post."

"We'll try the house first."

They got back on the trail. Stewart took the lead, calling back, "I know this pretty well."

The momentary warmth of the cabin had thawed Keene's chilled bones; now the coldness cut in again, more cruel than before. He called up. "Get along, Stewart — get along." The sins of men were many; in one form or another he had witnessed evil in all its grades, so that there was in him little capacity for surprise, no room at all for shock. He was neither surprised nor shocked now; what grew in him was a bitterness that would never have an ending until he met DePard. It heated him and boiled away all compassion.

They rode into a full-blowing blizzard, all the upper world screaming with it. At every aperture snow whirled down. Keene's pony sank into forming drifts; the pony's mane collected snow and slowly froze into solid hanks. Judging from the heat in the line cabin, Aurora could not have left it long before; therefore she was somewhere near, she was perhaps now riding ahead of him at no great distance. He called again. "Get going — get going."

Stewart said at last: "Here's the turnoff to the Bowley place. It's downgrade a half mile."

They stopped. Keene said: "What else around here?"

"The military post is six miles over in the rough country."

"They wouldn't try it. Too far tonight."

"Well, there's the Crews ranch. Not so far. But they wouldn't go there."

"Might if it got too tough." Then he said: "Possible that they'd try to get on to Broken Bit. That would be foolish but maybe they'd try it. This is too tough to be out in. If they're on this trail they're not much ahead of us. I'm going down to that Bowley place. You go to Crews's. If I don't find anything I'll come along to Crews. You stay there until I meet you. Don't break in on that ranch. Slide up and have a look first."

"What would you do if you ran into DePard at Bowley's?"

"Not more than one or two men with Aurora in the line cabin. Probably no more than that with her now — if she's at Bowley's. Meet you at Crews's."

Stewart called after him: "Damned easy to get lost tonight, Jim."

"I know where the house is," said Keene. "I passed it once."

The main trail had followed the ridge crest; this side trail dropped quickly, still crowded by pines. Presently the wind reached at him more forcefully and the racket of the night grew in his face. He came out of the trail into a flat open meadow which he felt rather than saw; he cut across the meadow and drifted against the shadow of a house; and now as before he circled the house and identified the opaque shadow of a barn.

He left his horse and moved against the back-sloping

wall of the barn and came to a broad doorway. Pieces
of the doorway teetered under his feet as he passed in;
and at once he touched the head of a horse. The horse
let out a startled blast and retreated. Keene stood dead
still, baffled by the cell of blackness. He heard the horse
step around and stop; there were no other inner sounds.
He murmured: "Easy — easy," and moved on, touching
the horse again. He ran his hand along the cheek strap
and felt the cold glass surface of the headstall ornament,
immediately recognizing this as Aurora's bridle. He
cruised through the darkness from corner to corner; but
this was the only horse. Knowing that, he turned from
the barn, struck broken house steps and reached forward
until he found a door. He tried the door, softly turning
a knob and feeling it give. He lifted his gun, steadied
himself on the steps and went through the doorway at a
jump.

The noise of his entry clacked onward into cold emptiness; he heard the echo die somewhere in distant rooms.
He said: "Aurora."

"Jim," she said, in a faraway, exhausted voice.

XIV

THINGS SAID AND UNSAID

HE moved over the room and stopped. He said: "You're alone?"

"Yes," she said. "Yes."

He heard her walking rapidly through a room. She struck a corner and cried softly to herself and stumbled on. Going forward, he met her in a narrow hall. He came against her and felt her arms slide around him, quick and hard. She was shaking. She started to speak to him but the words stuck in her throat. He spoke — and was afraid of what he would hear. "Nothing happened?"

"No."

He said: "How'd you get here? You were at the line cabin."

"They left me there with Red John. But he changed his mind and we came here. Then he left."

He said again: "Nothing happened, Aurora?"

"No — no. Don't think of that."

"It's all I've been thinking of. How long's Red been gone?"

"Not long. He said something funny to me, and left."

The excitement and the chill had broken into her reserve. She clung to him, trembling and pulling herself straight, and trembling again. He said: "Maybe there's a stove."

"I looked. There isn't anything."

He said: "I'll get the blankets from the saddles." Then he realized how close she was to exhaustion and loss of control. She tightened her grip on his neck and said, "Don't leave, Jim."

"Just out to the barn."

He stood still, waiting for her to let go and trying to find some line of reasoning which would explain Red John's departure. The foreman, he figured, might be somewhere in the neighborhood, expecting pursuit. He might have ridden for Broken Bit, knowing the girl could not leave this house in the storm. Wherever he was, he'd be back by daylight. Meanwhile the blizzard blocked departure. This was the only shelter.

She said, "All right, Jim," and dropped her arms. But she followed him to the door and remained there. He went across the yard, pulling his pony into the barn and unsaddling it. He unsaddled Aurora's horse as well, took the two blankets and moved around the barn and stumbled against a small pile of hay in one corner. He tried a match and caught a glimpse of a loft above; dropping the blankets he found a piece of a ladder leading to the loft. He climbed the ladder and tried a second match. There was a mound of gray, old hay in the loft.

He went down the ladder, returning to the house. She waited for him at the open door, badly shaken by the wind. She caught his arm, murmuring: "I'm sorry, Jim. I've had about all I can stand, I guess."

"Found a bed," he told her and led her across to the

stable. He searched for the ladder, he put her against it. "Climb up," he said. He went away from the ladder, hunting the blankets he had dropped; he got them, hearing her call from the loft. "All right. I made it."

He went up the ladder and tried a match — catching one short glimpse of the girl's dead-white face, the burned blackness of her eyes. The match went out. Wind cried along the roof and wind went all through the broken boards of the barn. Keene dug into the heart of the old hay in the loft and pulled her down. He took off his slicker and boots. He settled beside her, drawing the blankets and the slicker over them. He reached up and stirred the hay until they were buried in it. Her arms closed around him, her face was close to him, and the first real warmth since leaving the line cabin loosened him — the joined warmth of their bodies. Something went clattering across the roof; all the aged timbers of the barn swayed slowly, not far from collapse. She had ceased to tremble; when she spoke her lips brushed his cheek.

"I was deadly afraid of him. He came to the store a couple nights ago. That was unpleasant. Tonight he came back with DePard and some others. They took me to the line cabin. DePard said it was to make you follow me — he kept saying that. Then he went away with the other men, leaving me with Red John. DePard was to come back in the morning. But then a strange thing happened. Red John started the fire and I saw him get worried. He looked at me and I think he was more afraid of

me than I was of him. That was queer, because he had
always been so sure of himself. But he said something
about he being the man in trouble, not you. Then we
left the cabin and came here. I think he was afraid he
might be trapped there. It was a terrible ride. When we
got in the house I heard him walking around it — just
walking around and talking to himself. Then he said another strange thing. He told me to remember he hadn't
touched me. He wanted me to be sure to remember that.
Then he left — and here you are."

He was silent, trying to fathom the foreman's motives.
It was difficult to understand what had swung Red John
so quickly, so definitely.

She said: "You're still in trouble, Jim. Red John will
tell DePard where I am. They'll be back, they'll find
you. That's what DePard meant to do."

"Not tonight," he said. "Nobody goes anywhere tonight."

"But in the morning — "

"A long way off."

He heard her long, softening sigh. "How little it takes
to be happy. I was afraid of him, then I was cold — and
then I was alone in the house. All that wildness. Now
I'm warm, and that makes me happy. It doesn't take
much. That's your life, isn't it, Jim? A lot of trouble —
and little things to make you pleased."

He said: "You've had a hell of a time."

"The harder life is," she murmured, "the less people
ask of it. People who don't know fear or hunger or pain

want a lot. Those that face those things are happy if they have one small break. Terror makes us all very humble. How quick pride falls."

"Warm now?"

"And content," she said, gently. "Hear that wind. The blackest and bitterest of worlds is ten feet beyond us. It would kill us. But we are warm. Perhaps everything is really that simple." Then she added in a dark, troubled way, "No, not that simple. There's tomorrow, and De-Pard."

"A long way off."

"You never worry about the future, do you?"

"No use. All things come in time."

"So, then," she said, "it is today you love. Yesterday's gone and tomorrow isn't here — and it is just today that counts."

"Best that way," he answered. "Feels fine to eat when you're hungry, to watch the ground turn color when the sun goes down. Maybe to smell water when you're thirsty, or see lights shining over the flats when you're tired of riding. If you look too far ahead you miss what goes on now. You never stop to enjoy the present."

"But pretty soon the present is gone and then you are old and alone and what do you have?"

"That comes too," he admitted. "For me and for you, for everybody. Makes no difference, does it? The thing is, what can you look back on when you're old? What can you remember?"

"You're strange, Jim. You really believe that. But it

isn't so — for you. You want something and you look for something. Over the hill. Tomorrow."

After a long silence he said: "I guess I do."

"What is it?"

In his voice was the note of small surprise and odd wonder. "I don't know," he said.

She had asked him that question before, only a few days after first meeting him. His answer then had been the same as it was now. She remembered that he had added one other thing. She spoke of it now.

"But you'll know, when you find it?"

He lay still, her sweetness and fragrance close upon him, the weight of her arm on his shoulder. Her breathing blew gently against his cheeks; her lips moved, very near him. She whispered, "I'm afraid again. Tomorrow is never as far away as you think. I'm really afraid." In the beginning he had put his arms around her to take the chill from her body; now since she lay content and warm the need of it was gone, and what had been a natural and necessary act suddenly turned into something else. Within his arms was a woman and all the disturbance she could bring to a man — her beauty, her reliant will, the dreaming and lonely things which lay beyond her eyes, the impetuous moods suppressed but crying up through silence.

He drew his arms away. He heard her say: "What is it?" He held his arms still but he dropped his head forward, his mouth coming against her lips. Her arms were at his shoulders, still-placed. They pulled gently at his shoulders until some warning passed between them, and then she quietly repelled him. Her heartbeat was against his hands, strong and quick. She turned her head. She said: "Little pleasures, just for today. If that's a memory to look back on, Jim, I don't begrudge it. But you mustn't fool yourself. You're no man to be content with memories. You're going to be lonely after you cross the last hill."

"So will you, Aurora."

"There's a difference. I am more patient than you are." She brought her arms away and turned from him. "Good night."

He didn't answer. Presently she said in a gentle curiosity, "What is it now?"

"Thinking."

She reached back and took his arm, and pulled it over her. She held his hand. "Don't think," she murmured. "What good is that?"

One of the horses rubbed along the lower wall, the wind slammed steadily against the barn. Aurora's hand, holding to his, was warm and relaxed; she seemed to fall immediately asleep. This girl, he thought, had taken the heart out of him in more ways than she would ever realize. She revived old doubts; somehow she had made his life less important. He put the thought aside, considering DePard and Red John. He went slowly back over the night, trying to figure Red John; and at last thought he knew what had been in the man's mind. There was no other crime in all the frontier category as serious as that of troubling a woman. If DePard ever lost his battle and Broken Bit could no longer protect its men, Red John was finished.

He slept briefly, wakened by the shift of Aurora's body. He said: "Awake?"

"Yes."

"Do you have to stay at the ford?"

"That's my home. That's my last stand."

"Big world, Aurora."

"I've seen enough of it."

He said thoughtfully: "Sure. I've seen a lot of places I liked well enough to stay in. Never stayed, though."

"And never will. You're like my father." She put her hand on his shoulder and held it there; and again he fell asleep.

He had always been a man to wake at the first signal of daylight. Now when he opened his eyes he found Aurora kneeling beside him. Light came through all the apertures of the barn, cold-gray; the wind had slackened. Her cheeks were vivid red and hair lay loose around her temples. She had been watching him, she had been waiting for him to rouse; on her face was a sober, sadder thoughtfulness that vanished at once, to be replaced by a smile.

"Jim," she murmured, "when you grow old and speak to your children of your adventures leave this night out."

"Don't seem to see children in the plan."

"There'll be some woman," she said, "who'll gladly follow you wherever you want to go. But anyhow, I took your advice for one night. Today's pleasures for today. That's happiness. Now what?"

They went down the ladder. A long drift had blown through the barn doorway, crowding the horses into a corner. Outside the world was still and white, the tree limbs sagging with snow's weight. There was a half-wind in the air and the sky was gray, as though the storm had only incompletely blown itself out. Snow still fell. "Slow traveling," he remarked. "The trails will be two feet deep."

He saddled and helped her up. "This is the way it is. The Crews ranch is nearest. If I were certain it was safe for you I'd take you there, but it is hard to know what we'd find there. That leaves Stewart's across the valley. Or I'll take you to Spackman's."

"You can't show yourself in the open, Jim."

He moved from the barn doorway, quickly motioning her to pull aside. Short crisp echoes of a horse treading through drifts came forward; in a little while he saw Cleve Stewart appear on the meadow. Keene went into the yard. Stewart said: "You found her?"

"She's here."

Stewart groaned his relief. "My God. Now we've got to move. DePard's around here. I saw tracks up on the trail." As soon as Aurora came from the barn he called: "You all right, Aurora?"

Keene said: "Everything proper at Crews's?"

"Yes."

"You take her there," said Keene. "Keep off the big trail."

"Where you going?"

"That way," said Keene, pointing indefinitely toward the east. He was on his horse. "Get going," he said.

Aurora looked at him, troubled and silent. Stewart turned back into the meadow, calling, "Come on, Aurora. We're in a hurry."

She followed after Stewart. Beyond the house she turned in the saddle, as though to speak to Keene, and then she pulled the horse about and rode to him. She said, "Jim, do you have to — " and looked down at her hands. "Well," she murmured, "you started this habit." She lifted her eyes and she swayed in the saddle, offering her face to him; he bent over to kiss her, feeling the stir of her lips. She looked at him with the darkest, saddest glance and said: "I'll be at Crews's, or at the store. I wish — I wish I knew where you'd be." She wheeled and ran the pony after Stewart. Just before she entered the trail she waved at him; and then disappeared.

The morning was dull and biting and would get no better. He swung about, heading for the Short Hills country to the east — in that general direction where lay the canyon hideout. He bucked a trail through timber, saying to himself: "Leaving tracks a yard broad," and fell into an open meadow between rolling buttes. Aiming toward the slope on the far side of the meadow he heard a distant echo, thin and flat. He jerked upright in the saddle, sweeping all the open areas. To his right, near the Broken Bit road, he saw three men in motion. Two of them came toward him. The other was racing back into the timber.

Keene swung about into the trees he had so recently left. DePard, he realized, had him spotted and now would hang to his plain trail.

XV

MAN HUNT

COMING up from the Bowley house with Aurora, Stewart reached the crest of the ridge and discovered that some other rider had meanwhile passed along the main trail, headed in the direction of Broken Bit. Those tracks were deep-punched in the snow. "They're all through this country — DePard's crowd," he said. "We'll cut through the trees."

He left the trail to break a makeshift path through the pines. At places snow lay in drifts breast-high to the horses; in other areas the ground showed black beneath a thin crust. A mile more or less from the Bowley house both Aurora and Cleve were arrested by the sound of a single shot clacking along the dismal gray world. Aurora turned her pony around, crying out in the sharpest voice: "Do you think — ! Cleve, let's go back there!"

He saw the heart-squeezing fear in her eyes and then took his glance from her, grumbling, "I've got to get you to Crews's." They moved on. Five long minutes later he broke the silence with his irritated observation. "This is his fun, isn't it? He's the fellow who rode into it. Nobody asked him to. The big man that eats trouble for breakfast — "

"Cleve!" He rode doggedly ahead until she spoke again, and more gently: "Look at me, Cleve." He turned, showing her the blended worry and anger on his face. Her soft question took all the sting from her other words. "What's wrong, Cleve? You don't really mean that."

"No," he said, "I guess I don't." He rode with his head down, lost within himself, and when she saw that she had her quick contrast of the two men. Stewart took the world hard, he was at war with himself, he seemed always to face life with confused reflections. Keene was so unlike that. Were he riding in Stewart's place every sense in him would be sharp-focused, he would be alive to the day and the things it contained.

Cleve said: "What happened to you, Aurora?"

She told him the story of the previous night. He rode steadily into the timber, bucking the drifts, searching out the passable alleys. He rode stiffly, with his shoulders flung up; color stained the back of his neck. He said, more to himself than to her: "Red John. The world's gone wrong — and it's Red John."

After an hour's hard riding they came to the lip of a meadow and found the Crews ranch below them. Snow fell soft and steady; steam rose from the warm roof of the ranch house. A dog sounded from the far part of the yard and a man came from the barn with a rifle half lifted. Cleve wigwagged at him and passed on to the house. Portia Crews waited at the doorway; a moment later they were inside the house.

But Cleve Stewart remained by the door. "Well," he said, "I'll see you later."

Portia Crews asked: "Where are you going?"

"Why," he said, "I am a damned fool and I'm going back to find Keene."

"Cleve," said Portia, "do you think you should?"

"What you mean to say," he answered with a touched pride, "is can I take care of myself? I don't know. It will be interesting to find out. Things like that get in a man's head. You would suppose a sound education in the classics might shed some light on human behavior. I find it sheds no light at all on me. There is an end to the Socratic dialogue at last. It never was much good. The important thing, really, is to know if you can stand up and be shot at without making too much out of it."

"Cleve," said Portia, "don't go."

"Does it make any difference at all?"

"Yes," answered Portia.

"Ah," murmured Stewart with an ironic fragment of a smile on his mouth, "that's nice to know. Makes a man seem very masculine." He turned his eyes to Aurora, the smile disappearing. "What would you say?"

"I had hoped you'd help him," she answered.

It made him thoughtful. He stood tall before the two women, now again drawn into himself; a man who would always be gentle and never thoroughly acclimated to this life he had chosen. "Of course you would," he said, and added, "So long," and left the room.

"How much he has changed," murmured Portia, as much to herself as to Aurora. "When he finds he has courage it will please him. But if he should kill anybody to prove it, that will make him very sad." Then she said: "You're hungry and you want to clean up. You can use that room in the corner."

After Aurora had gone into the room Portia called at the kitchen: "Ed, cook up a breakfast." Standing at a window, she watched Cleve Stewart fade beyond the snow and thought of Keene with all her mind and felt his troubles with all her heart. As soon as Aurora came from the bedroom, Portia took her to the kitchen. She sat across from Aurora, distant and critical and harboring her resentments. She could never like Aurora.

She said: "How was it?" and listened to Aurora's story. Then she said, "Red John's chickens have come home to roost. He always was a lady's man — but he had to have a sure thing, no danger in it to him. Now he's in danger and he knows it. Somebody will kill him for what he's done to you."

"Who?"

"Why do you suppose Cleve went back?"

Aurora said: "Oh, I wish I'd known!"

"Why? To stop him? You can always start a man on something. That's any woman's gift. But you can't stop him. His pride gets up and there's nothing to be done. Why regret? You ought to be proud he's doing it for you. I'd be. It's lonesome not to be wanted."

"I know."

"How can you know?" retorted Portia. She gave Aurora a close, inquisitive look. "Wasn't it very cold at Bowley's last night?"

"We slept in some old hay in the barn loft."

"I see," murmured Portia and guessed the rest of it with a fertile, jealous imagination. The picture grew on her until she rose from the table and walked on to a window; it was an unbearable picture. For that one night, for that closeness, she would have given all she possessed. She grew hard and bitter, she was taunted by her imagination; she hated what she suspected. She said:

"For so cool and unapproachable a woman you have done very well."

"Perhaps," was Aurora's even answer.

"Perhaps!" cried Portia, coming back from the window. "Why set yourself up to a man as being too distant and pure to be touched? No woman's like that. You're not."

"No," said Aurora, "I'm not."

"Then why lie to him?"

Aurora said, very slow with her admission, "He knows what I am."

That answer tore deep into Portia Crews, it was fresh fuel to her jealousy. "Does he? Then why didn't you stay with him? All this trouble comes from you. That's why he's fighting DePard. But you have left him."

"I'd be in his way. I'd hold him back."

"I wouldn't leave him."

"I know," said Aurora and rose from the table. She went into the living room, Portia Crews coming after her. Standing by a window, Aurora saw the Crews meadow dip downgrade to the edge of Cloud Valley. Snow was a cottony screen shutting out sight of Skull Ridge three miles across the valley; the wind moved in slow and steady tempo. She said: "How far is it to the ford?"

"Seven miles."

"I think I'll go."

Portia said: "You've caused trouble enough."

"They won't catch me off-guard again."

"DePard's men are all around."

"If you'll lend me a gun — "

Portia said: "How can that store mean so much to you?"

Aurora turned about. "Didn't I tell you once? It's all I have. You don't know about that. You've never had to want anything very hard. You've always gotten what you wanted. I have lived in a hundred places, but none of them were mine. I have never known what it was like to be really safe and secure. The store is mine — it means everything."

"How can it mean more than a man?" insisted Portia. Hope brightened her and revived her interest. "Is it because he won't stay in one place?"

"He never will. If you want to give up every friend and every old thing you have lived with, if you want to follow him until you can't remember what last week's room looked like, if there's never any end to anything and never any chance of stopping, if you stand in some room, like now, wondering where he is and when he'll be back, if that's what you want, go ahead. Follow him."

"I would."

"I wouldn't."

Portia came near Aurora, facing her. She showed Aurora a soft, excited prettiness. She was anxious, eager, aroused by new hope. "But suppose he stayed here. Would you — ?"

"He won't stay," said Aurora in a small, tired tone. "Could I have my horse? Could you lend me a gun?"

Portia opened the door and yelled over the yard. "Bill, get Aurora Brant's horse." She walked across the room, into another, and returned with a Winchester which she handed to Aurora. The two of them waited in strained silence, full of speech but not speaking. A man came out of the snow and left Aurora's horse at the porch; he went back into the snowfall.

"Thanks," said Aurora. "I wish we could be friends. But that's never possible since we are what we are."

"I don't think you like me any more than I like you," stated Portia. "The truth is you don't love him. Everything he's doing for you means nothing. Last night — " the cruel feeling of that possibility showed in Portia's eyes — "last night he kept you warm. And what did you tell him then? Were you truthful with him? Probably not. You took his warmth and it meant nothing. Of course I don't like you!"

"Good-by," said Aurora and left the house. She stepped to the saddle, put the Winchester across her lap and rode downgrade. At the edge of the valley she looked back at the house now dim-shaped in the snow. In another hundred yards she was in a gray-white lost world, only the vague, black margin of the east ridge guiding her. As she traveled she thought of many things she wished she had told Portia; they were hot words rehearsed in her mind, they were angry and passionate answers. She was near crying, torn by a sudden uncontrolled rebellion at her own silence. She hated the impression she had left with Portia and in her mind was the recurring phrase: "I'm not like that. I'm the kind of a woman she is. But I can't ever afford to be that kind."

The three Broken Bit men, Long George and Len Teal and Snap, came out of the timber and sighted Keene in the open ground beyond the Bowley house. Long George clawed for his rifle and took a chance shot. Keene faded back into the trees, whereupon Long George said: "Here we go." Len Teal murmured: "Better be careful how we chase after that fellow," but obediently followed.

Snap called: "I'll go tell Grat," turning away. He reached the east-west road and found DePard a mile along it; DePard came on rapidly, summoned by Long George's shot. He had Red John and all seven of the other Broken Bit riders with him.

"He just came out of Bowley's old place," called Snap. "He's in those trees now."

"Alone?" asked Red John.

"Saw nobody with him."

DePard made a quick motion with his hand, slicing his party in half. Snap wheeled back with four of De-Pard's men. DePard sat hard and angry on the saddle. He stared at his foreman, not admiring Red John at all. "So he rode up the trail last night and got to Bowley's. You condemned fool, you'd had him if you'd stuck where I told you."

"Grat," said Red John, turned to pale fury by the words, "don't talk to me like that."

"You had him. You got cold feet and ran."

"I wasn't afraid of him," yelled Red John. He slapped his hand hard down on his leg. "Don't tell me that! Not of him and not of you. Not of any man alive! Don't talk to me like that!"

"You're a woman chaser," said DePard. "Never knew a chaser that wasn't soft as putty. What'd you run for?"

"Why didn't you stay with her?" shouted Red John. "You took her from the store. I didn't. If we ever get caught you're the man that dragged a woman into the hills, not me. You think I'm sucker enough to get stuck with that?"

"First I ever heard of your bein' worried about a woman."

"I know when to stop," said Red John. "I got sense. You don't catch me getting hung for woman-grabbin'. There's a lot of things a man can get by with. But that's one thing he don't talk himself out of if he's caught."

"Red," said DePard, "take these boys and go straight

down the Lost Man trail. Pinch in toward the Bowley house and don't make any racket about it. You'd better see you get this Keene or maybe you'll get hung yet."

"I didn't take her," flashed out the foreman.

"Red," DePard warned him, "don't throw off on me. I'm the man you got to watch out for. Don't worry about anybody else. Get along."

He watched Red and the two remaining hands swing into the timber; he listened to the grunting of their horses until the sound died, and thereafter he followed Snap's trail. One more rifle echo swelled through the steady fall of snow. He said, "Fine — fine," and gritted his big teeth together and plunged ahead.

Red John led his party up the slope of the ridge to the trail; he went along this main way until he reached the intersection of the trail leading west to Crews's. Deep holes showed the passage of a recent rider outbound from Crews's. Continuing forward, he came to the trail which slanted downhill to the Bowley place. All this area was chopped by previous riding and he stopped again, not sure of what had happened. Aurora, he believed, had gone back to Crews's; and it looked like somebody had gone with her. Not Keene, who was somewhere below, but another rider.

He was on the defensive from that moment, realizing other people now knew of his part in this night's business; it would be a story all over the flats within eight hours. He thought to himself: "I told her it wasn't my idea. She knows it." But he was rooted to the snow, full of fear and not knowing what next to do.

"You fellows go on down there," he said finally. "DePard's probably reached the Bowley place by now. There's somebody else floatin' around up here. I got to find out."

They dropped downslope away from him, disappearing around a bend. In that direction, farther off than the Bowley house and farther to the left, another small cold thin echo broke. Red John put his hands on the horn, dead-centered and thoroughly unable to come to a decision with himself. For when he fully realized how damning a story Aurora Brant would tell of him, he was seized by the paralyzing foresight of his own fate. This fear had come on him in the line cabin the night before. Watching Aurora, he had seen himself in her eyes, he had at last caught the enormity of his act. Fear had never left him since. Whether or not DePard won the battle with Keene and the homesteaders, the answer was still the same. There would always be somebody on the Silver Bow waiting for him. He was marked.

When he came to review the reputation he had the picture grew blacker and blacker. He thought of all the women he had known. They made a ring around him and they were smiling at him, mocking him and watching him slowly shrivel. Their laughter was a heartless, distant chiming. He groaned aloud and a stinging sensation crawled along his skin and then he knew he had to leave the country at the earliest moment. He was through here.

Seized by a terrible, unsettling need of haste, he muttered to himself, "Maybe it's too late," and the loneliest feeling in the world belonged to him now — the feeling of being hunted — and every corridor in the timber turned black and full of risk and for the first time in his life he lost confidence. "Got to get out of here," he sighed. His breathing worked deeper into his chest; he dragged in air and found it insufficient. He thought of the pass which, because of its elevation, would now be deep in snow. He thought of the valley lying westward, too open a stretch to risk. He kicked his horse into motion, but when he realized he had done it blindly he pulled up and took a hard grip on himself. There was really only one way to leave this country now. He would follow Lost Man, under the timber's shelter, cross the Silver Bow by dark and make a long run to the railroad. He would catch a train at Virgil, which was a water-tank stop east of Prairie.

It had to be the train; he had to put a thousand miles behind him as rapidly as possible. He swayed on the saddle and ticked the horse with his heels, sliding from the trail into the timber. Each forward yard tightened his inner suspense until every pine tree took on the shape of a gallows. If he was caught he would be hung. He groaned again, momentarily losing his self-control. There was nothing in him now but a pure dread of capture.

Cleve Stewart came to this cross-trail spot not more than five minutes after Red John had departed, and stopped to inspect the scuffed snow. His own tracks and those of Aurora were there; and others as well. The whole area had been crisscrossed by travel. Wind was rising again and snow fell slanting and thick, screening everything beyond twenty yards. Day's light had turned duller. Out of the broken country to the east came the distant sing of a shot. This, he thought, was far beyond and below the Bowley house; it seemed DePard had caught Keene's trail.

Aiming through the pines on a downgrade course which would bring him to the narrow meadow skirting the Short Hills, he found tracks printed before him; these he followed with an increased care. A kind of cold, growling sensation got at his nerves, and now in this cultivated and unsure man was an emotion which astonished him and which, because of his analytical mind, he tried to understand. In a way it was like looking back into the dim beginnings of his ancestral line and seeing the apparition of a squat and shaggy man whose little red eyes stared out from beneath deep sockets and a sloping forehead; a man with matted hair, crouching because he had not yet learned to stand, with nothing on his face but the feral instinct to kill for safety or for meat.

Every fragment of conscious philosophy Cleve Stewart owned denied the existence of that little shaggy man behind him. Yet there the little man was, his sly eyes peering out of a half covert, as though he had been following Cleve Stewart and would never cease to follow. Cleve shook the fancy away. Yet he said: "Perhaps we are all nearer to him than we think," and then he felt better; he felt prouder and tougher. Following the tracks laid down before him, he was less unsure; somewhere within him the spirit of the little man stirred.

These tracks threaded the timber and came to the edge of the narrow meadow; they made a crisscross pattern on the meadow and soon came back to the timber. Out in the meadow snow whirled steadily from the sky and Stewart saw nothing but the half-materialized outline of a broken ridge across the way. Somewhere in this day Keene traveled and somewhere DePard traveled; but now Stewart was isolated and at loss. The tracks paralleled the meadow, keeping within the trees. Following them, Stewart went on a hundred yards and saw the tracks double back in the direction of the ridge crest.

By now Stewart was pleased with his own courage. He had tasted something wild and bitter; the taste was good and a strange ambition stalked through him. He lifted his revolver from his heavy coat and held it on his lap; he moved uphill, searching the blind coverts of timber on either hand. The tracks led him to the height of the ridge and to the trail running north and south along it; and once again that unknown rider seemed to be swayed by uncertainty. Pursuing the trail three or four hundred feet, he had cut downslope again, aiming at the meadow.

"Like a drunk trying to walk a straight line," thought Stewart.

It occurred to him to give the tracks a closer inspection. Out of the saddle and on his knees, he looked into foot-deep prints and saw the clear stamp of the hoof mark, still uncovered by fresher snow; the traveler was at no great distance ahead.

Stewart got back on the horse. He drew a long breath, suddenly needing wind. To this point he had been on a comfortable chase, playing with the notion of pursuit but seeing nothing too serious in it. Now the possibilities of this pursuit hit him in the stomach. His face held a long, indrawn stiffness and he confronted himself with the old question again: What was he made of and how deep was his courage? He looked down at the gun on his lap and knew he wouldn't rest until he found that out; it was too late to withdraw.

He thought: "I'll stay off that trail. I'll get on his flank." He moved forward on the main trail; he came to a long bend and crouched forward in the saddle. Grayness swept through the trees in waves, an illusion produced by the steady drive of snow. Half around the bend, he heard the distant explosion of a gunshot; that turned him immediately downgrade to the narrow meadow. Reaching its edge he looked out into the snow's white scurry, saw nothing at all in the small area of visibility, and turned to the right. Within fifty feet he came upon the trail of the unknown rider; that rider had at last entered the open country.

Another shot beat back through the wind, originating from the far side of the meadow. Stewart scrubbed an arm over his stiff face; excitement began to sing in his nerves. Everything came to this moment and nothing else mattered. He drew a long breath and was afraid of himself, but the shaggy little man's red eyes were again watching him from some distant covert of time with a bright flame of interest. Stewart pushed out of the timber and started over the valley toward that general spot from which the shot had seemed to come.

XVI

AT ROPE'S END

FADING back into the timber near the Bowley house, Keene ran through the timber, parallel to the meadow, and came into the open again. The two Broken Bit men were dissolved shadows in the screening shimmer of snowfall. A shot rang out. He pushed at the horse with his spurs, sending it forward in labored jumps, until the gray wall of a ridge broke through the weather. Keene reached the ridge's first slope and passed into a side gulch; he followed the gulch a few yards, slid into timber and swung about. The two Broken Bit men's shadows had vanished.

He held the Winchester on his lap, waiting. Wind, growing stronger, trembled the pine branches overhead and shook stringers of snow on him. Somewhere in the meadow he heard a voice calling and then one Broken Bit man broke from the woolly smother. Keene flung up his Winchester, aimed low, and fired. The Broken Bit rider's horse dropped sidewise and the rider, flinging himself clear of the saddle, rolled on and on. Keene put a second shot near the man, hearing his wild, high yell. The man reared up, rushing back into the snow screen.

He heard the other Broken Bit man calling. From the head of the ravine a gun spoke in quick signal.

Keene dropped back to the side gulch, climbed a

short distance and cut to the east, returning toward the source of the signal shot. He arrived at a low point of the ridge, with the meadow below him. Standing against the dark wall of pines, he heard DePard's men calling but could not see them. Those voices drifted with the wind.

They came nearer. Keene reined his horse gently into the timber and stood fast. Below him the shadows of Broken Bit's men began to emerge. They drifted along the far side of the meadow, never fully taking shape; and over there they stopped. He heard their voices again. In a little while the voices faded and the shadows faded.

He came off the ridge into the meadow and now he had DePard in front of him, going away. DePard's crew had left a broad set of tracks on the snow and along these Keene drifted. The tracks circled gradually toward the east edge of the meadow. When he saw that, Keene pulled up.

Somewhere on his left a door squealed and a board fell against another board. Swinging about, Keene faced the unseen edge of timber to the west. Over there, closer than he had supposed, lay the Bowley house, and as he paused to consider that he saw a new set of shadows break the snow screen again in a ragged file. This was another party. One pace farther away and they would have been beyond sight; one pace nearer and they would have seen him. But they moved on and were gone. He heard a voice say:

"Try a shot."

The shot broke against the wind. The same voice said: "Here's tracks."

Listening closely to further sound from that area, he caught the brittle scuff of snow whose source seemed to swing with the wind. Keene shook his head. He bent low in the saddle to get the wind out of his ears and heard the sound definitely originate behind. What occurred to him then, even before he looked back, was that DePard had followed his tracks up the side of the east ridge and around into the open ground. He had cut back on DePard; now DePard had cut back on him.

He looked about, to discover at once shapes forming in the oatmeal thickness of the air. This would be De-Pard's main bunch following the tracks he had left behind him. They were moving slowly, turning more distinct in the day. DePard's voice yelled: "There!"

Keene clipped the horse with his heels, rushing away. A shot beat along the wind and DePard's continuing halloo sailed out of the rear. Keene swung to the right, looked back to find no shadow near him, and straightened forward once more. This unseen meadow was all in a moment crisscrossed by the hard-thrown shouting of men seeking contact and next he heard horses slogging along the snow not far away, and when he heard that he swung to the left with the intention of reaching the pines on the Lost Man side of the meadow. Making the swing, he came through the mists at the same instant another man raced up from a lower quarter of the meadow.

It was Snap. He saw Snap's red face stretch in surprise, he saw Snap's gun rise. Keene's pony slammed its shoulders against Snap's horse and the roar of the Broken Bit man's gun walloped Keene's face and drove at his eardrums. Keene had his Winchester half lifted and as Snap rolled back from the collision of the horses, Keene brought the barrel of the gun down on Snap's head and knocked him senseless from the saddle.

He was still moving to the left, now watching shadows move in. He straightened at once, with a great-lunged cry hard at his heels: "Keep him away from the trees!"

They had him boxed. He moved to the right, the pony plunging up and down in the drifts and making great labor of it. He lost the shapes on his left. Still veering to the right he reached the sharp eastern slope of the meadow wall and found no breach. The meadow, he guessed, formed a watercourse of the hills and would lead at last into the open country near the Silver Bow. Meanwhile he heard DePard's voice from a greater distance and thus knew he had temporarily escaped Broken Bit's encircling maneuver. Running on, Keene found a low notch in the ridge wall and swung at it immediately. The horse broke through a crust of ice into a creek, stumbled and caught its balance. Then Keene rose steadily into the ridge.

There was no timber within view. The ground beneath him grew increasingly rough and the horse, spending out its strength on the steep slope, began to falter. Keene dropped from the saddle and went ahead of the horse. He had lost all sound of men behind him; he had lost as well the general pattern of the country. In these broken hills there was no way of knowing what was ahead.

He came at last to a level rim and started over it, soon arriving at thoroughly impassable ground. Timber clung to the sharp edge of a rock barrier. Turning, he followed a ledge. The ledge grew narrow and within five minutes he came to a dead stop. The rock wall, edging in, pinched him off on the left. To his right was the edge of a canyon whose bottom was lost beneath the gray shadows and the snowfall.

He realized then DePard's smart maneuvering. The only way to escape this blind alley was to turn about and retrace his trail. That, of course, was out of the question. DePard was no doubt now coming up on his tracks. DePard had him bottled.

Keene kicked away the snow and got down on his knees, digging into the surface of the ledge. He got a chunk of rock and let it drop into the canyon. No sound came back to him. He dug out another rock, heavier than the first, and heaved it over the brink and thought he heard the answering splash of water. He had guessed that steady washing echo around him came from the wind; now he believed it came from a fast-running creek in the bottom of the canyon.

He had fifty feet of rope on the saddlehorn. He made a solid tie to the off stirrup of the saddle and flung the rest of the rope into the canyon. Flat on his belly, with his head hooked over the rim, he saw the yellow rope's end pay out through the snow and shadow and disappear. He jiggled the rope up and down, feeling it drag along the side of the canyon but unable to determine whether or not it touched bottom; and after listening to the creek he had no better estimate of the distance.

He gripped the Winchester and let himself over the rim, descending on the rope. Above him the horse stirred and for a moment he felt himself being dragged sidewise along the canyon's face as the horse started on the back trail. That motion presently stopped. Keene sank rapidly down, chest scraping the rocky outcrop of the canyon's face. His hat fell off, the sound of the creek reached up to him. At the bitter end of the rope he swung slowly, like the weight of a pendulum's arm, his feet touching nothing but air. The horse again moved and the taut rope, catching on the rough rim above, jerked him violently into the wall. He snagged his cheek against a stunted pine somehow growing in that impossible place.

Keene pushed himself far back from the wall with his feet and let go. Tight-braced for a long fall, he dropped immediately into a swift water that carried him off his feet and sent him sidewise against a niggerhead in the current. He gripped the niggerhead and stood erect, still clinging to the Winchester. The shock of the water took all wind from him. He opened his mouth wide and a guttering sound came out of his throat as breath returned; he was hip-high in a current hitting him like the edge of a board.

Steadying himself against the niggerhead, he gouged his boot heels into the slick gravel of the creek's bottom, stepped cautiously forward and found shallows before him. He came up to dry land. He came up also to the round face of a gallery cut into the canyon's wall. Looking into the gallery he saw the black ashes of a dead fire, a coffeepot and a frying pan.

This was the hideout to which Portia Crews had brought him two nights before.

A shot broke along the canyon, setting up a long and hollow drumming. Keene ducked back into the gallery. Looking upward, he saw the end of the lariat move out of sight, drawn away by men standing on the rim. Cold as ice, with water dripping slowly along his skin, he remembered there was but one exit from this gorge.

Passing down the narrow meadow, Cleve Stewart had the wind hard against his back and the tracks of the unknown traveler before him. For a while the tracks moved straight into the south, keeping to the middle of the meadow. Half a mile or more on, those tracks began to veer errantly, as though the man had been struck again by the uncertainty he had displayed previously in the pines. The tracks moved over to the Short Hills edge of the meadow, started up a slope and got as far as timber; here they doubled back into the meadow, crossed it and turned.

Cleve had nursed the thought that this might be Keene ahead of him. The longer he followed the trail the more sure he became that it was not, for Keene was too certain a man to leave that kind of print behind him. More likely, Stewart guessed, the fellow ahead belonged to Broken Bit.

The day was biting cold and this guess made him colder. Still, he was not afraid; realizing at last where those tracks might lead him, Cleve Stewart said to himself, as one man talking to another: "Well, this is it. You're in it now." If he came suddenly upon the Broken Bit man and if the Broken Bit man moved for his gun he, Stewart, would draw. There was one ticklish point, though, in all this reasoning. If he drew, should he fire at once or should he wait? If he waited the delay might kill him. He had been long enough in the country to have heard tougher men explain their philosophy of fighting. There was, they had said, a time for talking but a man had to judge when that time was past. How was he to know? He had never drawn a gun on a man. Keene, he thought, would know all this by heart.

He found more in Keene to admire at this moment than ever before. It was not a simple thing to fight. It was not easy to move blindly through snow, playing hide and seek with trouble. It took courage, but it took something more as well — it took a sound knowledge of other men, the ability to read in their eyes the things they would do; it took a hard-gained experience in all the clever tricks of living, an ability to listen into the wind, to read the patterns on the earth, to make a story out of dust and distant motion. As an educated man, possessing the prejudices of education, Cleve Stewart always had felt a certain contempt for men whose lives were confined to action; to him they were half blind, knowing nothing of the great and gentle philosophies which made life understandable.

But somewhere in the last twenty-four hours Stewart's world had come down about him; a complete change had occurred in him. The wisdom which came from earthy men, the wisdom of survival and bitter wind beating into a man's bones, of hunger suffered and thirst endured — this was the real wisdom, gained not from books or the tales of other travelers but personally experienced so that a man got it into his spirit and nerves and blood. A man had to know of what he was made. Knowing that, he knew everything.

To his rear and to his left one shot trembled in the hidden day. After a pause other shots broke in tumbling repetition. Stewart swung around, riding into the wind. He came against the high shoulder of the ridge on the Short Hills side, finding no easy way of climbing from the meadow. Plugging upwind, he caught no more sounds and therefore he stopped and waited out a long five minutes; and at last turned back to search for the trail he had abandoned. He moved away from the foot of the east ridge into the middle of the meadow and went slowly forward. Snow thickened and raced before the wind, closing about him and narrowing his vision. A shadow, very vague, showed ahead and he thought he had drifted against the trees on the Lost

Man side of the meadow. He pulled away to clear those trees, but the shadow seemed to move with him; and then, out of the driving gray-white wall, a rider came at him.

He was no more than a double length of a horse from this rider when he recognized the long, red-whipped face of Red John shadowed by his hat brim. He saw the chill shock in Red John's eyes and without need of thinking, without hesitation of any kind, Cleve Stewart flung up his Winchester.

Red John howled one formless word and pulled away. Red John's hand pointed and Stewart, weaving in the saddle, heard the beat of Red John's gun and thought he felt the breath of the bullet on his face. Stewart drove a shot at the foreman now sliding off into the pall; he knew he had missed and pulled the horse to a stop and fired again, this time at the pure wall of snow before him. Red John had vanished.

Cleve Stewart yelled, not knowing why, and gripped the Winchester hard with his hands. He had been shot at and he had answered with his own gun — and he was experiencing a feeling of ease and certainty he had never known; it was a sweet and whole sensation which changed him and made the world forever different. He yelled again and kicked his horse into a plunging run, trying to lift Red John out of the snow curtain.

Red John looked behind him and saw nothing; now he was half mad from thinking too long of his situation and he wasted one more bullet before taking control of himself. He moved to the right and came upon the high shoulder of the east ridge and discovered no quick way of leaving the meadow. He went along with his body bent forward in the saddle, exhausting his horse by the steady rake of his spurs. In his mind he saw himself swinging slowly at the end of a rope, with women — those familiar faces coming again before him — laughing at his broken neck. He heard that laughter in the wind, high and heartless and wild.

He slanted off from the ridge, aiming at the timber on the Lost Man side of the meadow. The trees, he now thought, would be safest. In them he might squirm and dodge his way to the Silver Bow and there wait until darkness came before crossing the ford. Behind him, in faintest echo, was the reverberation of firing. Before him a streak of darkness materialized in the steady flicker of snow. A voice said: "Who's that?"

Red John threw his weight about, he jerked the horse hard aside. Those shadows closed in, they emerged and became full bodies. He was at a dead stop, his horse confused and shaking; and he looked across the short space at the half-surprised faces of young Joe Spackman and the little group of homesteaders.

They had caught him, never expecting it; they were off-guard at the moment — the elder Spackman with his round Hollander's face loose in half-formed wonder, the Scotchman Comrie, Kilrain and Elijah Patterson, and other men he had never seen. They bulked before him, they made a half circle around him — silent and reflective and slowly pondering him.

Young Joe Spackman said: "Put up your hands, Red. I'm going to ride around and snatch your gun. Put up your hands."

In the rising wind was that wild, condemning laughter of women. It screamed against Red John's ears; he thought of their voices once so soft-whispering in his ears, he thought of warmth never to touch him again, he thought of Jennie Cannon and saw her face lift to him under the moonlight, half smiling and half afraid. That was his last thought except one, and it was his hardest thought.

Young Spackman said: "You're caught, Red. Do what I tell you. Put up your hands."

Red John had one hand in his coat pocket, gripping the solid butt of his revolver. He pulled out the hand, with the gun, and jammed the gun's muzzle into his mouth. He had started to speak, but those words, whatever they might have been, were blown everlastingly away when he pulled the trigger.

The homesteaders sat rooted, watching Red John roll from the saddle and drop; blood brightened the snow and turned quickly black. Comrie clenched his teeth together at the sight. Kilrain grew pale. The elder Spackman said in a sick voice: "Why did he do that?"

Young Joe, who understood what madness could be like, said: "He knew what was going to happen to him."

The older Spackman glanced at his son. "Why, I

guess he did," and continued to watch young Joe.

Comrie called: "Watch out — "

A shape broke through the thick mists. Young Joe reached for his Winchester and aimed it full on that shape; and dropped the gun as Cleve Stewart moved into view.

Comrie said: "You after him?" and pointed to the ground.

Stewart stared down. Day's cold had hardened his face beyond the ability to change expression. But because he was a reflective man, he sat long silent, thinking of those things which must have been last in Red John's mind. The great and wise philosophers, looking into the hearts of men two thousand years ago, and five thousand miles from this spot, had spoken of this thing, foretelling Red John's end. He looked up at the homesteaders and moved his shoulders slightly.

"Keene's back of us somewhere. DePard's got his crew there, pretty close to Keene. I've heard firing."

"Time's now to finish this," said Comrie.

"Come on then," said Stewart and led them back into the wind.

Big Jesse Morspeare, hard on Keene's heels the previous night, had reached Aurora's store and found it empty. By then the storm had warned him to take shelter but the store was a spot not to his liking and therefore he crossed the flats to the line cabin, which was the closest shelter, unknowingly on the heels of both

Keene and DePard. When he found the warm stove in the line cabin he sat long in the cabin's darkness, suspicious yet not wanting to risk the storm, his slow mind meanwhile plucking at the edges of the puzzle.

When day came he moved doggedly south on the ridge trail with Keene uppermost in his sullen head. At the Bowley turnoff he saw tracks and followed them to the house, finding nothing. Returning to the main trail, he moved south until he reached the east-west road, snow whirling soft and thick around him and the wind beginning to take on voice in the timber. A mile from the Broken Bit ranch he saw a shape rise through the making storm and in a little while he overtook Red John's horse, which walked slowly in the direction of the ranch. Blood lay frozen on the riderless saddle.

He towed the horse into the ranch, finding an empty yard and an empty barn. The cookstove was buried beneath a mound of snow, the Chinaman had disappeared. Morspeare sat in the barn, cold and troubled and useless. He knew nothing of DePard's whereabouts, he suspected the worst from Red John's saddle. Now alone, a masterless and unbridled animal, he brooded in sullen silence. Constantly he thought of Keene and because he was a man capable only of great loyalty and great hatred — no lesser emotions lying between those extremes — he saw Keene as the cause of all this ruin and his rage increased and left him with a savage, inarticulate longing to kill.

XVII

JENNIE

KEENE stood back in the rock gallery, listening to echoes beat along the narrow gorge. DePard's men were fifty feet above him on the rim, out of sight in the snowstorm, blindly firing down in hope of a chance hit. Wind rolled into the gallery and built up the ice-chill of his wet clothes. His legs and feet ached from cold; his muscles began to knot up.

The firing quit. Keene moved to the edge of the creek, knowing he could not stay here. The only exit was downgrade to his left and this exit, he realized, DePard would now have blocked. But he had to move on, warned by the frigid splinters of this weather driving into his marrow, into his vitals. This was not the smooth and lulling approach of cold death; this was pain biting at him, burning through him. He gripped the Winchester and fell into a spraddled run. His legs were thick and clumsy, his feet were granite blocks within his wet boots. He tripped over a snow-hidden boulder and dropped on his belly, sliding forward. He got up, angered by the fall and pushed by the need of haste, and at last fully conscious of the danger in his body. He continued to shiver as he ran; he stamped his feet hard against the snow. Sensations came up through his legs in slow, delayed waves. Pain quit, and by that he knew his feet were freezing.

He watched the canyon wall on his left, he watched the creek to his right. Presently the creek began to move away from him and the canyon wall took on a shallow pitch; the mouth of the canyon was before him, widening into the invisible meadow ahead. He was still at a steady running gait. Creek and canyon wall vanished; he was alone in the white-driving smother, the Winchester chest-high and slanted forward. In this windy, blind area he heard a voice rise and grow dim, and a shape came up from nothing and wavered in the snow screen. He ran dead at it, he fired at it and saw the shape sway aside and vanish. He continued forward at this changeless gait, with other gray shapes sliding along the edge of visibility and disappearing. A rider curved up from the right, the grunt of the horse stiff and deep in the wind. Keene turned the muzzle of the Winchester at the still unseen target and fired; a voice howled in full volume against the wind. That sound trembled in the storm and was blown away.

He pounded his dead feet hard into the snow as he ran. He was out in the valley flat, feeling nothing at all from toe to knee. Wind shouldered him, snow spatted against his cheeks and built ragged awnings on his eyebrows. He heard that same on-pushing voice come nearer. A rider rushed invisibly past; going on five yards, Keene saw the tracks of that horse. Men were circling in the storm, crisscrossing the area in search of him, and once more he heard them calling. One voice lifted high:

"Here's his trail!"

Beyond this area and beyond the sound of these voices Keene heard a shot, as though a detached part of DePard's outfit signaled from another quarter. Close by, a shot answered. He was, he guessed, three quarters across the valley but the long run and the pressure of the wind and the snow underfoot had him deadbeat. He took one long stride, lost balance, and went down. Flat against the snow he heard a horse grunt by; he resisted the impulse to lie still, he fought the powerful pull of exhaustion and rose to his knees and faced his back trail. In the distance another gun cracked — and as Keene rose to his feet, still gripping the Winchester, he saw a shape break from the wild, millrace run of the storm, head down and shoulders bent.

It was DePard, afoot. DePard had his eyes on the tracks Keene had left behind him; suddenly DePard lifted his face and discovered Keene before him. He took one more onward step and jerked to a complete halt.

He had lost his hat. Snow crusted his black scalp; it was a white rime on his cheeks, a sleeted braiding along his clothes. Without an overcoat, without gloves, he stood tough and impervious to the weather, his cotton shirt thrown open at the neck. This day's cold fanned the rich blood to his face; in his eyes was a bright self-certain flare. What Keene saw was an expression of supreme pleasure, a long-lipped grimace of satisfaction; the man's will was that fixed.

"Friend," said DePard, "you reached the end of the trail on a damned cold day."

In his mind there was no doubt at all, never a moment's uncertainty. He held a gun at the extended length of his right hand. Keene, slowly freezing in his tracks, called to his muscles and felt them slowly change the tilt of the Winchester. It was the longest moment of his life as he watched DePard bring up the revolver. He saw the snout of his own gun tip but he had no control over it; it moved in slow motion, beyond his power to hurry. He heard a shot and he felt the Winchester kick against his arm, but this was a faint feeling that came from a great distance. Across the interval, DePard's mouth framed a word; a strange anguish broke in DePard's eyes, an unbelieving shock. DePard bowed his head in one reluctant, bitter motion; he seemed to be looking at the revolver slowly pulling his arm down; he seemed to be praying at it. When he fell he turned aside and dropped with his face deep in the snow.

A yell slanted through the wind and once again there was the thump of a horse veering through this blind weather. Keene slung his gun around, firing at a shadow. The horse moved away. A gun exploded, quite near. The echo of it came to him as through a speaking tube:

"Keene!"

"Here," he said, in a small voice. He said again, no

louder, "Here." He retreated a few feet, passing De-
Pard. He looked at DePard.

"Keene!"

He stiffened in his tracks, he planted his legs —
wooden as pine poles — apart and got the Winchester
breast-high.

A rider passed within three yards of him, running on.
That rider yelled his name, and then Keene looked up
and saw Cleve Stewart suddenly above him.

"Why didn't you sing out?" shouted Stewart.

"I did."

Stewart bent on the saddle, intently staring at Keene.
He said, "What did you say?"

"I did."

Stewart noticed DePard for the first time and slid
from the saddle and bent down over the dead man; he
came back to Keene. He lifted a hand and caught
Keene's cheek flesh between his fingers. "Feel that?"

"No," said Keene. "Let's get over to the Bowley
house." He spoke with elaborate distinctness, fighting
the great weight of weariness. He was in need of sleep
and that need was hard to bear. He had his chin against
his chest and pulled it up with some difficulty, to find
that both Spackmans had ridden out of the murk. "To
the Bowley house," said Keene again. He wished to
make that clear. "I want to thaw out."

Cleve said: "Ride behind Joe."

Keene tried to lift a leg to the stirrup. He said: "I
guess I've taken on weight." Stewart got a shoulder

against him. Joe Spackman caught him by the arm. Keene rolled heavily as he rose; he took young Joe around the ribs with his hands.

Other homesteaders had drifted in. Stewart called: "Don't waste any time gettin' there, Joe."

Keene felt motion vaguely as the horse moved across the valley. They struck timber, young Joe calling back: "Where's that house?" Stewart rode ahead to lead the way. They came against the side of the barn and circled it and rode through the broken doorway. The force of the wind left Keene and a kind of long, velvet silence surrounded him and the last of physical sensation seemed to leave him. He sat on the horse's rump, unable to move and not concerned about it. He had his full weight on young Joe. Sleep was a soft bottomless hole into which he sank without resistance. From a distance he heard Stewart rapidly say:

"Get a fire going. Do it quick. Come on, Comrie. We'll get him down. We'll get his clothes off and slap hell out of him. The man's halfway turned to marble."

Morspeare heard a call in the Broken Bit yard and walked to the doorway of the barn. Snap and Len Teal rode through the snowfall into the barn.

Snap said: "Where's that Chinaman? I want some coffee."

"Chinaman's gone. Dig out the stove and light your own fire. What the hell you think I am? Grat comin' — Red John comin'? Where's everybody?"

Neither man left the saddle. Snap pushed a hand heavily across a scarred cheek; he had been bleeding at the nose, he had lost a front tooth. He said to Len Teal: "By God, I hate to buck this weather again. Can't stop at Crews's — not now. Or Stewart's. Nor any of the homesteaders'. Forty miles to town, Len. Hell of a long ways."

"Better start," said Teal. "They'll be comin' this way."

"Who's comin'?" asked Morspeare.

"I got some blankets over in the straw," said Teal.

"Let 'em alone," answered Snap. "We can buy fresh blankets at the next ranch we work for. Which will be a hell of a long ways from here. I don't want no more of this country. Gives me the shakes to think about it."

"Well," said Teal, "let's go." He looked down at the massive, slow-witted Morspeare. "You better get out of here. Them homesteaders will be up here pretty soon. Grat got killed by Keene. Red shot himself. Better go."

They rode into the weather, leaving big Jesse alone. He watched them vanish, not yet fully understanding what they had told him. He said: "How could Grat get killed? What'd Red John shoot himself for?" He turned it over and over in his mind; it was impossible to think of Grat being dead — it left a hole in the big man. It made him lonely, it destroyed the only solid thing he had ever known.

He stood in the doorway, scowling at the snow, painfully piecing together the scraps of information; and when he had the story gathered in his head he turned back into the barn and saddled his horse. Sitting up on the leather he looked around him; and then got down and walked over to a clean stall where Grat kept his belongings. Grat had left a briar pipe on a box. Morspeare took the pipe and held it in his enormous palm. He brought the back of the other hand up across his nose, sniveling like a boy. Afterwards he put the pipe in his pocket, returned to the horse and left Broken Bit.

"Grat," he said into the stormy, blank day, "I'll fix that for you. You was a better man than him. I'll fix it for you. Don't doubt that."

Later in the day he skirted the edge of the Crews ranch and watched its yard until he was satisfied Keene was not there. Near noon he drifted against the side of Stewart's house and crawled to a window, looking in. Past the middle of the afternoon, a gray ghost in the steady race of snow, he came quietly upon the lean-to of Aurora's store, finding only Aurora's horse stabled there. Keene hadn't reached here either. Big Jesse crossed the ford, moving on to Prairie City.

He was a lonely, disconsolate dog who had lost his master, but the devotion to Grat remained — the only devotion big Jesse ever had known. He said again in brokenhearted misery: "I'll make it right, Grat. I'll kill that man for you."

All the homestead men had come into Bowley's barn and now stood close by the fire built from hay and scrap boards. Wrapped in a saddle blanket, Keene waited for his clothes to dry. Heat began to penetrate his muscles and loosen them; heat traveled into him, thawing out distant recesses. Before they had let him come near the fire they had pounded circulation painfully back into his legs and face and that necessary punishment had left its aches. He was hollow with hunger but life began to run through him — he was whole again. His black hair still glittered with wetness, his face was rough with whiskers, and his eyes sparkled against the firelight.

"So he shot himself," said Cleve, explaining Red John.

Steam rose from Keene's drying clothes. Everybody crowded around the fire but the talk died out. Letdown was on these men — the reaction of fighting; they were looking back on what they had done and seeing themselves in a strange light. Watching them, Keene observed that these homesteaders, all good and faithful and honest men, were uncomfortably remembering what they had done. It was a way of living to which they were unaccustomed; that gray business troubled them and they were trying to forget it.

Comrie said: "We better go up to Broken Bit."

"You'll find nobody there," said Keene.

"Just the same," said Comrie, "we better go. It is a dirty chore better finished for good. I don't want to do this again."

"Once in one lifetime is enough," agreed the elder Spackman. Then he looked at Keene and closed his mouth, as though he might have said something to offend Keene.

"Yes," Keene said, "once is enough. I hope you never have to do it again."

"You think we might have to do it again?" asked the elder Spackman.

"No," said Keene. "DePard's dead."

"There's his crew."

Keene spoke out of his experience — the kind of experience none of them had, the kind he hoped they'd never have; for the reaction was on him, too, and he saw himself in that unlovely light which always came to him when riding was done. "They'll scatter," he said. "In a thing like this there's always a kingpin. When he's gone everything falls apart. There won't be any Broken Bit any more."

"You know what I'm going to do?" said Kilrain. "I'm going to give up my quarter-section and move across the ford to the valley. That's the place."

"Out of Egypt," murmured Keene, "to the promised land. Ten years from now that valley will be fences and houses, with trees growing up. It will be a pretty sight. I'd like to ride back someday and see it."

"You're not staying here?" asked Cleve, showing astonishment.

"Me?" said Keene. "What would I be doing with a home? I guess those clothes are dry enough."

He dropped the blanket to show a long red scar from

left hip to knee, the mark of his fall from the rope in the canyon. He got into his clothes.

Comrie said: "I think we better ride up to Broken Bit just the same."

"All right," said Spackman, though not liking the thought. Then he said to Keene, "Any time you pass my house, now and twenty years from now, there's a chair at the table."

"Why," said Comrie, "that is the least any of us can say."

The homesteaders moved to the barn doorway. Comrie turned back. "I am not a man to harbor sinful thoughts. Those men, out there dead in the valley, they need a Christian burial. We will wait until the storm breaks and come back for them."

Kilrain mused: "Him that was so proud — the De-Pard I mean — him that walked the earth and made the ground shake, 'tis hard to think of him cold clay. Wantin' a little less, he could have had the sweetness of his days and looked upon his cattle in content. Wantin' too much, it is nothin' now he's got."

"A man," reflected Keene softly, "is what he is. It is written in the book."

They were thoughtful and attentive but they didn't know what was in his head; they didn't really understand. He smiled, saying, "I'm hungry," and moved to the horse they had found for him in the storm; it was the same horse, it was Morspeare's. He rode up-trail with the group and came to the crest of the ridge. They turned south toward Broken Bit. At the Crews's turnoff Keene pulled out, Cleve joining him. The homesteaders stopped, looking at him; and Comrie rode back. He said: "You're leaving soon?"

"I expect."

"Well," said Comrie, "it will not be quite the same here," and put out his hand.

Keene shook it. He said to all of them: "So long," and moved down the Crews trail with Cleve. A dog charged across the Crews yard, loudly sounding. A man appeared through the driving snow.

"All over," Stewart told him.

Portia met them at the door. It was Cleve — always the reflective man — who saw the break of feeling in Portia's eyes as she looked at Keene. She said in an unsteady voice: "You're hungry, aren't you?" and turned toward the kitchen.

Keene called after her: "Where's Aurora?"

She swung about, the brightness of her eyes dying, the points of her shoulders dropping. She said: "She went back to the store."

They had a meal; they returned to the front room. Keene stood at the window, looking into the snow. Now that there was nothing to be done, he was at loose ends, he was tired and he was restless. That, he remembered, was the way it always was. He said: "I'll be riding."

"To the store?" asked Portia.

"I'll stop there on the way to town."

Cleve Stewart stood in a far corner of the room, forgotten by both of them. Portia came before Keene. She watched him for a long, deep-searching moment; she read him and, because she loved him, she knew him. "You're going, aren't you? Riding out as you rode in?"

"I suppose."

"Are you sure there's nothing here you'll regret leaving?"

He lifted his shoulders and made that do for an answer.

She said: "If it isn't here, Jim, you'll never find it anywhere."

"I think," he said, "you're right about that."

He turned to her with an expression half ironic and half regretful. It seemed his most characteristic attitude — somehow knowing himself for what he was, yet always touched by further hope. He gave her a straight glance, he really looked at her with a full and undivided attention. "So long," he said.

"So long, Jim."

He glanced across the room. "Thanks, Cleve. Thanks a lot."

"Sure," said Cleve.

Keene left the room, stepped to his saddle and turned from the house. In the space of five yards he had vanished behind the storm. Standing at the window, her cheek touching the cold glass and her eyes straining at the spot she had last seen him, Portia spoke in a dying voice: "How quick everything happens. How short the best things always are."

Cleve Stewart came across the room. He took her shoulder and pulled her around. She dropped her head to conceal her face; he put a finger beneath her chin and lifted it and discovered the glitter of tears in her eyes.

"Did he see that, Portia?"

"No," she said. "I waited until the door was closed, Cleve."

"I'm awfully sorry." He tried to smile. "How long since he came here? A week — a month? And the whole damned country's changed. Mighty queer."

"You've changed, too, Cleve. You know, I never used to like you. I guess you hid what you really were."

"Why," he said, "I guess I've grown up."

"That's a hard thing to do."

"Everything worth doing is hard."

She gave him a prolonged, interested appraisal. "Aren't you going down to Aurora's?"

She wished she hadn't said it, for she recognized the quick passage of hurt in his eyes, the rise of an old feeling and its dampening. "No, not tonight, Portia." He turned away. "When I was a youngster and came in wet and bruised my mother used to put me by the fire and make up a dish of popcorn. Funny how a childhood memory sticks. Whenever I feel tough I think of that."

"I'll make you some popcorn, Cleve."

It was middle-afternoon when Jim lifted the outline of Aurora's store and cabin through the storm and saw the light shining from the window. He shouted into the wind to announce himself; the door opened at once and he saw Aurora brace herself against the sudden rush of wind, her clothes pressed tight around her body. Her lips moved, saying something to him, but her face remained grave. He left his horse in the shed and went into the house. She closed the door; she put her back to it. Snow sparkled diamond-bright in her hair; light struck her eyes, provoking brilliance. She studied him over the long moments, distantly wise. She said:

"Is it all over?"

"Yes."

"I thought so. There's an expression on your face. It — I think you'd like some coffee."

He sat down at the small table. He put his arms on it, watching her move about the room. The coffeepot was already on the stove, in homestead custom. She poured a cup for each of them; she sat opposite him and now she was smiling.

"Is Cleve all right?"

"Everything's all right," he said.

"Perhaps," she corrected, "it would be better to say everything's changed."

"Cleve's a good man. If I were riding with a partner I'd like to have him along."

"But you don't ride with partners, do you?"

"I never have found anybody going as far along the trail as I go. Maybe I fall in with somebody but they always turn off along the line."

She said: "I was one of them. I rode a little way with

you. You kept me warm. That's going to be a happy memory."

She looked down at her cup. She sat idle and still in the chair, her face softened by inward things that were rich and warm and beautiful. She had never really shown him what she could be like. Except for the one moment in the barn loft he had never been permitted inside her guard. Yet he knew how strong, how deep and violent her imagination could be, how hot the fire of her spirit could burn. That glow now and then betrayed itself through the barrier she kept lifted.

She spoke in a voice that felt and shared his hurts. "They've bruised you. Somebody hit you on the face. You look very tired. Do you want me to cook supper now? I have extra blankets. I'll leave the storeroom door open to let in heat, if you want to sleep there."

Wind shouldered heavily against the log house and snow flattened on the window and dissolved. At three o'clock darkness was on the way.

"No," he said, "I'll ride on to town."

She rose from the table, moving back to the stove. She stood by it, turned from him. Her voice was very even and self-controlled and almost indifferent. "Riding on over the hill?"

"Sure," he said.

"For to see the world — the big wide world."

He had finished his coffee and got up. "You're all right," he told her. "Neither Red John nor DePard will be by this way again." This was as close as he could

cheerful. Young Joe sat in the saddle, fighting down one last small memory of Red John. Maybe, he thought, he never would really forget it; but still it was different than it had been a few days before. The acid-burning hurt of it had lessened. He was an older man and some things didn't look the same.

The door came open and Jennie showed herself before him. She said: "I thought I heard something," and looked at him, half-startled. "Maybe," she murmured, "you would like to come in."

"I just wanted to say," he announced, "that everything is all right. That's all I wanted to say. I mean, Jim Keene killed Grat DePard today. There is nothing more to worry about."

"Thank you," she said in a small, lusterless tone. "It was nice of you to come."

He looked at her, not knowing how to go on. At last, defeated by lack of words, he turned and rode into the snow. But then he swung back, seeing her vaguely through the storm. "Red John's dead too," he called.

She cried after him: "Joe — Joe!" She ran through the snow. He was near the Cannon barn; he wheeled against it and got down. She came to him, her eyes dark with fresh tragedy. "You didn't do it, Joe? You didn't?"

She was shaking. He opened the small barn door and pulled her into it. He said: "No, I didn't. He shot himself."

She went loose, her eyes fixed on some black and terrible thing far beyond him. She thought of it with a far-placed expression. She said dully: "I feel sorry for him, Joe."

He was angry and hurt again. "You loved him, I guess. That's why you asked me if I did it."

"Oh, no," she breathed. "Not that, Joe. I never did love him. I was — just — " She couldn't say more about it. She thrust it aside with a gesture of her hands. "But I couldn't think of you making your hands red, Joe. You're not that kind. You mustn't ever be."

"Jennie," he said, "what I came for was to say I wish it could be like it was."

"Nothing can be that way. Something's gone."

"Why now," he said, "maybe it is. But maybe not. If it was all gone I wouldn't be here and I wouldn't think of you. But I do. And what I think is that I can't help being here."

"Not me," she breathed in a half-crying tone. "How can that be, Joe? You'd remember — "

Maybe he would, he thought. But the hurt wasn't as hard to bear — and pretty soon it wouldn't bother him at all. He struggled with it, he gritted his teeth against it, the old longing to have her as strong as it had ever been. Once it had been very simple, but now it was not.

"Well," he said, "I want you, Jennie. That never changed."

She was openly crying. "You don't need to be kind — "

"No," he said, "I ain't kind. I'd of killed Red if I

could. But it don't make any difference, Jennie. I got to have you."

She put up her face to him. She exclaimed in one passionate breath: "I'll be good, Joe. I'll work so hard, I'll never look at another man — "

"Why," he said, "maybe you will look at other men, Jennie. I don't guess you can help that altogether. It is just the way you're made. But I'll know how to take care of that. I guess I've learned. That's what I really think."

She waited for him to take her. She trembled a little, her face lifted and ready for him. He stood back, not quite knowing what to do; and then Jennie, a spark of coquetry returning, murmured: "You can kiss me if you'd like to, Joe."

He took her in, awkward in this thing as he was in so many others; but he felt good about it, he felt powerful and certain of himself, like a man coming into his own. He held her gently, because he knew what she had been through and he wanted to tell her, this way, how he'd always be to her. But in a moment Jennie's lips and the wild strong flavor of her got the best of him and he wasn't gentle any more. He was young Joe Spackman, in love.

XVIII

"THIS WAY IT MUST BE"

KEENE reached town near six o'clock, darkness whirling
in with the snow and the turbulent wind. He put up his
horse at the stable. This was the same horse — Morspeare's — he had seized on his escape from Broken
Bit; the hostler, recognizing it, gave Keene a quick, uneasy glance. At the doorway, starting into the street,
Keene turned sharp about.

"Anything on your mind?"

"No," said the hostler.

Keene tramped along the walk, snow beating at his
back and cold's bitterness cutting through his clothes.
He was half exhausted from all that he had been through
and yet the old caginess, the quick sense for danger, still
moved in him. It made him swing about to challenge the
hostler, it was something which would never leave him.
This was what happened to a man like him, taking all
trust and security out of life. He moved through yellow
beams of lamplight, on through dark areas of shadow.
He crossed to the hotel and registered. The clerk gave
him a key and he climbed the stairs with his muscles
bunching against the weight put on them. His cheek
points burned steadily where they had been frosted;
they would be sensitive for a long time.

It was the corner room again, facing the bullet hole in the wall. That room's mustiness got in his nostrils, reminding him of a hundred other rooms along the course of his travels. He washed and rolled a cigarette, weary enough to sleep yet driven by the constant irritability which would not let him be still. He made one slow circle of the room and left it. He paused in the lobby, hearing the clatter of dishes in the dining room and made hungry by the smell of food. Men passed him, going to the dining room; a woman came in and her eyes touched him and held him a moment, and went on.

He crossed to the saloon and had a drink. Warmth folded around him. His body soaked it up steadily, never getting enough. The whisky loosened him and the grumble of men's voices in the saloon cradled him with a kind of comfort. He laid his money on the bar and watched the saloonman, Tim Sullivan, come forward. Sullivan's cheeks showed crimson in the shining lamplight; bright feeling danced in his green eyes. He shoved the money back to Keene. "Not in my place, friend. Your drinks are on the house. The girl — she's all right?"

"She's all right."

"And everything else is all right," murmured Sullivan, his eyes laughing. "That news came in ahead of you, friend. Whenever you want a drink come to Sullivan's place. But never offer to pay for it."

Small warning stirred through Keene. "Who brought in the news?"

"Why," said Sullivan, "some of the Broken Bit boys.

But I wouldn't worry about them, friend. They took the train out of here awhile back."

Keene rubbed the bar steadily with the ball of a thumb. He was trying to recollect what troubled him, what one thing lay unsettled and loose in the edge of his memory. Then he remembered.

"Morspeare — he's here?"

Sullivan said: "I ain't seen him. Well, friend, the world's yours. Whut you goin' to do with it?"

"I'll be riding on."

"Ah," said Sullivan and ceased to smile. "I am sorry to hear of it. That is the second thing which makes me feel bad. The first was Ben Borders' death. Well, it is a sentiment, maybe, but an Irishman's heart is like that."

Keene recrossed the street and had supper in the hotel. There was no need for hurry, and nothing to do; yet he ate rapidly, oppressed by the very idleness of his mind — the complete futility of the things he felt. He left the dining room and stood in a corner of the lobby, rolling up a cigarette. He watched people pass in and out, he was a shadow standing alone. If the storm died by morning he would be riding on; if it continued he faced the kind of day he dreaded — a motionless day in which his thoughts would turn back to the ford.

He moved into the street and faced the long, solid drive of snow. Two women passed him, both crying their words against the wind. He crossed the street, the gush of the saloon lights making a round yellow stain in the racing wall of snow. He came to the saloon doors and stood by them, pulled by the warmth and the cheer inside; what he felt was a loneliness that had never troubled him before. It was like a sense of loss, of something taken out of him and leaving him hollow. All his thoughts went back to the ford; as often as he pulled them away they returned arrow-straight to that cabin standing in the wild heart of night; warm within and holding all that meant anything to him.

"Well," he said aloud, "that was the way her father was. Pillar to post and hell to breakfast. That's the way I am, and that is why I left."

He skirted the saloon, continuing into the wind's strengthening push; he went nighthawking through the darkness and came to the entrance of the stable whose doors were three-quarters closed. He slid through the small opening into the sallow light of a single lantern swinging from a rafter. He was out of the wind but the coldness seemed greater because of the quietness here. The hostler moved uncertainly forward from the stable's black rear end.

"Don't want anything," said Keene and watched the hostler fade into darkness. Keene walked the length of the stable's runway; and turned about. The doors, he thought, stood wider than they had a moment before; and then as he moved toward them he saw the huge shape of Jesse Morspeare slide from an empty stall.

Back of Keene, in the darkness, the hostler cried: "Watch out!" The echo of his voice clacked barrenly through the stable and died. Keene had stopped, all weight on the balls of his feet. Morspeare was under the down-thrown cone of the lantern's strange glow; the big man's eyes showed red and hungry, they were the hating eyes of a deserted dog, expressive of everything and expressive of nothing. He made only one sound — a flat murmur in his throat — and his shoulders went down as he slapped at the gun in his holster. His arm came up with a great jerk. He fired at once, and too soon, the bullet spraying up the old spongy dirt of the runway.

Keene hit him with his shot; he hit the big man in the chest, the heavy wallop of the forty-five's slug driving Jesse one short step backward and half around. Big Jesse set himself, he called up all that massive power of which he was so proud and so sure. He had never doubted it and his slow-moving mind, fixed on one thing alone, never doubted it now as he fought himself squarely around to Keene and tried to lift the gun. It was a dead weight in his hand; the last of his strength went into the trigger and sound swelled like a dynamite blast in the stable and dirt slashed Keene across the knees. Looking across the space, Keene saw the big man's eyes go dead as they stared. He fell in a vast heavy sweep, never knowing — Keene thought — what had happened to him.

Horses pitched in the stalls. The hostler yelled out his fear. "Look out — look out!" Wind shook the stable and men ran through the doorway's aperture. Keene watched Sullivan bend over Morspeare and rise up.

"Friend," said Sullivan, "I didn't know he was in town."

Keene shrugged his shoulders. The place got suddenly crowded, the smell of burnt powder grew heavy; it clung in blued rings to the air. Somebody murmured: "Never could trust Jesse — never knew whether he was behind you or in front of you. He was sly like that."

Keene heard himself say: "He was DePard's man."

Sullivan, who knew men thoroughly, slowly nodded. "Why, yes, that's right. He was Grat's man. You got to give him credit. He never forgot that."

Keene went through the gathering townsmen. He shouldered his way past them and left the stable. People were still running up through the snow; they were dark, thin shadows around him in the rising storm. He cut into the hotel and walked up the stairs, the weight of his body heavier than before on his legs. In the room he discovered he still held the gun in his hand. He threw it on the bed. He turned up the lampwick to erase the dismal shadows of the room, he looked around at the faded and dirty wallpaper; and he saw again the bullet hole in the wall, with its inscription: "Ventilated by Smoky Jules from Medora. 1882. Forty-four barrel on a forty-five frame. Never bet aces in another man's game."

What made a man write his name in a dingy hotel room? Keene faced the wall, and knew why. Smoky Jules was a drifter with nothing behind him and nothing ahead of him. Nobody remembered him and nobody cared what became of him. So he wrote his name on the wall because he was lonely and his life empty, hoping that somebody might see it and remember it. Now Smoky Jules was a ghost walking the trail somewhere. All he had to show for his life was a name on a wall.

Keene sat on the edge of the bed. He rolled a cigarette and smoked it, bent over on the bed with his arms idle across his knees. He thought of big Jesse Morspeare. That was something in the cards, that shooting. It was in the book, but Keene pitied the man and felt no pride for what he had done. He felt small and sick — and useless. "That's the way it's going to be. Just like that. Every place and any place."

All the fun had gone. The trail didn't mean anything any more. Once there was a time when he waited for morning, so that he could ride; once he had been eager to top a ridge and look down at the next valley green and tawny under sunlight, with farther mists beckoning him on. It wasn't like that any more, it never would be like that any more. He had ridden too long. From this point on there wasn't anything to look for. He had left too much behind him at the ford.

Somebody climbed the stairs and moved slowly along the hall, past his room; and came back and knocked. He said: "Come right in." He had his back to the door and he didn't look up. He held his hands over his knees, smoke curling around his face.

"Well, Jim," said Aurora's voice.

He came off the bed in a single quick lift; and found her at the doorway. She wore a heavy coat and a muffler was wrapped around her head; and all he saw was the dark line of her eyes and a red small spot on each cheek. Snow covered her, slowly turning to water.

He said: "You didn't ride in alone, Aurora?"

She unwrapped the muffler, she unbuttoned the coat. She stood still, looking across the room at him; and he couldn't tell, from that ink-black coloring in her eyes, whether she hated him at this moment or whether she liked him. It was that kind of look, containing so many things.

"Yes," she said, "I came alone."

"You shouldn't ever do that in this weather."

Her shoulders lifted expressively. "If it is always going to be like this for us I suppose I had better get used to the worst of it now. Here I am."

"Aurora," he said, very slowly, "do you know what I am?"

"I know most of you, Jim."

"Then you should have stayed at the ford."

She gave him a half-angered glance. "Don't you suppose I wanted to stay there? Why did I let you kiss me? That was my last try, Jim. I thought it might be enough to hold you in one place. But it wasn't." Her voice dropped lower and lower. "So I guess it has to be this way."

"I didn't want to spoil the rest of your life, Aurora. That's the reason I left."

"Was it?" she breathed. "Was it really that?"

"You wanted a steady man."

She looked around the room. "How well I know rooms like this. A thousand of them. That's why I moved to the ford. The one thing I wanted above every other thing was to forget what this kind of a life was like. But here I am. Don't you know now why I came?"

He moved toward her. He took her arm and pulled her with him, across the room. He pointed at the bullet mark and the inscription of Smoky Jules. "There's a man like me. That's all he's got to show for himself. The fun's gone out of riding. Well, a man can keep going until he runs into something and leaves a big chunk of himself behind. Then everything after that is a matter of looking backward. This night's been the worst I've ever had."

"Jim," she said, and looked up at him, her face taking on light, "do you mean that?"

He was no longer alone. That made all the difference in the room, in the night, in his own body. He had been weary; he was no longer weary. He felt once more that old hope, that old flare of excitement. But without her he would never have experienced it; and this was how he knew he had ridden his last hill. He turned her with his arms, feeling the quick pressure of her hands forcing him back. She said, intent and anxious: "Don't fool yourself again, Jim. You could never be a homesteader."

"No," he admitted, "I didn't mean that. I was thinking of the rough country behind Bowley's. I was thinking of the Short Hills." Then he said: "Is that too far for you to move, Aurora? That's where I want to stay and make my ranch."

"No, not too far," she answered, and let the pressure die from her hands.

He stood back, humbled by what he knew about her. She smiled, a sweet and anxious receptivity on her lips. He looked fully through her reserve; it had dropped for him and he caught the strong, rich eagerness inside. So smiling, she waited for him and, growing impatient of waiting, brought him nearer with the pressure of her hands.